I'M SLEEPING WITH YOUR HUSBAND

A NOVEL

SHEILA MURDOCK

Blair West got the text no married woman wants to get.

And just in an instant, her marriage to tech mogul Langston West III is put in jeopardy, making her stress-free, billionaire wife lifestyle come to an end, and it is now replaced by a lot of questioning.

Because someone out there is determined to take her place because she sees herself as a better fit, and she will stop at nothing until the mission is accomplished.

Every woman is a suspect.

But Blair will do anything to hold on to her marriage and lifestyle, even if this means having to take matters into her own hands.

She has no idea what she's in for.

I'm Sleeping With Your Husband

A NOVEL

I'm Sleeping With Your Husband

A NOVEL

WHEN THE UNEXPECTED BECOMES EVEN MORE UNEXPECTED

SHEILA MURDOCK

ALSO AVAILABLE IN PAPERBACK

DIVESTED
Crystal
THE DIVESTED BWWM SERIES
SHEILA MURDOCK

The Vain Society
SHEILA MURDOCK

Entitled Woman
SHEILA MURDOCK

LAVONNE ON THE JOB
The Hair Salon
SHEILA MURDOCK

THIS MESS IN HIS STREET
A NOVEL
SHEILA MURDOCK

LESSONS Lisa
SHEILA MURDOCK

Billionaire Bliss
SHEILA MURDOCK

THE Club
A NOVEL
SHEILA MURDOCK

STANDALONES and STANDALONE SERIES
MORE to COME!

NIGHT SKY AFFAIR
A SHORT STORY
SHEILA MURDOCK

NIGHT SKY AFFAIR
A SHORT STORY
SHEILA MURDOCK

NIGHT SKY AFFAIR
A SHORT STORY
SHEILA MURDOCK

NIGHT SKY AFFAIR
A SHORT STORY
SHEILA MURDOCK

Holly's JOY
SHEILA MURDOCK

Passed UP
A SHORT STORY
SHEILA MURDOCK

SHEILA MURDOCK
A NOVELLA
BOOM!
INSTANT

short stories, novellas
MORE to COME!

I'm Sleeping With Your Husband
A NOVEL
WHEN THE UNEXPECTED BECOMES EVEN MORE UNEXPECTED
SHEILA MURDOCK

"Did you hear about the new woman in town?"

Mikena Rich was born with the right last name in more ways than one, and she uses it to the fullest.

Beautiful, slim, fierce in every way, shape, and form. She wins the all-around, hands down.

Women hold on to their men when she's anywhere near them.

Her competition is next to none, and when she's done with a man she's done . . . .

Then she's on to the next one.

And Kimiko Windsor is definitely on to her—as well as on to her husband—since she knows Mikena is definitely after her husband, the indominable billionaire Mr. Alister Windsor.

Mikena has not only brought herself to the land of men with outlandish amounts of wealth, bon vivant wives, and spoiled-to-no-ends children, she's also brought a lot of secrets, but one of these is the secret of all secrets and puts the man who she's after in more peril than ever . . . as well as the entire community of Savage Rivers.

SHE WANTS YOUR HUSBAND - COMING SOON

CHAPTER ONE

I'm sleeping with your husband. And you're not stopping me, and you're especially not stopping him.

Who the hell is this?

I tried to keep my classy etiquette, but I'd never received a text like this in all of the 18 years Langston and I had been married. It was a beautiful, classic fairytale marriage. A multi-million-dollar wedding with the fancy flowers, diamonds and jewels, and horse and carriage. No one had ever been to a wedding like ours. I felt like a star.

Now I felt like my star had officially fallen.

Hard.

But I would be a fool to believe that marriages were perfect, even though I felt mine was as perfect as one could be. I felt I got more than lucky. I married into a rare Black billionaire family having come from a middle-class family who could only dream of living like this, but it took only one of us to get in, and it was me, and that middle-class life became an instant and distant memory.

I thought I was invincible. I didn't think any woman could compete with me. I felt like I earned my right to be a part of the West family. They were the ones to be in with; and I'd made it. I'd made it in. I did whatever I could not to mess up my relationship with

Langston so it could get to where it had gotten to at this moment, but it was clear something got messed up along the way that would cause my husband to stray.

Was this a one-time thing?

I wanted to believe it was, but regardless, something was definitely going on. I didn't wanna have to do this, but I wasn't gonna sit here and be humiliated by some 304 that would be very lucky if I didn't show up at her front door.

Who the hell was this whore?

How did she get my number?

Who the hell raised this bitch that she would boldly text a woman to let her know she's sleeping with her husband?

My husband.

Wow, I just couldn't believe how many people's morals and values had really fallen, if they ever had any to begin with.

I got up out of my bed and walked over to Langston's bathroom. I could hear the shower water running as it sounded like a binaural ASMR video. I stood outside his door as I tried to figure out if I wanted to tell him about this text. I took another look at it.

I'm sleeping with your husband.

I took a deep breath, and sent a text back:

Tell me this to my face.

I waited for a response as I still stood outside of his bathroom as I *still* tried even harder to figure out whether or not I wanted to confront him about this. I'd never had to confront him about anything like this since the day we got married. Now the uncertainty about how long this could've possibly been going on and with how many other women? I didn't even wanna think these thoughts.

Name the place.

My mouth dropped.

Yes, this was one bold bitch who definitely had no real sense because she didn't have the slightest idea who she was fucking with.

I sighed since I honestly didn't know what I wanted to do about this.

I heard the shower water shut off. I walked away from the door and sat on the bed next to my nightstand. I quickly put my phone in the drawer.

"Hey, baby," Langston said as he emerged from the bathroom. "What are you doing up so early?"

"I really don't know. Sometimes I get up early like this. It's not unusual and it's not that early. The girls are already off to school so I thought I'd get started on my day as well."

"That's my baby," he said with a big smile. He walked around the corner to his wardrobe room to get dressed for work since he was going in late due to us being at a charity event last night.

But he went back out last night.

And he had no idea that I knew he had.

Charity Event: Last Night

"Welcome, Mr. and Mrs. West," Hector, the charity director, said to us.

"Thank you. It's a pleasure to be here," Langston replied in his robotic response with a smile, as we held hands and walked into the ballroom where the event was taking place. He looked at me. "I don't wanna be here for that long. I need to rest up for tomorrow."

"What's going on tomorrow?"

"Just work."

"Just work?" I asked, as I was confused because we'd been out pretty late a lot of times on a work night—as well as on a school night for our girls—and he didn't mind getting only a few hours of sleep as long as he was able to get just that, a few hours. "Important meeting?"

He looked around the ballroom as he checked out the atmosphere. "Yeah . . . important meeting."

"Lang and Blair, hey!" Astrid said, a family friend of ours, and she always referred to him as Lang just as I did most of the time. He was like a big brother to her. I only knew her because she hung out in the West family circles forever as well as being from a very rich family herself, so she had been in this lifestyle her whole life and was a genuinely nice woman.

"Hey, Astrid," Langston and I said, as we all exchanged pleasantries.

Langston kept looking around the room as if he was looking for someone. "I see Jamichael, baby. I'll be right back."

"Okay, honey," I said with a smile.

Astrid nodded with a smile, and then turned her attention towards me. "How are things going with the two of you?"

"Just fine," I genuinely replied, as I wondered why she was asking me this. "Why?"

"It's just that your smile was almost wiped clean from your face when he said he saw Jamichael and that he would be right back."

"That's because I don't see Jamichael anywhere," I informed her.

She sighed. "Neither do I," she admitted. "Haven't seen him at all since this event started and I've been here since it started. Maybe he just got here."

"Yeah, maybe," I said.

She smiled as she sized me up. "I love your dress. It's truly stunning," she said, in response to my Oscar de la Renta red rosette embroidered faille dress with slim straps and a flare hem, and I absolutely loved it.

"Thank you, Astrid," I replied with a smile as I kept my eyes glued to Langston.

"You always know how to put the best looks together when you come to these events."

"Langston makes it all possible. I don't take my life with him for granted, not at all," I reassured her with a smile as I still tried to keep my eyes on him, but he was now out of my sight.

"I know you don't, Blair. Lang was one of the most wanted men for a very long time before the two of you met. I knew you were the one for him when I noticed how you weren't fake like all of the other women he was involved with. I couldn't stand them. He said he never thought about marrying any of them, and he obviously meant it. But when everyone in his circle was introduced to you, we knew you were a real one, Blair, and you still are. I personally got no bad vibes about you, none at all."

"I really appreciate that, Astrid, and I can say the same about you and all of his family and friends. I didn't know whether or not I was gonna be received well by his friends and family, but when I was welcomed with open arms, I truly felt accepted and loved."

"Glad to hear it after 20 years, Blair. We don't hide how we feel about anyone we don't think is a good fit for our family and friends."

"It's a great thing you all thought I was a great fit for Langston like the way he thought I was for him."

"We definitely did," she replied with a smile. She looked around

the room as if she was also helping me look for Langston.
"Oooh! I see the adorable little boy that I sponsor. We couldn't
wait to see each other in person. Excuse me."

"Of course," I said with a smile. I continued on looking for
Langston as people stopped me to talk and take pictures with
them. It started to appear as if I'd come here alone.

"Ready to go?"

It'd appeared that Langston came out of nowhere.

"Where were—yes, sure. I'm ready," I said, as I clearly stopped
short of asking him questions that a wife who lived the life I
lived had learned not to ask. But even though I lived the life, I
wasn't blind, and I definitely wasn't stupid.

We held hands as we walked outside and into Langston's black
Rolls-Royce Phantom—a car we only took to events—as Chauffeur Charrod waited for us with the door opened. He was
Langston's longtime chauffeur and was genuinely a nice man
and dedicated West family employee.

"I didn't see Jamichael there," I informed him. I just couldn't
hold it in.

"You didn't?" he asked.

Charrod looked in his rearview mirror.

"No, I didn't, Lang," I said, since we were not in public. He
always wanted me to call him Langston when we were in public
since it sounded more professional. "You told me you saw him
so of course I wanted to see him and talk to him as well."

He sighed. "He wasn't there."

"What?"

"You heard me, Blair."

"Why did you lie?"

"I didn't lie. I thought it was him when I was looking around. I got close and found out it wasn't him. There were a lot of people there."

"Then where did you go for all of that time? I was looking all over for you."

Charrod kept looking in his rearview mirror.

"I was talking to various people, Blair, like the way I usually do. Mingling, you know? You're used to the same song and dance by now. I'm the largest donator to that charity, just like how I am to all of them."

I sighed. "I understand. But I felt like I was there by myself."

"I'll make it up to you."

Hours later, I woke up out of deep sleep.

2:42 am.

Lang was not in bed. I got up and looked at my phone. I went to the house app on it and swiped right to the main garage.

One of his cars was gone.

I stared out the window as it started to rain and watched as Charrod backed out of the garage in Lang's silver Rolls-Royce Cullinan with him sitting in the back seat. He not only drove us to events, he also drove him to work every day. I stared at the text once again, and called my best friend, Maxi Bailey, who was a private investigator. I'd never needed her on her job as much as I personally needed her now.

Some bold bitch was sleeping with my husband, and I was all too determined to find out who it was and what Lang had been up to, and just not up to last night, but what he'd been quite possibly up to for all 18 years of our marriage.

CHAPTER TWO

I stepped one foot out of my black Mercedes Maybach S 580 4MATIC sedan, popped open my red umbrella, and nervously got the rest of myself out of the car as Maxi's assistant, Yusari, held open the door for me. I didn't need to explain to myself why I was so nervous when all of the other times I'd come to my best friend's private investigation firm that it felt like I'd worked here myself, and Yusari always greeted me with her warm and enthusiastic smile.

But this time it was different.

And Yusari could see it in my smile that I was covering up something much bigger behind it, but I continued to smile throughout all of it.

I needed for Maxi to do something I didn't want to her to do, and I knew it was unethical and a conflict of interest since she was my best friend—I wanted her to investigate my own husband.

And I was serious.

I walked towards the door with a fake smile as I was donned in a black silk Balmain pussy-bow collar blouse, off white Galvan London flared trousers, and Manolo Blahnik BB heels on my feet. A Hermes orange crocodile Birkin 35 hung on the crook of my arm. I didn't dress to play; I had a legitimate appointment today.

"Hello, Blair. It's always nice to see you," Yusari said.

"Nice to see you, too, dear," I replied with a smile.

She sized me up. "You look beautiful."

"Thank you."

"You can go straight into her personal office. She's actually talking to one of the investigators in the break room."

"Thank you," I said once again with a smile.

I made myself comfortable in my favorite chair here in Maxi's office. I loved her office since she made it like she was at home, but had all kinds of investigative cases and pictures and paraphernalia on the walls and on her desk from going to conventions all over the world in here as well. I also loved the fact that she was living out her dream of being a private investigator after watching reruns of *Magnum, P.I.* while growing up since she was too young to remember any of it when the show was actually aired all throughout the 1980s, as well as not missing any episodes of the new version of the show in recent years, and freaked out when it ended so abruptly.

I already knew without her even saying it first, that I was hiring her for the case of her career.

"Blair, hey!" Maxi said.

I got up out of my seat and we hugged each other. "Hey, honey."

"Well, as usual, you look beautiful. I wouldn't assume anything is wrong. I would just assume that the two of us were headed to lunch for the millionth time," she said, as she sat down at her desk.

"I wish we were," I said. I shook my head. "Am I right to be doing this?"

"Yeah, I think you're right to be doing this . . . but I don't think I'm the right person to be doing this."

I sighed as I shook my head once again. "Don't start. You know I will pay you anything to find out who this bitch is. I sent you the texts she'd sent me earlier today as well as the whole exchange I had with her. I don't think she's gonna stop."

"Has she sent you anymore?"

I looked at my phone. "Not for right now."

Maxi sighed. "Look, Blair. I told you when you got involved with Lang that this was bound to happen sooner or later. Everyone knows that there's not a woman alive who would've turned down a date with Lang, much less a marriage proposal—and you're the one he proposed to."

I looked at my 18-carat solitaire diamond ring, an upgrade for being married for 18 years. "Yeah, I know, Maxi. I know accepting his proposal that I was accepting all of the problems that came with being married to a billionaire, a *Black* billionaire. The rarest of the rare. I just think now that Lang has hidden so much from me in these past 18 years, and I don't even know if I have the strength to know what all of it is, much less act on it."

"Then don't," she suggested.

"What?"

"Then don't, Blair. You heard me. Women would kill to live the life that you're living, and there are just some things you know that come with being married to a man like Lang."

"Like the constant cheating and lies and everything? The high jewelry to hide all the infidelities? Look, you know Lang and I have a real marriage, and we both know it hasn't been a perfect one. His family accepted me with open arms. He had more options in women than what he is worth, and he thought I was the one who was more worth it than all of them since I'm the one he asked to marry, and not only that, we've been married for 18 years with two children."

"Jodie and Lorie don't know anything about this, do they?"

"No, they were already off at school when the first text came into my phone. And that's just it. I still have two growing girls who are in their prime years as teens. We got Jodie's sweet sixteen party coming up and she's about to drive me insane with all of the shit she wants done for it. She thinks it's gonna be perfect. I told her nothing in life is perfect and is never gonna be perfect."

"When she gets older, she'll see that. But what she shouldn't see— and neither should Lorie—is your change in mood and attitude towards Lang because of this. You didn't show him the texts, did you?"

I sighed. "I came close; I was standing outside of his bathroom door with the phone in my hand. I suddenly changed my mind at the last minute. I just didn't wanna start the day off fighting. We have a date night tonight."

"Great. You did the right thing. He shouldn't know anything about it, especially since I'm the one who's investigating it."

"So you're really gonna take my case?" I asked with a lilt of excitement in my voice.

"Pro bono."

I smiled. "I love you."

"I love you, too, and I always will. But you need to stay out of the way and let me do my job. This is personal so I'm the only one who's gonna be working on it. I don't want anyone knowing anything about this. As much as I trust everyone who works for me here, I still don't trust them, especially when it comes to personal indiscretions concerning my best friend and her husband. But don't be surprised if it gets to those gossip sites because you just don't know what this woman's intentions are."

"And that's the thing. I don't want this bitch going around telling and showing people that she sent me that text, you know? And I responded to it."

"And why did you respond to it?"

"Because I wanted to know who the bitch is!"

"Calm down," she ordered. She knew me forever, and knew how fast I got heated up when something made me mad, and this text had me in a raging inferno right now, so much so that I was actually surprised I was able to calmly drive myself here in the pouring rain.

"I'm trying to exercise as much control as I can, you know that. It's just that you're right—I knew I was gonna get a text like this some time. But it's just the boldness and nerve of it all, you know? For her to say some shit like that and when I said I wanted to meet her somewhere to talk she's gonna tell me to name the place."

"Yeah, I saw the whole text exchange," she reminded me. "Look, my suggestion is that you don't respond to her anymore. It's just gonna make you mad and might even hinder my investigation. You know I will give you all of the info you need that I find out. I'll never let you down."

I smiled as tears welled up in my eyes. "I know you won't. But I forgot to tell you that he went out again last night after the charity event."

"He *what?*" she asked, as if she couldn't believe it herself.

"Yeah, he did. I woke up out of a deep sleep and found he obviously did the midnight creep. It was almost 3:00 am. Where the fuck did he go then? Especially when he had to work in the morning?"

"Did you ask him?"

"No, but I'm going to."

"Blair . . ."

"Maxi, I have a right to know. I mean, I told you how I couldn't find him for well over an hour at the charity event last night; I think it might have been even longer than that. He lied and said he saw Jamichael, but then just left me standing there and I didn't see him for a really long time after that. As I told you, Jamichael was never there; Lang admitted to me that he wasn't. He told me he was just around mingling. I think he left the event to meet up with that woman, and now she's harassing me with texts because she thinks he's leaving events to wanna be with her instead of being with me."

"Possibly. But if I can be honest, Blair?"

"Yeah, I need some honesty right now; I need *a lot* of honesty."

"I know you do, so here it goes. I just think that no matter what Lang says or what he does, I just don't think he'll ever leave you."

"I'll believe that if it really comes to the 'till death do us part' of our marriage."

"And you have every right to feel that way because you know I feel that way about my husband."

"Erwin is a great man, Maxi. You married the right one."

"And I believe you did, too."

"And I hope nothing changes my mind about that."

She nodded since she knew I was just gonna go in circles about this. "Well, you know I will start working on this right away since I just wrapped up a case a few days ago, and I gave my other cases to my other investigators since like I said, this one is personal and that's all they need to know."

"I know you're not gonna tell them anything, Maxi."

"Absolutely not. So, where are you headed after here?"

"I got a lunch date with Jamichael," I informed her.

She sighed. "And when was the last time you had a lunch date with your husband's best friend?"

"Years ago," I replied with a smirk. "It was when we all got together and had Erwin's birthday party there, remember?"

"Clearly," she said. "But that wasn't a lunch date, that was a party during traditional lunch hours." She sighed once again. "Blair, I know why you have a lunch date with him."

"Well, maybe I shouldn't say date since I only use that with Lang, so I should say lunch engagement."

"Same difference and you know it."

"Well, I love Jamichael's restaurant. He has the best Italian food since he's co-owners with a real Italian man who knows the ends and outs of Italian food, of course. I'm getting hungry so I gotta go."

"No getting carried away in talking about Lang and no telling him about me investigating your husband—his best friend—and who this woman could be that texted you about sleeping with him."

"You got it," I said with a full grin.

"Blair, *I mean it,*" she stressed with a firm tone in her voice and that glare in her eyes that only a best friend who really cared about me could give.

And I loved her for it.

CHAPTER THREE

"Here you go, Blair. I know the spaghetti and meatballs dish is your favorite," Jamichael said, as he sat down the savory plate of my favorite comfort food right in front of me as I sat in a private room in his restaurant. He didn't realize just how much I needed to talk to him and just how bad I really needed some comfort food right now.

"And that hasn't changed at all, Jamichael. Thank you," I said, and got ready to devour this plate of food, something that I usually got for dinner. "No one makes the classic spaghetti and meatballs dish better than this restaurant."

"Thank you," he said with a smile as I ate like no one was watching. He sat right across from me. "So, I must say I was surprised that you called me this morning and asked me could we have lunch together."

"There's a reason," I said, and continued to eat.

"Is everything all right between you and Lang?" he asked, as he stared at me. He hadn't even touched his food yet.

"I honestly don't know," I honestly replied.

"What's going on?"

I put my fork down and sighed. I needed to slow down from eating so fast anyway. "Well, I want to know first of all did he talk to you at any time last night?"

"No, I didn't talk to him at all last night," he informed me.

"Son of a bitch," I said, and took a sip of my water.

"Uh oh!" he said with a laugh. "Y'all were at the charity event last night, right?"

"Yeah, right. And he told me he thought he saw you there."

"No, I wasn't there at all. I had to get ready for today. As you can see, these days are really busy all the way up until almost midnight."

I shook my head. I dug into my purse and gently shoved my phone over to him. "Know anything about that?"

He looked at the text exchange between me and Lang's alleged bold lover. He gently shoved my phone back over to me. "I'm so sorry, Blair. I honestly don't know who sent that to you. Lang doesn't really tell me much if he's seeing someone because I think he knows I would tell you if you asked. I can ask him about it if you want me to, or have you already talked to him about it?"

"I came close this morning while he was in the bathroom, but I just couldn't get myself to do it. I keep trying to tell myself that I'm the one who's married to him and I just shouldn't go down to this bitch's level, but I already have."

"Well, I wouldn't say all of that, Blair. You were just responding to a bold text some thot sent you. Any woman would've responded the way you had and probably would've been a lot worse in her response at that. I don't think that thot has the guts to meet you anywhere, Blair. Those are the kind who talk so much shit but will never live up to it in person with anyone. But to be downright honest with you, I can't say for certainty that Lang did not sleep with her."

"And that's my bottom line. When women make claims like this, I have to believe them. So far, she hasn't shown me any proof that she has, but I believe that she has, you know? Even though I don't want to believe it at all. I swear some women have absolutely no respect for any women's marriages."

"That's because they have no respect for themselves," he concluded. "I really wouldn't worry about this too much, Blair, or not really at all. This woman is doing this because she wants your life—

what woman wouldn't? You have everything in this world going for you and have for 18 years now with two beautiful girls to show for it. But I know things have not been perfect because I've been a witness to it. You know my 20-plus-year marriage is far from perfect. So if Lang is willing to tell me anything about cheating on you then I will definitely let you know."

"Don't ever hesitate to tell me anything he tells you when it comes to him cheating on me because according to this text, it's clear he already has."

CHAPTER FOUR

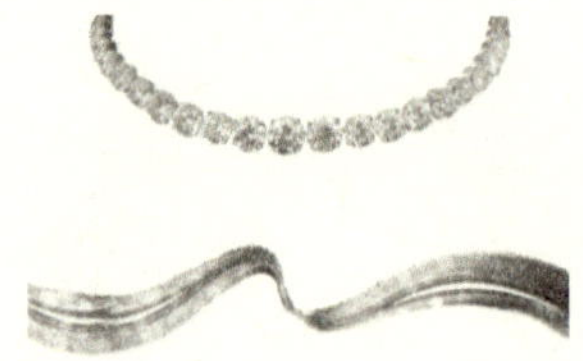

"You look beautiful tonight," Lang said, and took a sip of his wine.

"Thank you," I replied with a smile as I still looked at my menu while we were at one of his favorite steak and seafood restaurants for our date night. I looked up from the menu as he still glared at me. "What?"

"How was lunch with Maxi?"

"It was fine," I lied. "Nothing out of the ordinary." He nodded, and then kept his eyes on me as he took another sip of wine. I felt he was already on to me, and if he was, then it was finally time to tell him about the texts. "Um, I got a text this morning—"

"I got something for you," he immediately interrupted me. He signaled for Charrod to come over. Charrod walked over with a bag in his hands.

Van Cleef & Arpels.

Well.

I guess he knew what I was gonna ask him before I even had. He knew right when to cut me off.

"Thank you, Charrod," he said, as he stared at me.

"You're welcome, Mr. West," Charrod replied with a smile, and then nodded at me.

I nodded back at him with a smile. "Wow, VCA, huh? What did you do?" I said as I tried to chuckle to make it seem like a joke—but failed miserably. I couldn't even try to be funny about this . . . and I think he knew it.

He shoved the huge bag over to me. "I was gonna save this until we got home, but I think you would like it now since I think it would look good with your dress."

I nodded with a smile as I looked down at my jade green Leo Lin sleeveless V-neck Monica lambskin leather midi dress. I completed the look with a beautiful pair of Aquazzura Babe 105 green slingback sandals with beautiful sparkling crystal bows. I put the bag on the left side of me since we were sitting at a table in a private dining room, something Lang always requested at every restaurant that had these accommodations. I knew there wasn't just one item in this bag, and it pretty much told me without telling me that he was definitely out last night and definitely left the charity event to see this chick, and now I was getting the feeling it wasn't just one woman he saw. But if there was a possibility of more than one which there always was, well, then I was just focused on the one who boldly sent me the text, a text that I was now convinced he knew I wanted to talk to him about. "When did you pick these up?"

"I had them delivered them to my office this morning," he replied, and took another sip of his drink.

"You never get me anything for our date nights. What's the occasion?"

He stared at me. "Just because."

Just because you know damn well what I wanna talk to you about and you're trying to make it up to me with some high fucking jewelry; I'm no dummy, I thought. I put a smile on my face as I stared at the bag. I just didn't know if I wanted to open what was inside. I felt at this point he was doing everything he could not to admit guilt. It was clear he just didn't wanna talk about it; talk about something he knew damn well *I* wanted to talk about.

"What are you waiting for? Open your gifts," he demanded, and then took a sip of his water.

Gifts.

Yeah, before I even looked in the bag, I knew there was more than one item in here—and he confirmed it. He must've really felt guilty about what he'd done last night.

Twice.

I reached into the bag and pulled out three beautifully wrapped boxes. Yeah, he'd really done it this time.

"Start with that one," he said, as he pointed to one of the smaller of the three boxes.

I nodded with a fake smile as I took my time unwrapping it and opening it while I could feel him staring at me as he took swigs of his hard liquor. I opened the box to a beautiful pair of VCA Bouton d'or drop earrings which featured small round stones in 18 karat gold, chrysoprase—a gemstone which was a beautiful apple green color that did beautifully match my green leather dress—and onyx. Each stone had one beautiful tiny diamond in the center of it. "They're beautiful. They remind me of being in Jamaica." I opened the other box, a matching bracelet. I opened the last box, a matching necklace. "Thank you. This is a beautiful set."

"You're welcome," he said, as he continued to glare at me. He took another sip of his hard liquor. "Put everything on."

"Why?"

"Do I have to ask you again? Like I said before, I think the set looks beautiful with your dress."

I smiled, but I knew there was a reason why he wanted me to wear this set now. I did what he said. "How does it look?"

"Gorgeous," he replied. He got his phone out of his pocket and took a picture of me.

This completely caught me off guard since we never took pictures of each other on a date night since we considered it a private night for just the two of us.

He was definitely up to something.

. . .

Date night over.

I couldn't wait for this date to be over with, and after he'd given me my gifts, the night seemed to have dragged on and on. And I couldn't even finish my meal since I had a big lunch, so I decided to take it home with me.

"I have a long day tomorrow," he informed me.

"We didn't have to stay that late here then, you should've said something earlier. I would've . . . . *what the hell?!*"

Out of nowhere, we were completely bombarded by the media!

"MR. AND MRS. WEST! DO EITHER ONE OF YOU KNOW WHO THE WOMAN IS WHO'S CLAIMING TO BE SLEEPING WITH YOU, MR. WEST?" a woman from the media boldly asked.

Yeah, he knows damn well who it is, I thought.

Lang grabbed on to my hand! "Get these people out of here! *NOW!*" he barked at the staff, as Charrod tried his best to get us to the car.

"YOUR JEWELRY IS BEAUTIFUL, MRS. WEST!" another woman shouted out as cameras practically blinded me with their flashes.

"Thank you," I said calmly as I put my other free hand up across my eyes because the bright flashes from the cameras were so blinding as the media was smothering and almost knocking each other out of the way as they tried to get pictures of us, not to mention people who were just at the restaurant or bystanders who wanted to get their personal videos and pictures of us on their phones.

This was the first time this had ever happened in our 18 years of marriage. Never had we ever been in the spotlight like this, and it was the last thing I wanted to be in the spotlight about. People now knew everything I wanted to try and keep so private. There were no more secrets about this. My family's life was now on full display, and people were gonna do whatever they could to find out everything.

Just as bad as I wanted to find out.

Charrod rushed us in the car as the staff at the restaurant tried to hold back the media, but failed miserably as they were all up on our car as Charrod tried to honk his horn to get them off of it.

"Just drive, man," Lang instructed as he looked ahead. He looked at me. "Are you okay?"

"Not until I find out the real truth about what the hell all of that mess was out there for," I said. I looked down at my jewelry . . . and started taking it off as he stared at me. "The media was not out there for nothing, Lang, and you know it. What the hell is this shit about a woman claiming to be sleeping with you, huh?" I asked, as I tried so hard to pretend that I didn't get that text, and that Maxi was already investigating it.

Charrod looked in his rearview mirror as he drove us home.

"I don't know what they're talking about," Lang replied, as he continued to look straight ahead. He then glared at me. "And that will be the last time I talk about it."

CHAPTER FIVE

I stared Lang down as he snored in a deep sleep. We may have not talked about what'd happened after we left the restaurant tonight after our date night, but it definitely wasn't gonna be the last time we talked about it. Because now everything was out in the open for the world to see, and he knew it was all a matter of time before he had to tell me what he was hiding from me because he sure as hell didn't tell me that it wasn't anybody.

I got out of bed since I couldn't sleep. Luckily, I never seemed to have awaken Lang when I got out of bed. I walked out of our bedroom and down the hall and turned the corner. I could never get over how big and beautiful this house was. It was a total royal palace with everything anyone could ever want, all 40,000 square feet of it, built from the ground up when we got engaged and was ready when we were officially married. This was the part I definitely couldn't complain about, but not everything in the royal household was what people thought it would be, and tonight that was proven with my family being put on complete and total display.

And it all started with one damn text that had now turned into a text scandal.

I looked in on Jodie, our oldest. She was sound asleep. I went down the hall and looked in on Lorie, our second and youngest. She was also sound asleep. I knew by looking at them sleeping like this that their lives were not going to be the same since what I wanted to stay private was now all out in the open, and I was gonna do whatever I could to protect them.

I walked down one of the backstairs to the second floor and down the long hall to my office. I wanted to try and get away from the bedroom and Lang as much as I could. I closed my door and turned on my computer. I went to the search box and started typing:

Langston West and Blair West Secret Woman Text

It returned thousands of hits.

Already.

The first one listed was a social media famous woman with a show called Wild Black Tea with Beverly who already had a video up about us. I sighed and clicked it on:

<u>WILD BLACK TEA WITH BEVERLY</u>
THE TEXT SHOWN AROUND THE WORLD
BILLIONAIRE LANGSTON "LANG" WEST IS IN A HOT MESS!
MYSTERY WOMAN BOLDLY CLAIMS TO BE
SLEEPING WITH HIM! SENT TEXT TO BLAIR WEST, THE WIFEY!

"Uh, oh! Just when no one thought there was nothing going on with one of the world's wealthiest and hottest Black couples! Lang and Blair West have never been in the spotlight for anything messy, but that has all changed as of today, and admit it, everyone, we were *all* secretly waiting for something spicy to drop on this gorgeous Black billionaire couple, and now we finally have something! Hello, everyone, and welcome to Wild Black Tea with Beverly, I'm your girl, Beverly. If this is your first time here, welcome and I'm happy that you've joined us. If you like today's show there's plenty many more to come so hit those

Like and Subscribe buttons and the Follow button if you're watching this show on some of my other platforms because you won't be disappointed, especially now!"

She picked her teacup off of its tea saucer where she had a whole tea set out with her show's logo splashed all over each of the white pieces that had colorful small flowers sparsely painted on each one, and took a sip of her tea.

"Just remember, I am having a special sale on the tea sets starting now, just use the code LANGANDBLAIRWEST to get 25% off!"

"You're kidding!" I yelled out. "No she didn't!"

And in this moment, I realized just how much things had changed with my family. Nothing was no longer private like the way it once was. I continued to watch and listen carefully to what she had to say about who this could've been who'd sent me this text:

"Okay, when I personally got word on this, it was before Lang and Blair went out on a date night, something that they do a few times a month, it's been said. But I was told that Blair had actually received a text from this woman earlier in the day before her date night with Lang, but she, of course, refused to tell her who she was. What a damn coward, you know? How the hell are you gonna taunt a woman like Blair West with your foolish mess and then act as if you don't wanna say who you are? That's just on some cowardly mess, like I said. I mean, if you're gonna do it, be a woman and admit to who you are, but we haven't been able to find out who she is but it's like she wants us to know she's out there and that she's sleeping with Langston West III, the married multi-billionaire father of two beautiful girls, Jodie, 15, soon-to-be sweet 16; and Lorie, 14. I honestly think this is just very disrespectful and immature, but these women these days have never been taught respect and have no maturity—well, you know what you can blame all of that on!"

"Yeah, I think we all know that," I said, and continued to watch:

"Oh, and it's clear something is definitely going on because during their date night, Lang gave Blair a beautiful 3-piece set from one of my dream brands, Van Cleef & Arpels, and each piece is priced separately. I was able to get a great picture and videos of Blair wearing the set with that beautiful green leather dress she had on while those diamonds on those beautiful stones were sparkling like crazy, and was able to see that it was from their Bouton d'or collection. She had on three pieces from this collection, and it's priced as is from the last time I looked at the site because all prices are subject to change!"

Necklace: $105,000
Bracelet: $49,200
Earrings: $29,100

"Yes, everyone, and these are the base prices *without* tax! I know this is absolutely nothing to Lang since he's worth an estimated $7.3 billion, but it also shows that he is guilty of something because it's been said everywhere that he has never given her anything during their date nights, but then he does tonight? Right before the text goes public? She walks in without any jewelry on but her beautiful wedding ring and some diamond stud earrings, but walks out with a beautiful 3-piece VCA set on like that? But anyway, looks like we have a developing story here that's gonna get wild, so y'all know to keep it here for all of the tea!"

In a stunned stare, I couldn't keep my eyes off of the screen as she had the whole text exchange between that bitch and me displayed for the world to see. I knew that it all started with this bitch sending me the text and had probably sent it to a friend bragging about how she'd sent it to me—yeah, real mature if that was in fact the case. But what did I expect from some bitch who had probably done nothing but sleep with other women's husbands her whole life?

But I didn't care about any other woman's husband, I cared about mine, and I was gonna do everything in my power to find out who this was because now since this was all out in the open, this was taken to a whole other level. Sometimes I felt that things had to be taken more seriously than they were. I wasn't the type who was gonna ignore something like this. There was no way I was ignoring something that now everyone knew about because the last thing ignoring it was gonna do was make it go away. I knew Maxi was working on this right away, and I couldn't wait until she told me what she'd already found out.

"Blair?"

I jumped up out of a deep sleep. "What? What's going on?"

"What are you doing in here?" Lang asked.

I looked around and realized that I'd fallen asleep on my couch in my office. "I was working."

"On what?"

"Some event planning for the ABWS," I lied. Since I was the Affluent Black Women's Society's National President, a philanthropy organization, I did have a lot of responsibilities—but nothing so urgent at the moment that I needed to pull an all-nighter for.

"Well, Charrod and I are taking the girls to school this morning since their driver is on vacation for two weeks."

"Okay," I said, as I sat myself up on the couch. "Did they get their breakfast?"

"Yes." He kept staring down at me. "See you later."

"Lang," I said, as my head hung low.

He looked back at me. "What is it?"

I sighed. I just didn't have the strength to say anything about it since I'd just woke up. "Have a great day."

"You too."

Several minutes later, Lang got into the front seat of his SUV as Charrod was at the wheel and Jodie and Lorie were in the back seat.

"What's wrong with Mom?" Jodie asked, as Charrod pulled off and down the driveway.

"Nothing. She just fell asleep working in her office last night," Lang replied as he stared straight ahead.

"Like you do from time to time when you take us to the movies for Daddy-Daughter Date Night?" Lorie asked.

Charrod looked at Lang and smiled.

"Yes, baby, like I do when the three of us go on our date nights," Lang said as he looked back at her with a smile.

Several minutes later, they approached the school to a whirlwind of media!

"HERE THEY COME!" a reporter from the media yelled out!

Suddenly, the car was bombarded with a mob of reporters and blinding flashes coming through the lightly tinted windows from cameras as deafening sounds of the reporters tried to get something out of Lang as their microphones and cell phones knocked and scratched up against his newly bought black Rolls-Royce Cullinan.

"Dad! What is going on?" Lorie asked, as she looked frightened at the mob of media all around and over the SUV.

"Hello? Headmaster Henley?" Lang said, as Charrod had the SUV at a standstill at the grand entry of the school while a long line of cars waited behind them. He listened to what was being said to him by Henley. "GET THESE PEOPLE OUT OF HERE NOW! THEY'RE SCARING MY CHILDREN!"

"They're not scaring me, Dad," Jodie informed him. "I know why they're here."

Lang looked back at her. He sighed. "I knew the two of you were gonna find out. Damn social media! Look, since you know why they're here, you're under a strict order from me and your mom not to talk about it to anyone. *Anyone*. Not to your friends and not to your boyfriend. That goes for you too, Lorie."

"Okay," she replied as she stared out the window at the media as they were immediately dispersed from the SUV under the orders of Lang.

Charrod proceeded to slowly drive into the school's long spectacular entryway while a trail of luxury cars and SUVs followed in a line that was almost a mile behind them.

After getting out of the shower, a loud chime came into my phone. It was a text from Maxi:

Got some info regarding your case. You're not gonna wanna miss this.

I gasped as I texted her back:

I'll be right there.

CHAPTER SIX

"Okay, tell me everything. Don't leave anything out," I said, as I sat on the edge of my favorite seat in Maxi's office as a hot cup of Starbucks Pike Roast coffee sat in front of me, something Maxi already had waiting for me when I got here.

"You know I will never intentionally leave anything out, Blair. I actually could hardly believe this myself, and even had to confirm it," she said.

"Well, don't hold me in suspense! What is it?"

"Turn around," she said, and pointed up to the TV as she pressed a few buttons on her remote.

The TV mounted on her wall automatically went to surveillance footage.

"What is this video of?" I asked.

"The hotel that the two of you were at this week—the night of the charity event," she informed me.

Things just started getting very interesting.

I sighed. "I thought it looked familiar."

"I'm not gonna drag this out with you, Blair. I have a lot of video from that night since as you can see, their video surveillance is absolutely some of the best. It's crystal clear and in color, so I'm gonna cut through all of this."

"Okay, like I said, I know you did the work so once again, don't hold me in suspense."

"Video surveillance shows that Lang never left the building," Maxi informed me.

"What?" I shook my head. "*What?*! I just can't get myself to believe that. It's a big hotel; a big building. Big and old. He must've gone out a back way or something."

"I was able to get access to most of their surveillance for those hours that the two of you were at the charity event, Blair, and he never left the hotel."

"Then where the fuc—?"

"Blair . . ."

I shook my head as I crossed my arms in front of me. "Where did he go?"

She sighed. "Your answer is as good as mine."

I shook my head once again. "Now when I really think about it, I can honestly say I don't think he left the hotel, either."

"And like I said, that's some of the best surveillance, Blair. I was lucky I was able to get my hands on it. I looked everywhere on it and it never shows y'alls car leaving while the event is going on. In fact, here's some still pictures of the times it was parked there." She shoved the pictures over to me.

I looked at them carefully. I couldn't dispute that it was our car we took that night, with some pictures of Charrod even standing outside of it at times.

"It was parked there the entire night. Charrod never left in it nor did he take Lang anywhere in it and then return. Look at all of the time stamps on them. It was parked out in front of the hotel like it always is when the two of you are there for anything, and there was no video of it leaving anywhere except when the two of you left for the night."

"Well, Lang definitely left the ballroom and went somewhere, and that somewhere was definitely to one of the rooms in the hotel. Do you have a list of who was staying there that night?"

"Yes," she replied, and pulled out her iPad. "Here are all of the guests who were staying there that night. Management was able to forward me a copy of it. Let me know if you see any familiar names."

I put on my Chanel eyeglasses and carefully scrolled through the list, examining each name as I did. I felt like I was the one investigating my case for someone else. After minutes of looking carefully through the list, I had one thing to admit. "No, I don't recognize anyone on this list."

"Okay," she said, as I gave her back the iPad.

"But that doesn't mean Lang wasn't with someone that night. I honestly think he was up in some woman's room that night, and there are a lot of women on that list."

"Yeah, there are, that's why I thought at least one name looked familiar."

"No, unfortunately, none of them do, so Lang is lucky in that aspect."

She grinned. "Blair, we will find out who this is. Management actually told me that since it is a big hotel, they do have more surveillance they can give me since I am a private investigator, they just haven't gotten around to giving it to me yet."

"Well, whatever they can give you will be very helpful to me because now I believe he didn't leave. The pictures and the video from what I've seen of our car being parked there the whole time doesn't lie."

"No, this surveillance doesn't lie. I think it's already come in handy by way of the fact that he was still in the hotel the whole time. Like we all know, that's a big hotel with a lot of rooms."

"And he was up in some bitch's room while I was down there in that main ballroom by myself talking to people while wondering where he was for more than half of the night. I just knew he left, Maxi, I just knew it!"

"Well, it's clear he didn't leave at all, at least not the hotel. But like I said, management says they have more surveillance to send me of the elevators and of the floors as well. Wherever he left to go to in that hotel that night, he's gonna be somewhere on video."

"And I can't wait to see it since he told me he doesn't wanna talk about what happened last night after our date ever again. Tough shit. He's the one who started all of this. If he was just honest with me about not being happy or whatever then we wouldn't be going through this. I wanted to keep this private, now everything is out in the open. He knows he can't hide from this. Did you see the media mob him and my girls when him and Charrod took them to school this morning?"

"Yeah, I saw it," Maxi said as she shook her head.

"And then that Beverly tea woman is now talking about it? She has over a million subscribers and followers on her social media pages and she's even giving away tea sets for 25% off with the code LANGAND-BLAIRWEST!"

"You're kidding, Blair!"

"No, I'm not! This is why I wanna find out who this bitch is who caused all of this shit, and clearly it's the woman Lang saw in one of those hotel rooms that night because those texts started in the morning after that night. I never had any woman send me a text like that . . . *never*. Now I have a feeling he only wanted to go to that charity event that night so he could meet up with her."

"Sounds like it, but I will find out through surveillance where he went and quite possibly exactly what room he went to and whose name it was under for that night. But while I do, Blair, once again, *you know* not to interfere with my investigation because you know I will tell you everything you need to know. And try to do what Lang says about not bringing it up, either. It's clear that everything is out in the open about the texts and everything, but no one knows I'm investigating this."

"And they're not going to know. Oh, and another thing."

"What is it?"

"Have you been able to find out where he went that night *after* the charity event? When I got up in the middle of the night and saw from the house app that one of his cars was missing in one of our garages at almost 3:00 in the morning? Now *I know* I wasn't seeing things."

"You know I'm working on it."

CHAPTER SEVEN

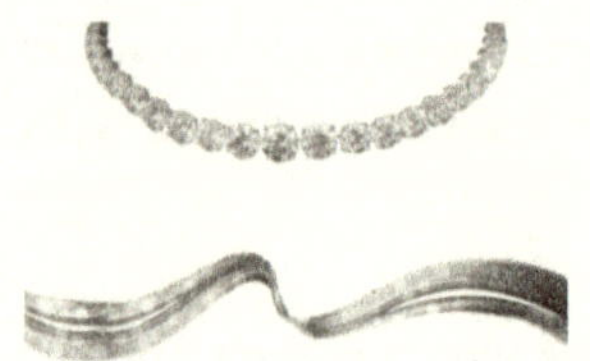

took a deep breath and knocked on Lorie's door to her study room.

"Come in!" I heard her say.

I opened the door with a big smile. "Hi, baby."

"Hi, Mom," she said with a smile as she was doing her homework.

I gave her a kiss on her head. "How was your day today?"

"Pretty wild before we even got in the main entry to school, but I'm sure you already know about that, huh?"

I sighed. "Yeah, I do. Your dad told me all about it."

"Mom, what is going on? Dad doesn't want us to talk about it and he told me and Jodie that you don't want us to talk about it, either."

"I don't," I reconfirmed with her. "Look, honey, I really don't know what's going on, either. It's just that we have people out here who just don't like seeing others happy and they'll do whatever they can to sabotage other people's happiness."

"Did Dad cheat on you?"

"Now who told you that?"

"No one."

"Lorie."

"No one, Mom, *I swear* they haven't. It's just that this sounds like something that has to do with cheating, that's all. I just hope it's not true."

I just didn't know what to say to her because this had everything to do with cheating, and she was just so innocent at this age she just didn't understand that her dad was not perfect. "Like I said, honey, don't talk about this to anyone, no matter how much you're hearing things. These are the times where you're gonna have to be strong more than ever now; you and Jodie. People are gonna do whatever they can to test both of your strengths and will play hard on your weaknesses. This is a private family matter no matter what people try and say. Unfortunately, people's private matters get put on public display all of the time for people's entertainment, and now our family became the latest victims of it. We'll be fine."

"I know we will, Mom. People know not to mess with us at school. Dad is the richest man at our school, and people treat money as power. I know a lot of people are afraid of him because of his size, and his wealth is even bigger than his size. He walked us into school today and it's like everyone was quiet and at a standstill. All he has to do is give an order and everyone will follow it."

I smiled with a nod. "Yes, your dad has a lot of power, but someone is trying to destroy it as you know, and we are not gonna let that happen."

"I know, Mom," she replied with a smile.

"Where's your sister?"

"I'm not sure. She might be in the theater room watching a movie for a class, that's what she told me she was gonna do."

"Okay. You finish your homework. I'll call you when dinner's ready in a few hours."

I headed to the theater room that seemed as if it was miles from here. When I approached it, the doors were shut. I opened the doors to the lights being turned completely off and I was completely disgusted by what I saw on the screen!

A porn movie!

The moaning and groaning and getting down on each other in a classic porn fashion and bad acting and even more bad music made it undeniably this type of movie!

I looked closely as I saw a head moving around as it sat on the love seat that was reserved specially for Lang and me when we watched movies in here. I approached it as I gasped as Jodie was giving her boyfriend Spearo a blow job!

"JODIE!" I screamed.

They both shrieked as it seemed as if they'd jumped right out of their skin!

"Oh, shit! Mrs. West! Oh, shit!" Spearo said, as he pulled up his school uniform pants so fast I honestly think he forgot to pull up his underwear first!

"I'm dead. I'm so fuckin' dead!" Jodie said as her head hung low.

"Turn that off . . . *now*," I ordered.

She picked her phone up out of the cupholder and turned the movie off.

I looked up at Spearo since he stood at six-foot-eight. "Do you have a ride home?"

"I'll call an Uber," he replied.

"And do it while you wait outside for it," I told him. I looked at Jodie. "Go to your room right now. I'll be up there in a few minutes."

I watched as they went in different directions once we all walked out of the theater room as I got on my phone to call Lang. I hung up before it rang.

Several minutes later, I stared sternly at Jodie as I shut her bedroom door behind me. "*That* was the movie you were supposed to be watching for class? Let me guess? For Sex Ed?"

"I haven't taken Sex Ed since freshman year. I got an A in it, remember?"

"Yeah, I remember, so don't try and change the subject. How come you didn't tell me Spearo was going to be here? You know you're supposed to call me or your dad when you want to have him over so one of us can be here."

"I tried calling both of you, but neither one of you answered."

I looked at my phone. She wasn't lying. She did call me while I was still at Maxi's while she told me what she'd found out about my case. I sighed. "You did. I see it on here as more than one missed call. Sorry about that."

"And I'm sorry about what I did, Mom. Please, *please* don't cancel my sweet sixteen party, *please*," she begged.

"You know you're in big trouble, Jodie. I am disgusted by what I saw you doing down there."

"But we didn't actually have sex, Mom, *I swear* we didn't. That was as far as we went."

"And how far would you have gone if I didn't walk in there, huh?"

She sighed. "I don't know, but we would've been careful."

"You weren't that careful, Jodie. You did this in the theater room where anyone could've walked in there since there are no locks on the doors, and you see how I did."

"I didn't think you were gonna be home until close to dinner."

I shook my head. "I don't know what I'm gonna do with you."

"Please don't tell Dad, Mom, *please*."

"I can't promise you that. I don't want you doing that crap in this house. You're too young."

"Everyone's doing it, pretty much."

"You're not everyone!" I snapped. I put my hand on top of my head. I felt a migraine coming on. "Look, I can't deal with this right now so I'm trying not to get as mad as I really am about it. I have enough to deal with."

"Like what's going on with that woman?"

I looked at her. "What woman?"

"The woman who claims to be sleeping with Dad. Mom, *everyone knows* she sent you a text stating this. I know you know what happened to us when Charrod and Dad drove Lorie and me to school this morning."

I sighed. "Yeah, I know, Jodie. I know all about it. So I'm gonna reconfirm to you what your dad told you and Lorie this morning—you are not allowed to discuss this with anyone, and I mean anyone. As much as people wanna make this their business, it's absolutely none of their business."

"I know it's not. My friends knew not to say anything to me about it, but I could tell they know because they were acting strange around me all day today and I knew why."

"Yes, they know, Jodie. They know. I just don't want people putting this family on blast for their entertainment, but they're already doing it that's why you have to be strong to take a stand against it; you and Lorie, and I know the two of you are very strong young ladies."

"We are. But do you know who this woman is?"

"I have no idea."

"Does Dad know?"

I sighed. "I don't know if he knows, Jodie, so don't ask him about it, okay? In fact, don't bring it up to him at all."

"Okay, I won't. I just wanna know if I'm still gonna have my party because everyone is looking forward to it."

I sighed. I couldn't believe that this family's private lives had changed overnight because of one bitch, and all she cared about was whether or not she was still gonna have her party. "I never said it was cancelled, but your dad still doesn't know what you did so that may change." I sized her up in her school uniform. "Wear your other uniform tomorrow since you have two of them because I'm taking the one you have on right now to the cleaners, so change out of it now and give it here."

She cracked a slight grin as she changed out of it and into her loungewear.

Minutes later, I walked down the hall to my bedroom when I received a text:

So, how does it feel to have the whole world know that I'm sleeping with your husband?

I stared at the text. I knew it was from this bitch, but from the very first time she'd sent me a text I knew I could never respond to her again if she started sending them to me again . . . and it was all a matter of time before she had, and the time was now. I forwarded the text to Maxi as Jodie's school uniform hung in the crook of my left arm.

My phone rang in less than a minute.

Maxi.

"Did you get it?"

"Yes, I got it, Blair. Yeah, this is one bold bitch who wants you to know that she's not gonna stop doing what she's doing, huh? Especially since the whole world knows about the first text exchange."

"Yeah, she may be bold right now, but she's not gonna be bold when I get a hold of her."

"Blair. Now you know I don't want you confronting this woman about sleeping with Lang when I find out who she is; let the authorities handle it."

"They're not gonna do anything, Maxi, and you know it. Some bitches need to be put in their place because I have a feeling this isn't the first time she's done this."

"I have a feeling you're right, but I don't want you getting in trouble over all of this, it's not worth it. However, it is worth it to find out who this is because I believe she is not gonna stop until you do."

"Yeah, a classic coward. She can talk all this shit through a text but doesn't wanna confront me face-to-face about sleeping with Lang; telling me to name the place where we can meet the very first time she contacted me. Even if I did, the bitch won't be there."

"Probably not, Blair, but there are other ways of finding out who she is, and I think I'm getting close to doing it."

I perked up. "For real? What have you found out?"

"Well, I don't wanna discuss this with you on the phone and I wanna be sure so let me do a little more work."

"Okay, it's just that you're getting me excited now, especially now since this bitch contacted me again. I need something to get excited about after what I saw earlier here."

"Uh oh! What happened?"

I sighed. "I caught Jodie and Spearo in the theater room watching porn with Spearo all laid back on the love seat—the one Lang and I sit on when we're in there—while she was sucking his . . . his . . . *spear*!"

Maxi busted out laughing! "Never heard it called that!"

"I'm trying not to get too graphic."

"I appreciate it! But please, go easy on her. She knows what's going on and you all don't need any stress on yourselves more than what you already have. I'll give you a call later when I get more info on these other surveillance videos—and just when I thought they gave them all to me."

"I can't wait to see what else they can show. I hope they got his ass on video walking directly to her room because to me it's now clear that he went to some bitch's room that night and stayed there for more than half the night, and I doubt it was work related."

"Work related of a different kind, obviously."

"Yeah, obviously." I looked at my watch. "I'm gonna go help Chef Forrest with dinner. I like doing it because it takes my mind off of things."

"Do what you need to do, honey, and let me do my work here because this is definitely getting more interesting."

"It is. Talk to you later."

"So, anything interesting happen today besides what happened this morning before school started?" Lang asked, and then took a sip of his drink, and then continued to eat as he stared down at his plate.

I glared at Jodie.

"Mom, *please*," she mouthed to me as she pleaded hard with me as she clasped her hands together in a praying pleading hold.

"No, nothing with me," Lorie said with a smile.

"Just had lunch with Maxi again," I said, and glared back at Jodie.

"Again?" Lang asked. "Wow, Blair. You've been having lunch with her a lot lately."

"I've had the time," I replied with a fake smile.

He nodded as he chewed his food. He took another sip of his water. "Jodie."

She froze as she was about to put food into her mouth. "Yes, Dad?"

"How was that test for Business Law?" he asked.

I looked at her as I raised my eyebrows.

"It was easy. I got an A on it," she replied with relief all heard in her voice.

"That's my baby!" he said with a big smile and continued to it.

I stared at Jodie as I could literally still see her breathing heavy. I knew this was gonna be a long dinner, especially for her.

And it was over just like that.

"If you're done, Jodie, then go and help Maritza with the dishes," I said.

"Why does she have to help her with the dishes?" Lorie asked.

"Yeah, why does she have to help her?" Lang asked, and then took a slow sip of his drink.

Everyone was now staring at me.

"Go on," I told Jodie.

She got up with her plate and went to the kitchen with no arguments.

Several minutes later, Lang was in his office working. He'd called me in here to talk to him. He took off his glasses as he stared at me. "How come you're putting Jodie on dishwashing duty?"

I sighed. "She knows why."

"Well, I don't know why; Lorie doesn't know why."

"It's none of Lorie's business."

"But it's my business," he informed me as he glared at me. "Clearly, you're making her do something because she did something; something pretty bad. Something so bad you didn't want to tell me. So, what did she do?"

I sighed as I sat down at the front of his desk. I looked up at the beautiful TVs mounted behind him. "She didn't want me to tell you."

"Too bad, I'm her dad."

I sighed again. "I caught her in the theater room with Spearo watching porn."

His facial expression was of disbelief for a second, then it turned into a grin. "We've all watched porn. We first started around their age and even younger."

"Yeah, I know. I'm no saint. None of us are. But now I'm a mom and have been for 15 years and I don't want that garbage in my house. If my mom or dad caught me watching it, I would've gotten a lot worse than having to do the dishes."

He chuckled. "Yeah, me too." He raised his eyebrows as he stared me down. "But I have a feeling you're not telling me everything."

"I caught her in there polishing his spear."

He busted out laughing!

My mouth dropped in shock! "Lang! How can you think this is funny?!"

"I've never heard it put like that!" He shook his head as he still laughed. I honestly didn't think he was gonna take this to be funny, but then again I did say it in a way he wasn't expecting, but he knew exactly what I was talking about. "I guess the boy's name ain't Spearo for nothing!"

"Lang! Be serious! We're talking about our daughter, here!"

"Yeah, I know." He let out a sigh as he sat back in his chair. "Well, Blair, she was gonna start doing it sometime. We can't keep sex away from her forever. No, I don't like to think about the fact that my daughter is sucking her boyfriend's dick at 15—but she's doing it. Hell, I lost my virginity when I was her age to a 17-year-old senior girl who went to the same all-girls high school you went to."

"Yeah, and what a coincidence because I lost mine when I was 16— weeks after I got my driver's license—to a boy who went to a co-ed religious school that was practically right next to the all-girls religious school I went to. I was only there my junior year."

"And after that you scratched the fuck out, huh?"

"Sure as hell did!"

We laughed.

I sighed. "I just want her to be safe. She's only 15 with her whole life ahead of her and is definitely one of the most privileged girls in this world, especially for a Black girl. I just don't want her doing anything she doesn't have to do."

"Well, apparently, she wanted to do it."

"I don't want them doing it in this house."

"Blair, they're gonna do it wherever they can do it. You know how it is. We've been those ages and had done it numerous times wherever we were able to do it."

"Don't remind me."

"Well, I won't say anything to her about it."

"Good, because she thought if I told you that you would be so mad you would cancel her sweet sixteen party."

"Of course I'm mad about it, but I'm not cancelling anything . . . unless she ends up pregnant."

"And that's exactly what I told her. I just want her to be responsible and not careless. It's just too much of this shit now more than ever with these girls, social media, and this baby mama culture shit. I don't want my Jodie or my Lorie a part of it."

"And neither do I."

His phone rang. "I gotta take this call . . . in private."

I nodded with a smile and walked out of his office and shut the door behind me.

Yeah.

Right.

CHAPTER EIGHT

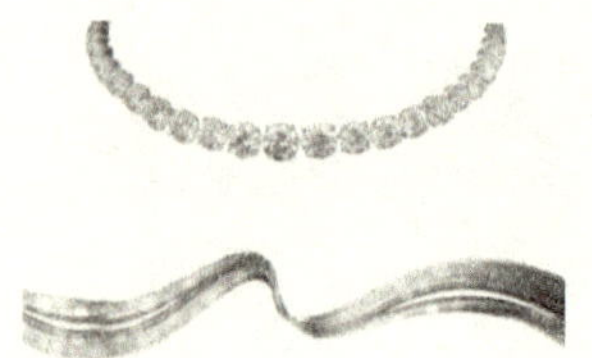

Without any arguing, I went into my office and looked to see if the tea woman had something to say about what'd happened today:

<u>WILD BLACK TEA WITH BEVERLY</u>
DADDY LANG AND TEEN DAUGHTERS MOBBED BY
MEDIA IN ROLLS-ROYCE SUV COMING IN TO
SCHOOL
YES, IT HAS OFFICIALLY STARTED, EVERYONE!
WELCOME TO THE WEST MESS!

"And I know you're all probably asking, 'What?! All of this over a text?' Yes, all of this over a text! It shows just how fascinated people are with a Black billionaire family like the West family who were very private until this happened. The fact of the matter is, there are very few in this world that are like them, especially with them being Black. Whoever this woman is who sent this text did start a big mess in the West household! I wish I knew who she was, but as of today, she still hasn't responded to me since I put out a public request for her to contact me so I can get all of the tea as to why she did this because there has got to be a reason behind it. Usually, you wouldn't want anyone to know that you're sleeping with another woman's husband, but this chick texted the wifey and that's a no-no-NO!"

She picked up her teacup off of the saucer and took a sip out of it. She put the cup down as she shook her head, and then took a bite of her croissant sandwich.

"Some women out there have no damn shame and I mean no damn shame—what a damn shame!" she laughed, and then took another sip of her tea. "But word has it that Daddy Lang was mad as hell and cussed out the headmaster of the most prestigious high school in this state—probably in the world for that matter—about the mob of media this morning, and I admit I saw it firsthand because yes, your girl Beverly was out there! Oh, yes, I was! And let me tell you something, you all. That Rolls-Royce SUV was one of the most beautiful SUV's I have ever seen . . . ever. Shows you just how some people have it like that out there, but all is definitely not well in the land of sunshine, blue skies, bluebells, and butterflies—okay, let me stop!"

She ate some more of her sandwich, took another sip of her tea, and shook her head.

"I'm telling y'all, being close to all of that action today was something to see, and I had to be all up in it because your girl needs to get the best tea she can get when it comes to the West Mess, as I'm now officially calling it! And you could practically hear Daddy Lang yelling obviously at Headmaster Henley through all of the chaos with the windows rolled up and lightly tinted and all, and it showed that I was in the thick of all of it! And I could've swore he told us all to fuck off—but I can't confirm it. Sorry, Lang, we're just getting started on this and I am here for all of the mess and all that ish!

"Oh, and before I get out of here as you all still look at the videos and pictures my assistant and I were able to get of today at the school, there is definitely something going on because Blair has seen her best friend Maxi Bailey more than usual, and we all know her BFF is a PI—private investigator. Yeah, I think we can all put two-and-two together when it comes to this! So stay tuned so you can hear all of it straight from me because I'm gathering info right now that if confirmed is gonna be spilling all of the wild tea!"

"You're not gonna know shit!" I said, as I shook my head and then got off of the computer. I got on my phone and called Maxi.

"Blair, hey. What's going on?"

"Hey, Maxi. I just got done looking at that Beverly woman, the one who says she's got all the wild black tea or whatever."

"Yeah, everyone knows who she is. What about her?"

"Well, as you know, she's talking about me and my family and was out there when Lang took our girls to school this morning."

"Doesn't surprise me. But I'm sure she couldn't get anything out of him just like everyone else, huh?"

"No, she couldn't get anything out of him and she admitted that, but she claims to be gathering information about my family, Maxi. She mentioned you as being my best friend and she knows you're a PI."

"A lot of people know what I do, Blair; stop being so paranoid. She doesn't know I'm working on your case; all she can do is assume that I am."

"But you are."

"But she doesn't know that nor can she confirm it with anyone. I have given my staff instructions on not to answer or give me calls that have to do with you because I know they're just trying to get to you through me, and you know that's not happening."

"I know it's not, Maxi. I just don't want your investigation—that you're doing for me for free when you can be working on other cases— to be blown because of someone like her."

"Relax, Blair. Nothing is gonna be blown. I'm the best at what I do, you know that or else you would not have asked me to take on your case."

I smiled with a sense of relief. I trusted my best friend. "I know, Maxi."

"But she's not the only one who has gathered information, if she wants to claim she really did that."

I jumped up out of my seat! "What did you find out?" I started to pace nervously around my office. I went to the doors and opened one of them and looked both ways down the hall, and then closed the doors and locked them.

"I take it Lang is not around, right?"

"Nowhere in sight."

She sighed. "Look, I got more video of the night the two of you were at the charity event," she informed me.

"You did?!" I asked, as if I didn't believe that she could get any more of it, but she told me they had more to send to her, and she obviously now had it in her possession. "So . . . . ."

She sighed once again. "Blair, you're gonna have to come in here and view this yourself. I need for you to be present to confirm what I'm seeing on it."

"Oh, no! I don't like the sound of this."

"No, you're not gonna like this at all, and I just don't wanna go into detail with everything with you over the phone since I just got this footage no more than an hour ago and I've been reviewing it and taking my own notes and gathering information—*real information*—unlike that Beverly and all of those others."

"What time do you want me there tomorrow?"

"The earliest you can get here."

CHAPTER NINE

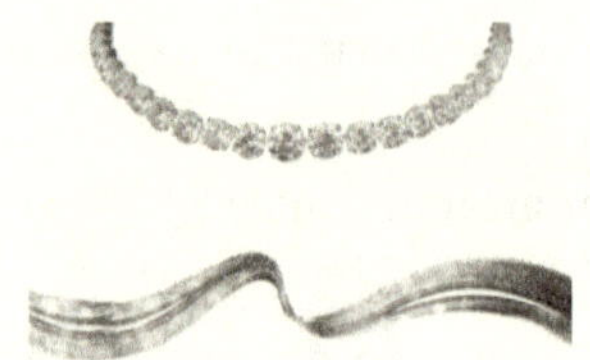

It was 5:00 am. I was up before my girls and Lang were. I sat here in my car in the parking lot of Maxi's firm as I waited for her to get here while a downpour of rain and light rumbles of thunder sounded off in the sky. I actually thought she would be here by now. I checked my phone to see if she'd called me. Not yet.

I looked in my rearview mirror and saw the headlights of a newer model Audi. The car pulled up next to me as I continued to watch it since the windows were deeply tinted. I saw the door swing open and an umbrella pop up and head over to my car.

It was Yusari.

I could see her infectious smile as she waved for me to come out of the car since she was opening the door which was what she did when she knew Maxi would be running late.

"Good morning, Blair," she said as she still smiled at me, and then turned and opened the door.

"Good morning," I replied with a smile. "It's storming like crazy. I'm sorry I came here so early, but Maxi told me to get here as early as I could, and since she said that I actually thought she was gonna be here by now."

"Well, she usually doesn't get here *this* early, but she told me that you would probably be here this early so she told me to get here early to meet you here. But even I didn't know you were gonna show up this early, though!" she said as she laughed.

I laughed as well. "Well, she's got me curious about my case and told me to get here as early as I could. Do you know what it is she wants to tell me?"

"Not at all. She's not discussing your case with any of us," she informed me, as she hung up her umbrella on the coat hanger rack. "You can go to her office. I'll get the coffee started. I also ordered some fresh breakfast pastries as well since I knew Maxi had you coming in early. They should be here soon but there's probably a delay with them getting here because of the storm."

"Sounds great. I'll be waiting," I said with a smile, and headed to Maxi's office.

I turned on the lights as well as the TV and sat down in my usual seat. I could smell the coffee brewing as I was too curious to know what she'd found. Her desk had all sorts of papers all over it. I didn't know where to start or just exercised patience until she got here.

Fuck that.

I got up and started snooping.

I looked through papers as I tried to keep them in place but didn't see anything that looked as if it was related to my case. I couldn't believe I was actually doing this, and I already got tired of doing it. I didn't wanna get caught by Maxi snooping all over her desk, so I sat back down as I tried very hard to keep in mind that I was a client here now before I was her best friend, and she obviously meant business with my case just as much as I did and wanted her to.

I took out my phone and checked my messages and emails, and there was one from Jodie stating that she and Lorie were just leaving to go to school since I left messages on their phones to let them know that I was coming here very early.

My phone rang.

Lang.

"Hey, honey."

"Blair, where are you?" he asked.

"I'm at Maxi's office," I replied. I had no reason to lie.

"What the hell are you doing at her office this early? It's almost 6:00am. I'm in the car waiting for the girls to take them to school. Did you tell them you were leaving this early?"

"Yes, Lang, I told them. I sent them a text."

"And you didn't send me anything. And you still haven't told me why you're at Maxi's office at 5:00 in the damn morning. You can't be having coffee and breakfast pastries with her this damn early."

"Well, I just couldn't sleep, Lang. It's nothing, okay? You know how much I like going to her office. I feel like I work here."

"You might as well."

He hung up on me.

I sighed as I shook my head. I didn't have to tell him anything, especially since he was the reason why I was here. And in a lot of ways, I think he had some idea why I was here; he just couldn't prove it.

Minutes later, Yusari came in with my cup of coffee. "Here you go, Blair. Maxi just texted me and told me she will be here in a few minutes. She had to drop her son off at school today when her husband usually does it, plus, this weather and all."

"I know," I said with a smile. I took a nervous sip of my coffee since I couldn't wait until Maxi got here so I could hear what she had to say and show me what she had to show me. I couldn't sleep at all last night thinking about it despite taking a double shot of cherry Nyquil. "Thanks for the coffee."

"You're welcome," she replied with a smile and closed the door behind her.

Jodie and Lorie got into the back seat of their dad's black Rolls-Royce Cullinan SUV with Charrod at the wheel.

"Girls, did your mom tell you why she was going to Maxi's so early today?" Lang asked.

They looked at each other.

"No, she didn't tell me," Lorie said.

He nodded. "Jodie?"

"No, she didn't tell me, either; just that she was going," Jodie replied. "Why?"

Charrod looked at Lang.

"Just wanted to know," Lang replied. He sighed and shook his head. Charrod pulled out of the garage and drove down the long driveway. "I wish this storm would let up." *In more ways than one,* he thought.

Several minutes later, they arrived at the school with the media respectfully across the street where the cops and school security made sure they stayed. They yelled questions at Lang while they drove up into the entryway of the school.

"Are they gonna be out here every morning?" Lorie asked, as she looked back at them.

"Probably," Lang said as he shook his head. "There's nothing I can do about it except keep them off of the school's property so they're actually in their rights to be here. The minute they step on the property and start asking students and staff about the two of you and especially trying to talk to the two of you, then they're in violation."

"I know, Dad," Jodie said.

Her and Lorie got out the car less than a minute later.

"Have a nice day, girls," Lang said with a smile.

"Thanks, Dad. You too," they replied.

He sighed as he watched them walk into school as other students stared at them as they walked into school as well.

"So, why do you think Blair really went to see Maxi this early?" Charrod asked, as he drove out and off of the school's property.

Lang continued to stare at the media as they drove by them as they shouted questions at him. "I need for you to take me somewhere first before I go into work since I don't have to be there this soon. Hell, I own the damn company."

"Okay. Tell me where."

I sipped nervously on my coffee and then gobbled down my second breakfast pastry as the door flung open and Maxi walked in.

"Good morning, babe," she said with a smile, as she had a breakfast pastry in her hand with her black Louis Vuitton On The Go GM bag on her shoulder as her coffee sat on her desk where Yusari had put it just minutes before since she knew she was gonna be here soon.

"Good morning," I said.

We hugged.

"Wow, I see that you are serious about your case, and I can't say that I blame you," she said, as she took a bite out of her pastry and then a sip of her coffee while she still had on her long tan Burberry Kensington Heritage trench coat, and I coincidentally had the same one in black that I wore today. She put down her breakfast and took off her coat and hung it up on her coat rack. She looked down at all of the papers on her desk. "You weren't trying to go through this mess, were you?"

"No, Maxi. You know me," I lied.

"Damn right I know you," she said with a grin, and then took another sip of her coffee.

"Maxi!" I said with a slight laugh. "Look, I couldn't sleep last night since you told me you have something else you need to show me, and I'm dying here in suspense. I felt like I've been sitting in here all morning."

"I just know you felt like you have, Blair. I can tell how serious you are about your case, and I can't blame you for it. This has gotten worldwide attention now. I wish it didn't get to this point but it's now where it is and we just have to deal with it, right?"

"Yeah, right. So, what else did you find out?"

She picked up her remote and pointed it to the TV since it was already on. This prompted me to turn around and look at the TV. "I was able to get the surveillance footage of the elevators and the floors. Keep watching."

I watched as Lang walked out of the ballroom and walked a short distance down the hall . . . and stepped into one of the elevators! "That son of a bitch! He *never* left the hotel! He *never* left!" I looked back at Maxi as she stared back at me. I could tell she really felt sorry for me.

"I'm so sorry, Blair. It's clear my suspicions about him never leaving the hotel are now officially confirmed when I noticed that the car Charrod drove the two of you in that night never left the front entry of the hotel. I knew Lang was around in there somewhere. Keep watching."

The surveillance then cut to him being on the elevator. There was no one else on there with him. When the elevator stopped, it didn't show what floor he was on.

"Do you know what floor he stopped on?"

"I have no idea. It's clear the surveillance doesn't show that particular side that's inside of the elevator. I think if it did it would've gotten a clear view of it."

"Fuck!" I said as I shook my head. But I continued to watch as the surveillance picked up on the floor where he'd got off of the elevator and headed down the hall. He made a right down a long, wide hall then a left—and stopped in front of a door. I stood up as I saw him scan the QR code on it and open it. "What the fuck? Maxi, what the hell is going on? It's clear he had access to this room!"

"Yeah, Blair, it's clear that he did. You didn't see anyone open the door for him. I think he paid for this room and just put it in a woman's name. You told me you didn't recognize anyone on that list I showed you the first time you were in here about your case, did you?"

"No, I didn't recognize any of the names at all. It was clear he probably paid for the room and put it in her name because of course he didn't wanna put it in his name. Asshole."

Maxi grinned. "Remember, all of this was going on when you were down there in the ballroom at the charity event."

"And he creeped the fuck out to go up to some whore's room and paid for it. This was obviously planned, Maxi. I don't think she would've been there had there not been the charity event going on."

"Yeah, you're probably right, Blair, even though we can't prove it." She shuffled through some of her papers on her desk. She picked up one and looked at it, and then put it back down. "Keep watching," she told me once again.

And I did exactly what she said. My eyes were completely glued to the TV as I watched as Lang left the room, got back into the elevator, and went back downstairs. The other surveillance picked him up as he got off of the elevator and headed back to the ballroom. There was also surveillance of him and me leaving the charity event for the night.

"I see that they definitely got us on surveillance leaving for the night, and definitely got him leaving the ballroom alone and going up to someone's room and staying there for practically the entire time the charity event was going on. Luckily, I had Astrid to talk to as well as others, and they were even asking me where was Lang because they hadn't seen him in a while. Now I have proof that he left the event and went up to that whore's hotel room during it."

"Yeah, he went to someone's room, Blair, but it's unfortunate you didn't recognize anyone on that guest list for that night. If you did, I think I could have actually solved this very fast, and it would've been one of the fastest cases I would've ever solved."

"No, it's very unfortunate that I didn't recognize anyone on that list," I replied as I shook my head. "Damn, Maxi. This is real. This is fuckin' real. He really is cheating on me, and I believe that bitch is not gonna stop taunting me about her sleeping with him. These texts started happening that night, so I know it was that bitch he saw during the charity event. You got to find out who she is."

"And you know I will, Blair."

There was a knock on the door.

"Come in!" Maxi said, as she turned off the TV.

Yusari walked in. "Maxi, David has questions for you about the new case he's working on."

"I'll be right there," she said. She got up. "I'll only be a few minutes."

"Okay, take your time," I replied with a smile.

Maxi closed the door behind her.

I stared at the papers sitting on her desk. I knew she'd shuffled them around, so I knew they were in a different order now. And I knew she'd shuffled them around because she was obviously looking for something. I looked towards the door to see if she was gonna come back in, and then quickly got up and went behind her desk and got a good look at the papers. I gasped at what I saw one paper had said that was sitting right on top of a pile:

POI – Person of Interest "CS" Cordelia Sharpe Rm. 2609

I couldn't believe this! I knew she was leaving something major out when it came to whose room it was that Lang had gone to. I didn't even remember seeing this woman's name on the list, but it was obviously on there. I was serious when I said I didn't recognize anyone's name, but she was gonna recognize me. I took a picture of the info with my phone, and quickly sat back down.

Maxi walked back in less than a minute later. "Sorry, that took a little longer than I thought."

"Um, Maxi, I almost forgot I have a nail appointment in a half hour. I better get going since it's still storming pretty hard and it's across town."

"Oh, okay. Sorry to have held you up."

"Do you have anything else you need to show me?"

"Not right now. I'm still working on where he was when he left y'alls house in the middle of the night. I'm getting close to some information about it."

"And you know you can call me 24/7/365 when you do."

"You know I will."

Minutes later, I got into my car and drove straight to the hotel.

CHAPTER TEN

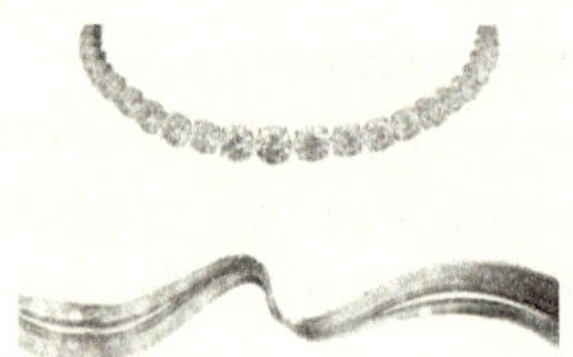

$\mathcal{I}$ arrived at the hotel. And I admitted that it looked different during a stormy early morning than it did on the beautiful clear and calm night we went to the charity event. I immediately took the side street and went to the back entry of the hotel and into the parking lot attached to the hotel. There was no doing that luxury of valet front-of-the hotel parking with one of our cars on full display. Today was a much different day.

I found a spot close to the entry into the hotel and parked there. I knew this room was on the 26th floor so I wanted to be able to get on the elevator and not have to be on it for that long while it ascended to the top floors. I looked in my back seat and saw my Burberry black baseball cap. I grabbed it from the back seat and put it on since my hair was already in a bun. I knew there were cameras all around here catching surveillance of everyone's every move, and there was no way I could avoid them.

I got out of the car and walked inside the hotel and to the elevator. This hotel was downright opulent in every way, shape, and form. The Regalis Montemar was 150 years old. Yeah, very old. My hands practically shook as I pressed the button to go up. I looked every which way I could, and it was dead quiet in here and not a person in sight. This pretty much confirmed to me that I was here very early.

I practically jumped when the door opened to no one in the elevator. I didn't expect it to be full, but I didn't expect it to be empty, either. I guess I was here pretty early and especially on a weekday. I pressed 26 and it started to ascend to the floor I knew Lang was on during the night of the charity event.

What the hell was I really doing?

I had to do this. I wanted to do this. *I needed to do this.*

I just felt that women who do what this bitch had done to me needed to be confronted about what she did because it was already affecting my family, and I was willing to take my chances in finding out who she was myself and confronting her about why she sent me such a nasty, bold text. And that was just the beginning.

Fuck!

The elevator came to an abrupt stop.

I lowered my head since I didn't want anyone seeing who I was. I didn't know if it was gonna be one person or several, but I was about to find out in a second.

The doors slowly opened . . . .

To one of the hotel maids with her large cart of cleaning materials.

"Good morning," she said to me with an enthusiastic smile.

I was glad someone seemed happy.

"Good morning," I said with a smile as I tried to keep my head down. I panned my eyes to the left since her cart was practically pushed up against me because the elevator was small since this was an old hotel. I could hardly believe my eyes.

Hanging from her cart was a lanyard and attached to it was a scanner to get into the rooms!

I suddenly became a person I never thought I would become.

I took the scanner and put it in my coat pocket. I looked up at her as she continued to smile as she looked up at the numbers as they continued to climb to the floor she was waiting to get off on.

Ding!

It was the 25th floor!

"Have a nice day," she said to me.

"Thank you. You too," I replied with a smile as I still had my head lowered.

Holy shit.

That was close!

Ding!

The 26th floor.

I took a deep breath and got off the elevator on my search for the only room on my mind . . . Room 2609.

I felt like I was walking around on this floor for several minutes. I felt already that I was gonna sweat off all of my Jo Malone Nectarine Blossom & Honey cologne, my absolute year-round favorite. I tried to remember when watching the surveillance that when Lang got off of the elevator, he made a right—so I naturally did the same—and then made a left down the hall. I had a feeling I was on the right floor, and I knew that Cordelia Sharpe was still here in a room that my husband paid for because if she wasn't I knew Maxi would not have written down her name as a person of interest.

I walked down the hall a little bit more. I turned and looked to my right . . . .

2609.

I started shaking.

Just what the fuck was I really doing here?

I didn't wanna answer that right now because now I was here. I drove for almost a half hour in very stormy weather just to get here because I had to see for myself who this bitch was. I got even more lucky at a chance in a million with a maid coming into the same exact elevator I was in with her cleaning cart and having her scanner that she used to get into all of the rooms she cleaned up hanging from her cart when I personally thought it should've been hanging like a sacred necklace around her neck. I guess I never looked like a suspect that would steal it from her.

Never trust anyone.

Talk about taking rare chances and acting on a one-in-a-million, one-hundred percent opportunity.

But I was here, standing in front of room 2609. My hands shook as I pulled out my phone and made sure that this was in fact what Maxi had written down. It was. I put my phone back in my purse, pulled out the scanner from my coat pocket, listened closely at the door to see if there was anyone in the room, and put the scanner up to the code.

A green light flashed twice, indicating to me that it worked!

I pushed down the handle as I looked to my left, and then looked to my right as I saw a couple coming around the corner! I rushed into the room!

They missed seeing me by *seconds*!

I was in.

The lights were all off. The bed wasn't made. It was clear that the maid who I'd stolen this scanner from hadn't gotten to this room yet if she worked on this floor. The bathroom door was closed. I knocked on it.

No answer.

I slowly pushed down the door handle and peeked inside.

No one was in here.

Cordelia obviously wasn't here. And I wondered where she went so early in the morning?

I checked out the surroundings including several pairs of expensive high-end designer shoes like Christian Louboutin, Valentino, and Jimmy Choo—just to name a few—that were scattered on the floor. I glared at another very expensive item—a $4,850 Louis Vuitton My LV Heritage Horizon 70 rolling luggage with thick pink and green stripes going right down the middle of it along with the initials "CS" right in the middle of the stripes.

"CS".

Cordelia Sharpe.

I knew I was officially in the right room.

I searched around for anything I could find that connected her to Lang, but all the while making sure I didn't touch anything.

The door opened!

"Who the hell are you?!" a woman standing right at the door asked me as she held a cup of hot tea and a small bag of food in her hands. "What the hell are you doing in my room?!"

CHAPTER ELEVEN

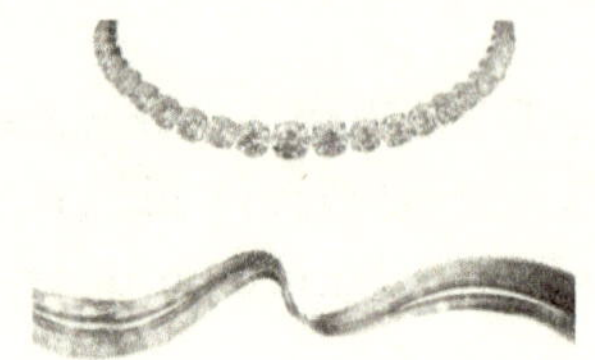

"**S**hut that fuckin' door right now," I said as calmly as I could, since I didn't know if these walls were soundproof or if anyone was gonna walk by in a second.

She stared at me as she did exactly what I'd told her to do. "Who the hell are you?" she asked again.

I shook my head. "You know *exactly* who I am," I replied with a hard-hearted look on my face.

And here I was, standing face-to-face with the bitch who was sleeping with my husband.

"No, I don't know who you are. I've never seen you before in my life," she said, as she was frozen in the same spot. I think she was genuinely shocked that I was actually standing right here in her hotel room and was confronting her about the text she'd sent me.

I shook my head. I knew this bitch was lying. "You've seen me, bitch! And you've *definitely* seen my husband!"

"Don't call me a bitch! I don't know who the fuck you are and what you're doing here inside of my room!"

"Don't you mean *my husband's* room? Since he paid for it? But of course he put it in your name."

"Excuse me, but I paid for this room myself," she informed me.

But she never said she didn't know my husband.

I shook my head once again. "Yeah, you look my husband's type," I said, as I checked out her very light skin, long dark natural hair, and slim body. A Chanel medium black classic bag hung from her right shoulder.

I knew she was being taken care of.

By him.

"Look, lady, get the fuck out of my room before I call security," she threatened. "How the hell did you get in here and talking all of this shit about me and your husband?"

"So, it is true, huh?"

"What is true? Look, I don't wanna have to do this—*don't make me do this*—but I don't want any trouble from you and your husband. You're fucking crazy!"

I continued to stare at her no matter how crazy she thought I was and looked to her. "No, *you're the one* who's fuckin' crazy by messing around with a woman's husband and then taunting his wife—*me*—about it! You wanna taunt me now, bitch? Huh? Yeah, you're not so tough when you're unexpectedly confronted!"

She pulled a gun out of her purse!

"Get the fuck out of my room you fuckin' crazy fool! GET OUT!"

I threw my hands up in the air in shock! Now I knew I had to get the fuck out. And I was the one who was crazy? "This isn't over, bitch! It's not over in the least bit!"

"GET THE FUCK OUT OF HERE, YOU CRAZY BITCH!" she screamed!

But I knew I was pretty much cornered and had to get by her to leave the room. I picked up a large black Christian Dior Lady Dior bag sitting on the table and threw it at her!

She screamed and a shot was fired at me before the bag knocked the gun out of her hands! "BITCH!" she yelled, and came charging towards me!

But she slipped and fell and hit her head hard on the floor!

I breathed heavy as I stared at her. She wasn't moving. I looked at the floor as there were personal things from the bag I'd thrown at her scattered all over it. Her cup of hot tea was spilled everywhere. I picked up her driver's license:

Cecilia Sinclair.

"CS".

My eyes couldn't get any bigger as my hands shook as I once again looked over at her luggage.

"CS".

I felt like I was gonna pass out right along with her. I breathed heavy as I pulled myself together, took one last look at the woman I thought was Cordelia Sharpe, and exited the room.

CHAPTER TWELVE

<u>WILD BLACK TEA WITH BEVERLY</u>
A WBT BREAKING NEWS EXCLUSIVE!
WOMAN FOUND DEAD IN LUXURY HOTEL
SAME HOTEL LANG AND BLAIR'S CHARITY EVENT
TOOK PLACE

"Okay, let's get right into this story, y'all! For those of you who are here for the first time my name is Beverly, and I speak on the wild Black tea more than anyone out there. And I just have to say that when I heard about this story, I had to report it because I definitely believe there is some foul play involved in this. And you know when I say something is a WBT—Wild Black Tea—exclusive, that means you are seeing this story on my channel—*and only on my channel*—for the very first time because I have access to the kind of sources all of the other tea people out there don't have."

She poured tea into her teacup and took a sip.

"Okay, let's get into it because there is a reason why I'm talking

about this story. And this seems like it's some pretty wild shit
because the hotel authorities tried to keep this a secret for business reasons—protecting the hotel, I understand—but you
know they know damn well that people who work there were
gonna find out about it, and what my source who works at the
Regalis Montemar Hotel told me was that a 38-year-old woman
was found dead in her room in the late afternoon when
someone reported that she didn't show up at a seminar she was
supposed to be the keynote speaker at in the early afternoon.
She has been identified as Cecilia Sinclair, a CEO of a
cosmetics company, something like that. She was married with
two children—a girl and a boy. None of them were with her on
this trip. She just checked in to her room last night, that's what
my source had told me. My source also told me that there
appeared to be a fight in the room because there was shit scattered everywhere, including a spilled cup of tea—literally—on
the floor. *I swear* I'm not making this up!"

She grinned and took another sip of her tea.

"So there was obviously someone else in that room with her
who obviously killed her, but her initial cause of death has not
yet been determined, but I think we can all determine that
there was some kind of struggle in there and something
happened between her and someone who was there who obviously got in there and got out of there real fast as they knew
they should've!

"Okay, so you're all wondering what the hell does this have to
do with Lang and Blair West and the fact that the charity event
they went to was held at the same hotel that this murder
happened in? Nothing at all. I see absolutely no connection, but
it did happen at the same hotel and I wanted this reported
because hotels are always covering up shit when bad things
happen there, and this especially caught my interest since it
happened to a Black woman—and a very affluent one at that. I

believe they kept it out of the media because they don't want to lose business, but a woman loses her life in there? How is that fair? Well, this hotel I'm sure already has a lawsuit against it from Cecilia's husband as it should, but most of all, who was the person in that room with her? Oh, we're gonna find that out eventually because I know someone who works in the department of the surveillance security! Stay tuned!"

"*B*lair."

I immediately shut down my computer as I still stared at the blank screen.

Lang walked towards me as he stared at me. "What's wrong with you?"

"What do you mean what's wrong with me?"

"You hardly said a word at dinner; you barely touched your food."

"I just wasn't hungry, that's all."

He sighed as he sat on one of my sofas. "How come I have a feeling you're not telling me the truth?"

"I am telling you the truth, Lang. But if you wanna know the truth even more, I just feel like this shit is not gonna go away when it comes to whoever this woman is who keeps harassing me with these texts."

"I told you I didn't wanna talk to you about this anymore."

"And that's exactly the problem, Lang. We haven't talked about it. I think we need to talk about it."

"Then what about it, Blair? What the hell do you want me to do?"

"Tell me who she is," I said, as I had never given him more of serious look than I'd given him now.

"I have nothing to tell you."

He got up and left.

Tears welled up in my eyes. I knew he was lying. And now there was a dead woman out there because I went to her hotel room thinking she was the one who he was cheating on me with, only to find out it was not her after all.

But I didn't kill her.

Things were now taken to a whole other level, a level that I never thought they would be. And this incident involved me.

I looked at my phone.

Langston West Sex is the BEST! Can't wait to do it again!

I breathed heavy as I tried to control myself the best I could, but ended up throwing my phone across the room.

CHAPTER THIRTEEN

20 Years Earlier

"Maxi, *you know* I have a sociology exam tomorrow. Why do you wanna come to this club tonight?" I asked, as she drove us to the hottest club open during the week, Escape.

She laughed. "You know why, Blair. Besides, I'm coming here to celebrate the A+ I got on my criminology exam, *and* the best night to come here is on a Wednesday night because it's Ladies Night, and when it is we get one free drink."

"No thanks, I don't like that cheap shit they serve for free. I think it's offensive that they would serve it for this night. Shows us what they think of us—well, at least it shows me—that they can't even give us a good, quality drink even if it is for free."

"Well, it's not the best stuff, so at least it's free."

"Yeah, you got that right, but they should respect us more and give us something worth coming here for to get for free."

"So true!"

We laughed as she found a place to park. I felt like this place was out in the middle of nowhere, but it was in the middle of a business area that was very quiet around this time of night, but anyone could tell when Escape was open on one of these nights, especially on Wednesdays which was undoubtedly the best night to come here, because cars were parked everywhere since this was a small club that was in a mini mall.

We walked in but missed the time deadline where we had to be here to get in for free so we had to pay the $5.00 cover charge which was half of what it usually was since it was ladies night. This place was packed as 50 Cent's "In da Club" played throughout it which had the dance floor just as packed as the bottleneck crowd that wasn't dancing on it. I didn't wanna tell Maxi, but I hated coming here when it was this crowded because it always made me nervous—especially with the tragedies that'd happened in other nightclubs recently— besides, the thick cigarette smoke was always nauseating to me and anything else people smoked that they thought they could get away with having in here. There were no tables open to sit at, and the bar looked impossible to even get near it. I already wanted to leave as I tried to mentally study for my test tomorrow.

Maxi took my hand and led me to the bar. I wanted to yank my hand away from hers and call my sister to come get me to take me home even though Maxi and I lived together. I saw very fast that turning 21 and getting into a club legally that I was in fact not missing anything, just as everyone who'd been my age before me had told me.

"It's crowded as fuck in here! I thought we were actually getting here pretty early!" Maxi said, as she pushed her way to the bar, and surprisingly, people made room for us.

"It's a little too crowded if you ask me. It wasn't that serious for me to come here tonight. I just can't stay that long because of the exam I have tomorrow."

"I know, that's why I wanted to get here early so we wouldn't have to stay here that long. I don't wanna be here all night, either. I just thought it would be nice to celebrate my A+ on my exam."

"We could've celebrated back at our apartment, Maxi. There was no need for us to go out," I said, as I tried to get her to wanna leave, but it was clear she wasn't hearing me. Being at the club was her thang, her getaway. In a lot of ways it was mine as well, but I just didn't wanna be here tonight since I just didn't wanna come here every night it was open, and especially when it was this crowded.

We got our drinks with Maxi getting her staple—a Sex on the Beach, and me just getting a Pepsi—and we made our way around the club as people still enjoyed themselves and the music. Suddenly, a couple got up from a booth table, we immediately seized the opportunity and sat down practically faster than they got up.

"Okay, now *this* was just plain luck," I acknowledged.

"Yeah, you're right, it was," she replied with a smile, and took a sip of her drink. "I had a feeling about going this way instead of going the other way!"

"Glad you did!" I said as I looked around. "Why does it seem so crowded in here tonight more than usual?"

"It really is. This is really the only club that's open in the middle of the week and has a ladies night at that. There are almost ten women here to one man."

"It's usually always like this on any night at a club, Maxi. Even though we're only 21, we should definitely know that by now."

"Yeah, I know it by now. I also know that I'm always seeing the same people here, too, male and female. And even if we go to a different club, the same people show up there as well."

"That's for sure. Remember how we thought it was gonna be so fun and exciting going to clubs that were 21 and over? And now here we are. Ain't nothing different from the teen clubs we went to in high school, except the serving of alcohol."

"My brother warned me about it, and now I have to say I believe him!"

"Me too!"

We continued to laugh, but there was something serious I wanted to talk about, and I was actually glad now that we were in a public place because I didn't know how she was going to take what I had to say.

"Um, Maxi?" I said.

"Yes?" she said, as she bobbed her head to the music.

"I'm thinking about not going back to school for the fall semester," I informed her.

She looked at me as if I'd just given her some devastating news. "What? Blair, are you serious? Why?"

I shook my head. "I just don't think things are working out for me there. I don't even know if college is even for me after all because it's not for everyone."

"Well, you're not everyone, Blair. You're Blair Claxton. A very beautiful and smart girl. I never thought I would be hearing this."

I sighed. "Maxi. I didn't say I was quitting school permanently; I just need to take some time off because I don't even know what I wanna do. I'm not like you being set on being a private investigator. I said I wanted to do that, too, at one point. Then I switched to communications, and then to this and then to that. I honestly don't know what I wanna do and I thought I would by now. I'm only 21 years old. Am I really supposed to be this confused about what I wanna do with my life?"

"Not at all. A lot of women got married and had kids right out of high school. They never even gave college a thought or even a chance. But times have changed, Blair. You don't have to follow what everyone else is doing. College definitely isn't for everyone. I just don't want you making bad choices because I think both of us have done pretty damn good at not making them so far, although we're not perfect."

"Yeah, we got through high school, didn't we? And we'll get through other things. I know I'm in my third year in college and I just feel like if I haven't figured it out now about what I wanna do then I need to take some time off and work until I do. My sister immediately went to work out of high school since she said college was not for her."

"Like I said, it's not for everyone. But don't your parents want you to finish since they did?"

"Yeah, they do, but it's my life, not theirs."

"That's definitely true."

Maxi and I finished our drinks at the same time, and minutes later, one of the bartenders brought over new drinks for us. We both exchanged looks of confusion.

"Um, we didn't order a second round," Maxi told him.

"I know. He ordered them for you," the bartender let us know.

Maxi and I looked to where the bartender pointed, and we stared into the eyes of one of the most gorgeous guys I'd ever seen. I mean, he was so gorgeous I could not put it into words, and I just didn't know if he was interested in me and was just being courteous by buying Maxi one as well since she was sitting with me, or he was interested in her and was being courteous by buying one for me just because I was sitting with her.

"Fuck! He's fucking fine!" Maxi said.

"He is," I replied with a smile.

"Have you ever seen him here before?"

"No, I can honestly say I haven't. Remember, we don't come here every Wednesday."

"But we've been here enough where I would definitely remember him because any woman would remember him."

"You're right about that!"

We laughed as I looked up and he was headed to our table!

"Oh my god, Maxi! He's coming over here!"

"It's about time!" she said with a nervous laugh.

But he wasn't alone. He approached our table with a friend.

"Hello, ladies," he said, as he stared at me.

"Hi," Maxi and I said in our sweet, flirty voices.

"I'm Langston West III; Lang for short. This is my friend, Kamden."

We all exchanged pleasantries.

"Please, have a seat," I said.

Langston sat next to me, and Kamden sat next to Maxi. Looks like this was gonna be a great night after all.

"So, we've never seen the two of you here before. Is it y'alls first time here?" Maxi asked, and took a sip of her drink Langston bought us.

"It's not my first time, but it's my boy's first time," Kamden said with a smile.

"He's right, it is," Langston said. "I see what I've been missing since it is my first time; what I've *really* been missing." He smiled as he sized me up.

I didn't know how I felt about him doing this, but he was hot as all hell, but realistically, I just didn't know how far this was gonna go with him.

"Told you, man, that this place is the ultimate escape! They named it this for a reason!" Kamden said, and took a sip of his drink.

"They sure did," Langston said with a smile. His eyes wandered into the crowd, and then focused back on me. "So, what do you ladies do for a living?"

"We're college students," Maxi answered for us.

"And some fine ones at that," Kamden said with a smile.

"That's for sure," Langston agreed as he kept his sexy stare on me.

"Thank you," Maxi and I said once again in our sweet, flirtatious voices when men complimented one or both of us.

"What do the two of you do?" I asked.

"I own a tech company. Been in business for five years," Langston replied. "My man right here works with me. We're partners."

"That's great," I said, and I really meant it. "I like to see more Black-owned tech companies."

"They're out there, but we're the best," Kamden said matter-of-factly.

"I'll drink to that," Langston said, as they touched their cups together.

Maxi and I smiled at each other.

I looked at the time. "I'm really sorry but I gotta get going. I really need to study and rest up for a big sociology test I have tomorrow afternoon."

"Then what are you doing here?" Langston asked with a grin.

"Maxi can answer that for you," I said as I glared at her.

She grinned back and took a sip of her drink so she wouldn't have to answer.

"Well, where do you live? I can take you home. Did you drive here?" Langston asked.

Maxi looked at me and raised her eyebrows.

"No, Maxi did. We live together," I informed him.

"Go on, Blair. I'll be just fine," she said as she looked at Kamden for assurance.

"She sure will be," Kamden replied as he put his arm around her.

I started to get up which prompted Langston to get up. "See you later. Nice meeting you, Kamden."

"Nice meeting you, too, Blair," he replied with a big smile.

Langston slapped hands with Kamden. "See you tomorrow." He let me go ahead of him as we made our way through the crowd and had finally made it to the front door.

And I couldn't help but notice just how many women were checking Langston out. I felt lucky already.

"LANGSTON! LANG! LANGSTON!" a female voice could be heard shouting through the crowd.

I looked back at the door as we walked through it and outside where just as many people hung out waiting for closing time. "Did you hear someone calling your name?"

"I didn't hear a thing," he replied as he stared straight ahead. "It was loud as hell in there like a typical club always is. C'mon, my car is over here."

I followed him over to where his car was as a crowd cleared the way for him to get to a yellow Lamborghini Murcielago. "Is this your car?" I had to ask with a sound of surprise I just couldn't hide. And it just slipped out.

"It's my car," he confirmed with a smile and unlocked the doors and opened the passenger's side door for me.

"Thank you," I said, as I couldn't believe this was actually happening. And just to think I didn't even want to come here tonight.

He got in on the driver's side and pulled off and out of the parking lot as all eyes were on us. "It's brand new for this year. Always wanted one."

"Business must be great," I said with a smile, as I took in this ride because I just didn't know if I would ever be in this car again after tonight.

"It is. And being a Black man with an athlete's build, I'm always mistaken as one so people automatically assume that's how I got this car."

"They're ignorant," I replied. "Not every Black man is an athlete and does not have to be to get cars like these and live a great life."

"I'm glad you see that, Blair. I like you already," he said with a smile.

I smiled back at him.

"So, where do you live?" he asked.

Now seeing that he was for real, I didn't really want him to know where I lived even though he offered to take me home. "You're going in the right direction. It's pretty out of the way from here."

"I'm going in the direction of my home as well. Do you want to come to my place instead for another drink?"

I stared out the window. Now he was pretty much showing me what he had in mind the whole time. "Sure," I said anyway, as "Come Go with Me" by Teddy Pendergrass came on the radio.

He smiled as he looked at me. "Love this song."

"Me too. Old school is the best."

"There's nothing else like it."

Now I was really wondering what he had in store for me once we got to his house. But I had to admit that I was enjoying a ride I never thought in a million years I would be taking with a gorgeous man I met at a club I patronized regularly and wasn't even gonna go to tonight if it wasn't for Maxi's pushiness. Now I'm glad as hell that she pushed me!

But what was I really doing?

I would know that once we got to his house if this was a good decision to leave with him or not.

CHAPTER FOURTEEN

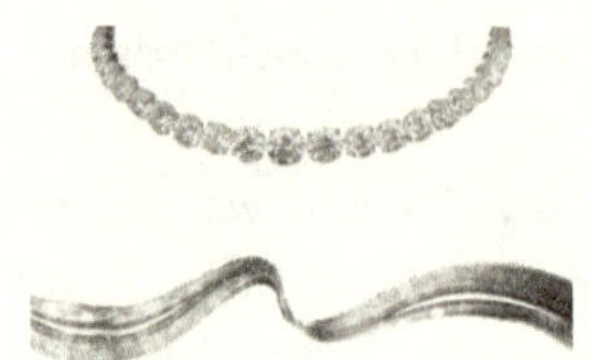

I checked out the beautiful surroundings as I had my window rolled slightly down as a gentle warm breeze came into the car while the night sky was filled with stars. And I felt like a star being in a car like this.

"So, what are you studying?" he asked me.

I chuckled. "I honestly don't know. A little bit of everything, I guess."

He laughed. "A little bit of everything. Interesting answer."

I sighed. "That's because I honestly don't know what I wanna do. I thought since I would be in my third year that I would know by now, but I really don't. I'm constantly changing my mind and I hate that I'm always doing it. I just can't seem to settle on anything. I was just telling Maxi before you bought us a second round of drinks that I'm probably just gonna take some time off from school because I really feel I need to at this point. I'm 21 years old and I feel like I've been in school since I was 2 years old."

He smiled. "Sounds like you do need to take some time off. Nothing wrong with that."

"But I'll have to get a job."

"To buy some more of those fancy bags you got, huh?" he asked, as he stared at my Louis Vuitton Murakami black multicolor pochette on my lap.

"Yeah, I believe in working hard for what you want, but I paid for this off of one of my many credit cards which I regret getting them because I have a hard time paying them off now. I had no business buying it because it cost a few hundred dollars, but I just had to have it since these pieces from the Murakami collection are very hard to get your hands on. They're the hottest bags of the spring and summer and I think it's gonna be like this for years to come."

"It's definitely an eye-catching little bag, that's for sure. But is there something wrong with having a job? You don't like to work?"

"Well, I've never had a job. I didn't have one in high school because I didn't have to have one since my parents both worked —and they still do—and provided a decent living for me and my younger sister. They also had saved enough since we were born to pay for our college tuition until we graduate, well, just me now. My sister's only 18 and just graduated from high school last year and she said college just wasn't for her, so she works full-time at a clothing store."

"You have a younger sister? Is she as beautiful as you?"

I blushed. "She's beautiful."

"Wow," he said, as he kept staring at me at a stoplight. "I was gonna ask you how old you were until you told me."

"Yeah, I'm only 21 years old, but I already feel like my life isn't going anywhere."

"Now don't say that. Your life is just beginning. You're young, beautiful . . . and I assume single?"

"You assumed right. I haven't had a boyfriend since high school."

He nodded with a smile as he made a turn, and we seemed as if we were in a very wealthy area very fast.

"Um, how old are you?" I asked, as I checked out these huge homes. I'd never been in this area before.

"28," he replied with a smile. "Am I too old?"

"No, I don't think so. Not at all."

He nodded once again with a smile as he concentrated more on the road, and then made a right into a guard-gated community but pressed a button on a remote to go through a side-gated entry. I immediately saw for myself as we slowly went up the road that he definitely lived a life most people could only dream of, and he was only 28 years old. He was obviously doing something right; something very right.

I tried to suppress a gasp when he pulled up into a circular driveway of one of the most beautiful homes I'd ever seen up this close in person. There was no doubt to me that he was for real. Very real. We weren't even inside his house yet and I couldn't wait to tell Maxi this!

He parked in the front of the house as I still sat in the car in amazement.

"Is there anyone else here?" I asked.

"Not a soul," he replied with a sexy smile. "I live alone."

He opened the front door and my mouth almost hit the floor. I felt like I'd just walked into the front doors of a king's palace. I always dreamed of a double staircase with beautiful, fancy black French wrought iron spiraling down them, and standing on these white marble floors that I could pretty much see my reflection in made me not want to take another step.

"Should I take my shoes off?" I asked.

"That's not necessary," he said with a slight chuckle. "A lot of people do ask that."

"I bet," I said with a smile.

"C'mon to the rec room," he said.

I followed him through this beautiful house as I took in a life I could only dream of living. He had so much already at his young age, but at the same time, it seemed very lonely if you didn't have anyone special in your life to share all of this with. And I had yet to find out if he had anyone because he never told me he didn't, and that was also a red flag to me when it came to a potential serious relationship.

He turned on the lights to his state-of-the art rec room, and it had everything a person who loved to entertain could want and more. A huge screen TV, bar, pool table, and a very impressive and sharp organized collection of DVDs—*everything*.

"Wow, this looks better than Escape. You could give them a run for their money by having a Ladies Night over here. I bet all of the women will come over here in droves instead of going there."

He laughed. "Now that's what I *don't* want," he informed me. "Escape can have and keep all of that."

"You just like picking women up from the club and bringing them or her here, huh?"

He grinned and then broke out into a chuckle. "Sometimes." He went behind the bar. "What do you want for a drink?"

"Just some water," I said. "I have an exam tomorrow, so I don't need anymore alcohol. Two was enough. I don't want any hangovers."

"I understand," he said, and got me a bottle of water out of the refrigerator behind the bar.

"Thanks," I said, as I sat on the couch facing this huge TV. I still couldn't believe I was over here.

"You're welcome," he said with a smile. "So, since you're only 21 and a college student but don't know if college is for you after all, where do you see yourself 20 years from now?"

"*M*rs. West?"
I looked around to Maritza staring at me. She literally snapped me out of my trance from the past. "Yes?"

"Maxi is here to see you."

"Thank you," I replied with a smile. I continued to look out the window in my office at a storm that seemed as if it would not let up as the rain came pounding down faster and harder. And I'd caused just as much of a storm now since a woman I thought Lang was cheating on me with was now dead, and even though I didn't physically kill her, she was dead because of me being somewhere I had no business being after all.

Maxi came walking in the room minutes later. "Good morning, babe," she said to me, as she had her work bag with her. She was going into the office in the afternoon since she said she had something else she wanted to show me, but I just didn't know if I wanted to tell her what I wanted to tell her.

"Good morning," I said with a weary smile.

We hugged.

She looked back at me as we headed to my conference room which was inside of my office but had its beautiful separate double glass doors which were already open for her to walk right in. It had a beautiful white marbled conference table with matching chairs that seated twelve, and 100-inch TV mounted on the wall at the other end from where my seat was. "Love this room. If I didn't have to be at the office all of the time, I would talk about your case all of the time in here."

"Yeah, I get a lot of use out of it when I wanna have the private ABWS meetings. And I would definitely prefer for us to talk about it all of the time here. I feel it's the ultimate privacy."

"It most definitely is," she said, and took one of the pastries I had waiting for her, as well as a cup of coffee. She took off her coat and sat down, and started pulling things out of her bag, including her computer.

I sat at the head of the table which was my normal seat as she sat adjacent to me on the left. "Do you remember when we met Lang?" I asked as she tried to get organized.

"Of course. It was 20 years ago. My goodness, has it really been that long?"

I smiled. "It most definitely has. And I will never stop thanking you for forcing me to go there that night because if you didn't, I feel my life would've turned out very different."

"I just knew there was another reason why I wanted to go besides acing that criminology exam and forcing you to come with me. But it was definitely a memorable night."

"And you still haven't spoken to Kamden since, huh?"

"Damn! That's a fuckin' blast from the past! Sure haven't. We just sloppy-drunk fucked and that was all there was to that potential relationship. A one-night stand at its finest. But I personally think it was the wrong move for him to quit working with Lang. He lost billions because of it."

"Well, Lang told me that Kamden decided that the tech industry was not his thing after all and he really didn't contribute much at all to growing the business, either. He just more liked the idea of owning it with Lang. Lang was all about the business and growing it and he was serious and wanted someone just as serious. He told me numerous times since we'd been together that he was gonna fire him, and I think Kamden knew it, so he quit to pursue his real dreams of being a rapper —but that clearly didn't work out because he was horrible, even though I never told him that and neither did Lang. He got into music producing but just produced music for a bunch of talentless people who were desperate to be on an album cover and to be stars, and that went nowhere. I don't know what he's doing now."

"And who cares? I really dodged a bullet with that one! I could sense that in him, too. Well, at least one of us hit the jackpot that night."

I sighed. "Yeah, but you know it hasn't been everything people think it has been, but I will admit I would've never imagined in a million years that I would be married to a Black billionaire before he even became a billionaire—but it happened. And everything seemed like it happened so fast between me and Lang after that night. I slept in one of his guestrooms that night and he took me to school the next day; I took that test—got a C+ on it—and I was happy with that grade since I was flat-out tired of school at that point. He asked me to be his girlfriend only after two months of dating, and his family welcomed me with open arms. I didn't go back to school in the fall as I thought about not doing, but it was for the last reason I thought it would be for—because I didn't have to. All I had to be was a great girlfriend to Lang, and I was that and everything he wanted and more. We got engaged within 6 months and married in just two years after meeting each other."

She smiled with a nod. "It was like a fairytale, Blair, and I witnessed it from the start. A lot of people were envious of you, especially the women."

"But everything was already in motion for Lang to make it as far as he has. I'm glad he wanted to share his life with me and let me continue to build with him as well as us starting a family so we could create that generational wealth, and we have."

"You most certainly have, Blair," she said with a smile.

"But some woman wants to take it all away from me."

"And you're not gonna let her do that because if she hasn't by now, she's not going to."

I nodded as I focused back on the present instead of constantly thinking about the past because the present was definitely gonna determine the future, especially now. But I just didn't know if I wanted to ask her if she'd heard about Cecilia Sinclair, especially since Beverly had already talked about the story.

"Um, can I see that list again of the people who were guests that night at the hotel when the charity event was going on?"

"Absolutely." She pulled it up on her iPad and gave it to me.

I put my eyeglasses on and carefully examined it this time, much more carefully than I did the first time . . . and I saw a name:

Cordelia Sharpe: Room 2609

I completely missed her name the very first time, but if I did see it, I still didn't recognize it. I only knew about it because I was snooping on Maxi's desk and saw that she'd written down that she was a person of interest.

I checked over the list one more time. There was no Cecilia Sinclair anywhere on this list. She really did check in that night before, making it obvious that Cordelia checked out probably that same morning.

I was one day late.

"Any names ring a bell this time around?" she asked.

I sighed. "No," I informed her, and gently shoved her iPad back to her.

She stared at me as she put it on the left side of her. She looked at the TV. "Turn it up!"

I stared at the TV as I turned up the volume on it:

"My name is Omar Sinclair. I'm standing here in front of the Regalis Montemar Hotel for a reason everyone knows all too well. I believe my wife, Cecilia Sinclair, was murdered right in her hotel room at this hotel across the street from where we're all standing. Sources have told my lawyer that there was a struggle in the room, but no one had seen anyone or heard anything. I call bullshit on that. Someone walked into that room and murdered my beautiful wife, and now have left her two children without a mother. They are inconsolable. Whoever has any information about my wife's murder needs to come forward now with the information they have. It's not an option. Thank you."

Maxi looked at me. "Did you hear anything about this?"

"No," I lied. I could barely get it out. I felt sick. I knew I didn't kill her, and I was hoping that the truth would come out about that. I changed it to another station.

Lang sat in his office as he'd just got done watching Omar's plea to the people watching him on TV. He continued to watch as the media asked him questions as his business partner and friend Rodney Moore, who now made up the Moore in West-Moore Tech, Inc., stood next to his desk and watched it with him.

"Damn. That's messed up. These hotels will do anything to cover shit up, and you know they're really doing it since she was a Black woman, although she looked mixed."

"Did you know who she was?"

"Not at all. I saw the story for the first time on that tea woman Beverly's channel since she reported on it before this mainstream media did. My wife watches Beverly all of the time and showed it to me. Everyone seems to be talking about it on social media just as much as they're talking about who's been sending your wife those texts about sleeping with you. Can't believe this happened at the same hotel you both went to for the charity event."

"Yeah, that's what I can't believe," he replied, as he stared at the TV. His personal phone rang. He looked at it. "I gotta take this call, man."

Rodney nodded. "By all means," he said with a nod, and left the office. He shut the door behind him.

Lang answered his call. "Hello? Yeah . . . yeah, I saw it. We need to talk."

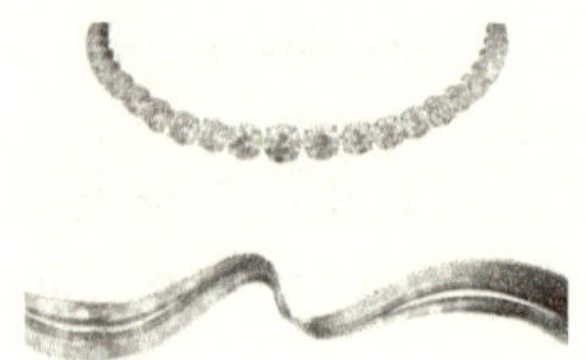

CHAPTER FIFTEEN

I continued to stare at the TV in my conference room as Maxi talked on the phone to one of her investigators about a case completely unrelated to mine. I couldn't believe that Cecilia's case was now in the mainstream media—and I had everything to do with why it was. I had gotten myself into some deep shit over something that absolutely did not have to happen. I owed it to Omar and his kids to own up to what I did and explain what really happened in that room and why, but in this case, I was now the fuckin' coward.

Maxi shook her head as she hung up the phone. "Why be an investigator if you can't properly investigate? Sometimes I wonder why he got into this business, especially since he graduated from Harvard."

I cracked a smile. "No one does it like you, huh?"

"Well, I absolutely try to do my best to try and make sure the best gets hired to work at my firm, but some can definitely slip through the cracks," she said, as she continued to look at her computer. "Speaking about what'd happened in that room to that woman? Cecilia Sinclair?"

I stared at her. "Yeah? What about it?"

"Since hearing about it, I requested surveillance of the morning she was murdered to see who went to her hotel room because it could have some connection to your case I'm working on even though I don't know that for sure. They said they will try and get it to me today."

I felt faint. I tried to cover myself up as much as I could, but now she would probably know it was me who went to the room. Everything was fitting with the room number that Cordelia Sharpe had, and that she checked out the morning or afternoon before Cecilia Sinclair checked into the room that same night before, and me confronting the wrong woman the very next morning after Cordelia checked out and Cecilia checked in. Maxi was really on her job with my case in wanting to find out who this was who went to room 2609 that morning since she knew Cordelia was in the room prior. She knew whoever "killed" Cecilia Sinclair was after Cordelia Sharpe.

Fuck.

Maxi looked at her computer. "I got the surveillance," she informed me.

I was almost visibly shaking. "You do?" I squeaked out.

She nodded as she kept looking at her computer. "This is the surveillance from you and Lang's penthouse that night of the charity event—the one you think he went to?"

For some reason, I breathed a big sigh of relief to myself. "Yeah, I think he did go there, so it shows him there?"

"I'll send you the link so you can put it on the big screen," she said.

Minutes later, we were watching the security surveillance from the penthouse on the mounted TV.

"Pay attention to the time," she told me.

"Yeah, he was definitely there at 3:00 in the morning just as I suspected. That's a private elevator that goes up to the penthouse as you know," I said, as I watched Lang ride in the elevator—alone—up to our penthouse. "I just don't understand why he went there that late. It had to be because of another woman. *I know* he saw another woman that night."

She sighed. "Looks like he did, Blair. Keep watching."

I shook my head as I watched as the time stamp stated that it was 1:39 am, and it showed a woman riding up our private penthouse elevator! "I knew it! I knew it! She wore that big hat and has her hair up in it for a reason because she obviously knows there are cameras in there so it makes me believe that she's been there before. She was up in my family's penthouse for almost two whole hours before he got there—*two whole hours*?! What the fuck was she doing in there?"

Maxi shook her head. "Your guess is as good as mine."

"But I knew what he mainly did with her and why he left that late when he knew I would be in a deep sleep. Yeah, he got me—he got me the best way he could—while I was in a deep sleep."

"So, you don't recognize her at all?"

"No, I can't see her face at all so I don't know if I would recognize her or not, but now I'm getting the feeling that this was a different woman than who he went to see at the hotel."

"It's definitely a different woman, Blair," she informed me.

I looked at her. "How do you know that as an absolute fact?"

She sighed. I knew she wanted to tell me something. "Blair, I'm gonna ask you one last time. *Are you sure* there was no one on that hotel guest list you recognized?"

"No, I didn't recognize anyone. Why are you so adamant about me recognizing anyone on that list?"

"Because I was able to find out the room Lang went to that night."

"What?!" I said, as my voice practically echoed throughout the room.

"Yeah, I was able to find out through a lot of research. Do you know a woman by the name of Cordelia Sharpe?"

It had never gotten as real as it had right now.

"No, never heard of her. I saw her name on the list, but I didn't recognize it."

"She was the main person of interest on the list, Blair. I sought her out because I found out when Lang went to the 26th floor, there was nothing but older couples on that floor for that night; got their names and private info from the hotel staff since they know I'm a private investigator, so they fully cooperated with the investigation. She was the only one who fit who Lang could've potentially saw, and I found out that he did in fact go to her room that night of the charity event because there's a different camera angle on the floor when he arrived at the room which clearly shows the room number—2609—but she was not at the door when he opened it." She looked at her laptop. "They said they would send me that footage after I reviewed it on a private link they sent to me to look at it, but they have yet to send it personally to me for my records."

"I believe you," I said. But I knew what was done had been done and there was nothing I could do about it.

"But I honestly think someone was looking for Cordelia and could've mistaken Cecilia for her. I mean, what are the odds of that happening where two people—back-to-back—end up with the same hotel room with the same initials? Not likely, but it does happen and obviously happened in this case."

"Did she pay for the room herself?"

"She did," she confirmed. "I haven't found out much about her, only that she is from out of town, so I don't know what she was doing here. She was obviously here on business."

"Yeah, here on business with my husband."

She grinned. "I'm trying to find out more about her, Blair, you know I am."

"Yeah, you know I know, and you know I always appreciate it. Everything you're doing for me I appreciate it."

She smiled. "I know you do," she said as she typed on her computer. "I just sent you links to her social media pages. Most of them are private, though."

I pulled them up on my computer. "Yeah, she looks like Lang's type. He's never dated an unattractive woman in his life . . . or fucked around on me with one. Looks like she's pretty well off, too . . . and married to an owner of a string of Black banks across this country and they have four kids? Has her own educational business? So, what the fuck is she doing fucking around with my husband?"

"Your husband is one of the richest Black men in this world, Blair. Most women, if given a chance, would mess around with him no matter what their marital status is."

"But how could she be so damn bold and taunt me about it, though? When she has her own damn family at that. Why can't people just be happy with who they're with?"

"That's a great question. It just seems like living how well they live is never good enough and they don't realize it's much better than how most people live in this world."

"It is. I know I don't take for granted who and what I have, and I don't want to lose who and what I have to this bitch or any bitch who can't be happy with her status in life."

"I know, Blair. But you don't have an ordinary husband, especially with him being a Black man, so if any woman gets that chance to be with him and he unfortunately gives in, then they're really not gonna have any problem giving in to temptation. Hey, Erwin is my husband and has been for 15 years. He may not be a billionaire, but he has a great job and I have great one and we have great kids and live very well within our means . . . so it helps to have a best friend whose husband *is* a billionaire!"

"Maxi!" I said with a laugh.

She laughed as she started putting her things back into her bag. "Well, let me get going. I promised my staff lunch today and I rarely do that, plus, I need to work more on your case at getting more information. I haven't done much field work on it since the surveillance systems that they've sent to me have really been helpful, but I'm really waiting on that other surveillance now of who went to Cecilia's room thinking Cordelia was still up in there."

"Do you think it was Lang? You know, since he knows I'm on to him about this?" I hated putting my own husband in my place, but he was the one who put everything in motion for all of this to go down to begin with.

"Well, the surveillance will definitely show me whether or not it's him since it showed him going to her room the night of the charity event and leaving it, so I know if they have that kind of footage then I know they got it of him going to her room again. Since the receipts are the receipts since she was confirmed to have paid for everything, maybe he thought she was still there. We'll find out who it was, Blair, I promise."

And this was one thing I was hoping she wouldn't find out. All I could hope at this point was that I covered myself good enough from the cameras because she was gonna get this footage whether I wanted her to or not, and there was no way I was gonna be able to intercept it at all.

CHAPTER SIXTEEN

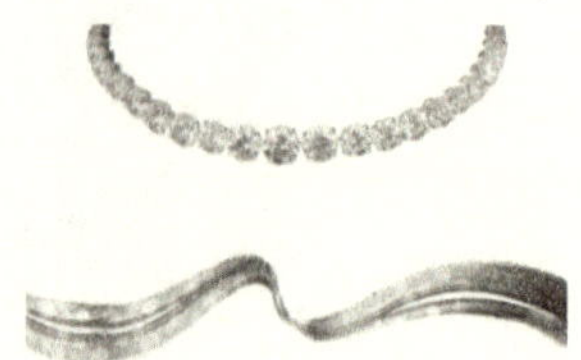

"I've always meant to ask you something," Spearo said, as him and Jodie laid in bed together in her bedroom.

"What's that?"

"How come you've never been to my house?"

"I don't wanna go in that neighborhood, and I couldn't even if I wanted to. My parents won't allow me to, it's too dangerous."

He sighed as he shook his head. "It's not dangerous, Jodie."

"Well, tell that to them. I'm gonna be getting my driver's license soon and hopefully the car I want when I have my party, so I'll probably be able to sneak off to see you."

"*Sneak off?* If you have to do that then it seems like you're ashamed to be with me, Jodie."

"What makes you think that?"

"What do you think? C'mon. Don't answer a question with a question. I hate that shit. We've been together since the middle of sophomore year and you've never been to my home. We're juniors now in case you didn't know. You've never met any of my family and neither have your parents. They know about you and know we go to school together. They think I'm lying about you being my girlfriend despite all of the pictures and videos we share on our social media pages with us showing proof that we're in a relationship—and a serious one at that. I'm lucky to be going to that school since I got in all because of basketball, but the first reason was to get a great education."

"And you're getting the best of both worlds. I just can't go to your home, Spearo, especially now since I'm still in deep shit with my parents for what my mom caught us doing in the theater room that day. I don't wanna get in trouble with them again."

"Then what am I doing here?" he asked with a grin.

"They never said I couldn't see you again and especially have you back over here."

"Your parents know I will never let anything happen to you."

"Yeah, but something still can, Spearo, you know that."

He sighed once again as he looked up at the ceiling. "So, what is up with what's going on with your parents and that woman and her texts?"

"Nothing that I know of. They really don't talk to me and Lorie about it at all. I can tell they never talk about it with us around as if we don't know what's going on. The shit is everywhere about what's going on."

"Yeah, you got that right. But it looks like your dad scared the kids at our school enough not to bring it up to you and Lorie, and no one has asked me about it either because they know not to. Do you think they will ever find out who started all of this?"

She shrugged. "I have no idea. I mean, it's not like it's having such a drastic effect on my life or Lorie's. All I care about is my party and I don't want anything such as this stupid shit about a text some bitch sent to my mom about sleeping with my dad to ruin it."

He grinned as he had his arm around her as she laid her head on his chest. "There's more to life than a big super sweet sixteen party, Jodie."

"I know there is, but that's their problem having to deal with that crap; I don't want anything to do with it. Why should I suffer because of it? Or Lorie?"

"Well, I don't think the two of you are suffering; not living a billionaire lifestyle you're not, especially as young Black girls. But stuff will affect you no matter how much money you got. Your mom seems pretty stressed about it and your dad does, too."

"They'll work it out," she concluded. She looked up at one of her three 55-inch TVs mounted on her wall, and saw a car headed into the front entry of the home! "Get up! Get up! My mom is coming up the driveway!"

Spearo jumped up out of the bed as if it was on fire! "Oh, shit! Don't wanna be caught again! Shit!"

Jodie grabbed her phone. "Hello? Maritza? Could you come to my room and make up my bed right now? Yes, right now!"

I walked up the stairs and down the hall and came up on Lorie's study room. I waved at her since I could tell she was watching something on her TV that was clearly related to her homework; she smiled and waved back. I walked down the hall some more and came up on Jodie's study room where she was in it with Spearo as it appeared they were actually working instead of engaging in other activities more pleasing to them.

"Hi, Mom," Jodie said with a smile.

"Hi, honey. Hi, Spearo."

"Hello, Mrs. West," Spearo said with a smile.

I walked away and then looked back and noticed how Jodie's side zip on her uniform skirt was open! Buttoned at the top but wide open as if she forgot to zip it after using the bathroom or . . . . I shook my head as I went straight to her bedroom and saw how her bed was perfectly made. "She thinks she's fooling me. They think they're fooling me. Probably was just in that bed having sex before I got here and had Maritza or one of the other maids make it up," I mumbled to myself. I sighed and went to my office.

<u>WILD BLACK TEA WITH BEVERLY</u>
OMAR SINCLAIR, HUSBAND OF THE LATE CECILIA
SINCLAIR, JUST PUT IT ALL OUT THERE!
"DAMN THE HOTEL'S REP, I WANT ANSWERS AS TO
WHAT HAPPENED TO MY WIFE"

"And can you honestly blame the man? His wife goes on a business trip and she ends up dead in her hotel room at the very old and prestigious ritzy-tizzy Regalis Montemar Hotel, a hotel that has been around since 1873—that's 150 years, y'all! And they're not gonna go out of business because some Black man wants to know how his Black wife ended up dead in one of their rooms —real professional, motherfuckers! There, I said it! This man has every right to know what happened to his wife in that room that day because they are clearly hiding shit from him, all because they don't wanna lose business or even worse, go out of business since the hotel has been standing there in the same spot for 150 years, and you all can imagine how much shit has went down in it, including people who ended up dead in it for whatever reason and no one did a damn thing about it. This man is owed answers, so yes, your girl Beverly is all on his side in finding out who murdered his beautiful wife and left two beautiful children motherless. There is so much more to this and you know I will be on top of this just like I'm still on top of the Lang and Blair text scandal so keep those pots steaming and that tea flowing!"

I turned off my computer as tears welled up in my eyes. I was still a fuckin' coward about turning myself in and at least giving Omar the honest answers that he wanted and deserved, but due to what was going on, I knew no one would probably believe me about what really happened in that room because only one of us walked out of it alive, especially because of the text scandal that's going on right now. I didn't wanna be involved in any type of scandals—none of this shit—but here we were, and it was all Lang's fault why everything had went down the way it had and was still going down, and it turned me into a person I never thought I could or would be.

My phone chimed in with a text:

It was you! It was you! Turn yourself in!

I dropped my phone on the floor. I started to feel sick. Someone knew it was me who was there at the hotel that day. They'd already seen the footage. The footage of me going directly up to Cecilia's room thinking Cordelia was still in there. That Beverly chick said she had connections to the hotel's security surveillance department, so I knew it was either her or someone else taunting me because I have not changed my number, even though it was not and had never been publicly available. My hands shook as I called Maxi.

"Blair, hey! What's up?"

"Um, Maxi, have you gotten that surveillance yet of the person who went to Cecilia's room the day she was found dead?"

"No, I haven't gotten it yet and I know that for a fact because I just checked a few minutes ago right before you called. Why?"

I sighed. "No reason. I just wanted to know. I gotta go help Chef Forrest with dinner again. I'll talk to you later."

"Okay, babe. You know I'll let you know as soon as it is sent to me."

"I know you will."

I hung up as I stared at my computer's screen. I just couldn't tell her about the text I'd just received because she would've asked me a million-and-one questions about why this person thought it was me, but since she confirmed to me that the room was Cordelia's before it was Cecilia's, then knowing it was me was pretty self-explanatory.

Another chime came into my phone. I looked at the text:

We can settle this out of court. What do you say?

CHAPTER SEVENTEEN

"Hey, Blair. How are you doing?" Blythe said, my one-and-only sister, as she sat her stunning Hermes Kelly 35cm shiny porous crocodile bag in electric blue with palladium hardware on the table in my conference room in my office. I gave the bag as a gift to her for her 30th birthday eight years ago, and she still carried it every day to this day.

"Hey, honey," I said with a smile.

We hugged and kissed each other on the cheek.

I was on my computer working on a new project for the ABWS, but I was doing more lurking at gossip sites about me and Lang, as well as waiting on Maxi to get back to me with that surveillance footage, something someone claims to already have and know it was me.

She poured herself some coffee, and then took one of the breakfast pastries. "Mmmm, this is soooo good. You have the best personal pastry chef. It's funny how fast I got used to eating good when you first met Lang."

"Are we gonna go down memory lane?" I asked as I still lurked all over online. And I hated myself for doing this because, once again, all of this shit had turned me into a person I never thought I would be.

"Not if you don't want to," she said with a grin.

"Lang sent you over here, didn't he?"

She sighed. "Yes, and no."

"And what the hell is that supposed to mean?"

"Yes, he called me last night to come over and check on you this morning since Nathan and I just got back from Cyprus. He's worried about you, Blair, and so am I and so are Mom and Dad. Have you spoken to them?"

"Yeah, I have—but just over the phone. They take as many vacations as you and Nathan and my nephew do."

"And you marrying Lang made this all possible, Blair. When the two of you took your vows and he promised not only to love and protect you and take care of the future family the two of you created, he promised the same thing to our side of the family. He hasn't disappointed us— none of us—at all. He wasn't even a billionaire yet."

"But he still had a nine-figure income," I reminded her.

"Yeah, I know. But where would we all be if it wasn't for you meeting him 20 years ago and marrying him 2 years later?"

"I don't wanna think about it," I said, as I checked my emails. "The fact is, things took a wrong turn in our marriage somewhere for him to do this shit to me and now I have no idea who this bitch is. She's caused a lot of fuckin' trouble already, trouble that should not have been caused."

"Like what?" she asked, and then took a sip of her coffee and a bite of her pastry.

I shook my head. "I don't wanna get into it. I'm trying to get some normalcy restored back around here. It's just that Lang and I have the 25th Anniversary Gala coming up in celebration of his business being open for 25 years, and to top it off, Jodie is *still* driving me fuckin' crazy about her sweet sixteen party as if it's gonna be the best damn thing in the world many times over."

"For her it is, Blair. Come on now. We were both that age. We both knew how exciting it was when we turned that age and was able to get our driver's licenses."

"I failed my driver's test on my 16th birthday, remember?"

"Yeah, but you got it a few weeks later and already had a new car waiting for you," she reminded me with a smile.

"I know. But I'm not thinking about the past right now, Blythe. I'm thinking about now and now my family is put in a light that I don't want all of us in at all and it's all because of some bitch who wanted to let the whole world know that she's sleeping with my husband." I glared at her.

"What the hell are you looking at me like that for?"

"Whoever's doing this to me doesn't happen to be one of your ratchet-ass friends you've been knowing since high school, is it?"

She gasped! "What? Blair! Why the hell would you bring any of *them* up? I haven't been out with them since I got married over 10 years ago. They were a bunch of jealous-ass, toxic bitches who were yes, jealous of you because you met and married a man who ended up becoming a rare Black billionaire, and I'm your younger sister so that meant my life changed for the better as well."

I grinned. "Just wanna make sure."

"If it is one of them, Blair, I think I would've found out by now because they can't stop talking on social media about a whole lot of nothing. All of them got babies and aren't married and some of them don't work and are so depressed and unhappy so that's why I had to cut them off in terms of in-person socialization because no, I did not like the things they were saying about you and everything. I honestly think they're talking about you a lot—especially now since this text scandal —but they're probably doing it in person or through private messaging and chats or groups or whatever because I notice that I seem to be left out of a lot of what they're doing online lately as well as in person, and I honestly don't care. I'm glad to be away from all of that toxicity and in this life with you. I have made new friends because of it, but I'm really not that close to them because they seem to be some haters, too, because they know you're my sister and who you're married to."

"Yeah, it's the billionaire wife lifestyle. Anyone who's a family member of mine also gets treated like me. Guilt by association at its finest. But I'm glad you're away from those old friends, too. You don't need that shit. All you need is one good friend like the way I have Maxi. She said hi, by the way."

"Tell her I said the same," she replied with a smile. "Maxi is truly one of a kind."

"That she is." I sighed. "But even though she's investigating my case pro bono, as you know, there's something I just can't tell her."

Her eyes widened where it reminded me of when she was young, and I would tell her something I didn't want her telling anyone. "What is it, Blair?"

I sighed once again as I tried to brace myself for what I had to tell her. "Blythe. *No one* knows this, okay? This has *got* to stay between you and me."

"You know I will never say anything, Blair."

I nodded. I picked up my phone and went to the text and shoved my phone over to her. "I received that text last night."

It was you! It was you! Turn yourself in!

She gasped! "What the hell is this shit! Blair, *are you sure* you have no idea who sent this to you?"

I sighed and shook my head. "No, Blythe, I have no idea who sent this to me. Not a clue."

"Do you think it's the same person who sent you the one about sleeping with Lang?"

"I honestly don't know. I think for some reason it is. I know the bitch who sent me that text that was seen around the world was probably sent on a different phone that the bitch rarely uses because a lot of people have more than one phone. I don't, but Lang does, of course. I just have a feeling now that this is not the same person, but then again, you just never can tell."

"Yeah, I see the other one on here, too."

We can settle this out of court. What do you say?

"Have you thought about settling out of court?"

"Not a chance. This person cannot prove that I did anything."

She kept staring at the text. "Okay, I'm confused. What is it that this person is accusing you of doing?"

"Killing Cecilia Sinclair," I blurted out.

She shrieked as she quickly put her hands over her month. "What the fuck, Blair?! How the hell did Cecilia Sinclair get involved in this? I heard about her murder and that it happened at the same hotel as the charity event you and Lang went to that night, but I didn't think . . . oh, my god! *What the hell* is really going on, Blair?"

"This person who sent me this text is lying, Blythe, and that's all you need to know for right now. I just need to get myself together about all of this."

"Have you talked to your lawyers?"

"Not at all because I haven't done anything to get them all involved in this," I said, as I tried to throw her off of the fact that I had something to do with Cecilia's death even though I witnessed that it was a freak accident, an accident that would not have happened if it wasn't for me going to that room thinking she was someone else and accusing her of being Cordelia. "If anything, Lang is gonna need to get his lawyers ready."

"For what, Blair?"

I shook my head. "I know I'm talking crazy but I'm just not in the right state of mind right now. I guess I do need some family around me to get my head straight about things again because I'm just really fucked up right now where I'm thinking really crazy thoughts."

"Well, I can understand that all of this is making you crazy because you and Lang used to be a private, quiet couple until some bitch wanted to cause some drama because she doesn't have shit going on in her own life. Do you really think she slept with him?"

"Yes," I replied without hesitation. "The last thing Lang is is perfect, Blythe, you know that. I may be living a life that most women can only dream of living, but I haven't been stupid and naïve to anything since living like this. I have to be on top of my game with everything, but it shows you that no matter how on top of your game you are, how great of a wife you are and how well you're raising your kids, your husband will still find a reason and a way to stray."

"Yeah, unfortunately, that's what they do, especially one with Lang's power and status. It's too bad he did what he did. How long do you think he's been sleeping with other women?"

"Since we met," I honestly replied. "But who was I to say anything? I can't change the way a person is, they have to want and change for themselves. I just knew that some woman was gonna taunt me one day about her sleeping with him; it was all a matter of time. I just wish I knew who this bitch was because it's clear to me that it's more than just one who is."

"How do you know that for sure?"

"Because Lang left the charity event that night to see some woman who was staying at the hotel, and then he went back out again to see another woman in the middle of the night at our penthouse. I believe it's between these two women who are taunting me, I just don't know which one it is."

"Sounds like it, Blair. I'm sure Maxi will give you all of the answers you need."

"Well, she's really working hard on my case. I honestly think Lang may know something is up with being investigated because of course he knows Maxi is a PI."

"So, if the woman who was in the penthouse that night who he went to go see is in fact a different woman—and I think she is, too—because why would she leave a hotel to go to a penthouse hours later?"

"Yeah, that's true, but you just never know."

"True. But like you, I think it's a different woman. If this is a different woman, do you have footage of her coming to or leaving the penthouse because I know the elevator that goes up and down from it is y'alls private elevator."

"Maxi was able to obtain footage of a woman going up to the penthouse that night we went to the charity event, and it was past midnight. So she was obviously granted access by Lang to go up there because that elevator is guarded 24/7, so I'm definitely waiting to see if a guard at the time could give Maxi a better description of her or not. She showed me the footage of her riding up the elevator and she had on some short, tight-ass white dress with her fake boobs busting all out of it while wearing some huge floppy black hat on her head with her hair up in it because she knew there were cameras in there and Lang probably told her to disguise herself as much as she could from them, but not to make it too obvious that she was. But those guards know me and know he's married."

"Yeah, it most definitely sounds like it. I'm sure Maxi will give you all of the answers you need as to who these women are, and I say women because I believe there is definitely more than one."

"Yeah, Lang's definitely sleeping with more than one or two or hundreds."

"Blair . . ."

"Just being honest. It's just that none of them have ever done this shit by actually contacting me and admitting that they are. It's obviously something about this bitch as to why she's doing this shit and wants me to know what she's doing with him."

"Yeah, but it's clear this coward-ass bitch doesn't want you to know that bad since she's acting as if she doesn't wanna show her face."

"And when she shows her face she's gonna see my fuckin' fist up in it."

"Blair! Don't talk like that. You know damn well you're better than that. I know you're upset right now and you have a million things to do and everything, but don't go flying off the handle and doing something you will regret doing."

Too late, I thought, as Cecilia Sinclair was always on my mind and was already haunting me like a perpetual bad dream, but it was now my wide-awake reality. And I just didn't know if I could even tell Blythe that I was the reason why she was dead, because even though she was my sister, I didn't even know if she would've believed me about exactly what'd happened.

Several minutes later after Blythe had left, I received a call from Maxi.

"Hey, Blair. I got some more footage of the woman on y'alls penthouse elevator that night in question. I was just reviewing it and I'm gonna send it to you right now so you can tell me if you notice anything in it because it clearly shows her leaving. I think there's something obvious that you're gonna notice, though."

"Send it to me."

CHAPTER EIGHTEEN

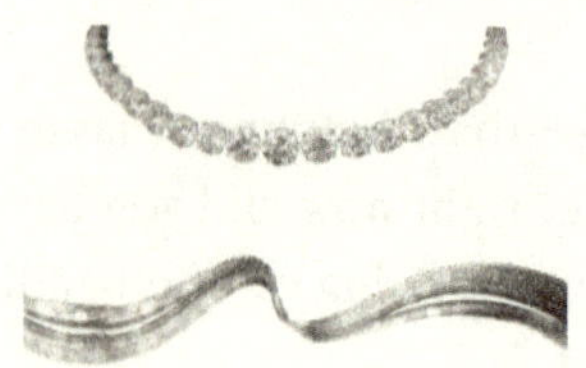

"Okay, I have it up on my screen and I'm turning it on right now," I said, as I had the latest video Maxi had sent to me of the woman who was in Lang and my penthouse that night. I noticed that the video started off with her getting on the elevator as she was leaving for the night. I also noticed that she had a shopping bag in her hands, as well as something else. "She's got a pair of shoes in her hand, and a very nice pair at that. In fact, they're so nice that I recognize them as a pair that I have in my closet, I just have them in a peacock blue-green color."

"I knew you would recognize those shoes, Blair. Of all shoes, I remember going shopping with you at Jimmy Choo when your SA brought them out for you to see."

"And I was gonna get the pink ones that she has in her hands but have a lot of shoes similar in that style," I said, as I shook my head since I knew Lang had in fact given this bitch a nice gift—a pair of $1,995 Jimmy Choo Saeda 100 pumps all embellished in multicolor candy pink crystals. "Well, it's clear that he's buying this bitch gifts, so at least she can get something good out of it for bussing it wide open for him; I don't know about the other one."

"Regardless of if he's buying the other one gifts or not, it still doesn't make it right."

"Damn right it doesn't make it right," I said, as I watched as the elevator descended down to where the parking garage was. I noticed how she got off on this floor. "Do you have footage of the parking garage?"

"I already requested it because of course since they have security driving around in it 24/7, they also have surveillance inside of the parking garage as well."

"Let me know when you get it," I said. "Yeah, but as I see, the bitch is still covered up where there is no way I can see who she is."

"Yeah, it's like she knows the routine, all right. Again, I can't even begin to say how sorry I am, Blair, that this is happening to you."

"Well, I'm lucky to have you on my case because I just wouldn't trust anyone else. Since Lang is a billionaire, they would've probably asked for money from him in exchange for them to tell me that they didn't find him cheating on me."

"Yeah, and a lot of PI's have done that shit and have had their licenses either suspended or expelled. That's the epitome of unethical practices and they know it."

"That's why I wanted you and only you working on this case."

"And yes, I think this is already the case of my career. Keep watching."

I did what she told me to do. I noticed how the elevator was back up at the penthouse. The doors opened to Lang getting on it about 10 minutes after she did—the time stamp was 3:06 am. "Yeah, I'm noting the time on here. Yep, that's about the time I woke up out of a deep sleep and noticed he wasn't in bed and got on my phone and checked the house app and noticed one of his cars was gone out of one of the garages."

"So this is proof that this was where he was, Blair. You got proof that he was with a woman during the time you were sleeping and was just leaving when you noticed he was gone. Do you know what time he got back home?"

"Probably a little bit after 4:00 am. He just got right back into bed as if he was just in his bathroom as I pretended to be asleep. I was up and wide awake since I noticed his car was gone, but of course when he walked into the room I pretended to be asleep. Hours later, he got up and went into his bathroom and took a shower—probably another one because I'm sure he took one at the penthouse—and that's when I was standing outside of the bathroom armed with my phone ready to ask him about the text that I'd received so early in the morning. Now I'm starting to believe it was that bitch who was on the elevator than the one who was at the hotel who sent me that first text about sleeping with him."

"It's possible, Blair, and I'm still waiting on the phone records to see if I can trace whose number it is, but it might be one of those burner phones she's using because she does know how easily she can be traced with any other phone that you can do more than call and text on."

"Yeah, true. I believe a hundred percent now that she's using one of those burner phones because she would not be texting me like this on her regular phone."

"I don't think she is or would be, either. And if it is in fact a burner phone she's using, then there is no way to trace it, Blair, since people just discard them when they're done with them, and they're pre-paid phones that you can buy anywhere."

"I know, so I'm not expecting to catch her that way, believe it or not. I know there are other ways, I just wish I knew how."

"Well, that's where I come in and why I'm investigating this. No one can do the job I'm doing."

"You're doing a fantastic job so far, Maxi, but I also wanted to know is have you received the other footage from the hotel? The one of the person going to Cordelia Sharpe's room?"

"No, I still haven't gotten it yet. I'm gonna have to put in another request to have them send it to me if I don't receive it soon because no, it should not be taking them this long. I know they have millions and millions of footage in their vaults, but if they were able to get the other footage from there that I'd requested in a reasonable time then I should've gotten this by now."

This was probably the only time that I was breathing a sigh of relief that she hadn't received it yet. I'd hoped that it was either lost or erased because I knew my best friend would have some kind of sixth sense that it was me going to Cordelia's room if she saw the footage, even though I tried to mentally prepare myself in the fact that I would've tried everything I could to convince her that it wasn't me.

A chime came into my phone, indicating to me that I'd received a text:

So, what's it gonna be? Or am I gonna have to tell that tea woman Beverly what I know?

I started breathing heavy. I pounded hard down on the keys as I texted this person back:

And what is it that you know?

I braced myself for their response:

That you killed Cecilia Sinclair.

CHAPTER NINETEEN

<u>WILD BLACK TEA WITH BEVERLY</u>
TEA ALERT! TEA ALERT!
THE LANG AND BLAIR WEST TEXT SCANDAL CASE
HAS BEEN TAKEN TO NEW HEIGHTS!
A PERSON HAS INFO ABOUT BLAIR THEY'RE ONLY
SHARING WITH ME!

"And I'm only sharing it with y'all! Whew! I can't believe that this is happening! At first, let me be honest, y'all, I didn't think this case was going anywhere, but then I received an email that I believe to be very legit tea on Blair West herself! Man! Now, just to let all of you know, this person, of course, wrote to me under complete anonymity since they claim to be close to Blair and close to the case, but of course they're not giving me any more info than that! Well! It's more info than what I've received recently! This is about to get good, y'all! I knew things were too quiet so I was wondering when some tea—some big tea—was gonna be spilled about this case, and it's gonna be real soon!"

She poured tea into her teacup and started drinking it.

"Okay, since I've only received this one email from this person —and I'm respecting their wishes by not posting the email publicly for everyone to see—it just says that, like I said, they're close to Blair and close to this text scandal case and says that there is definitely a connection between Blair and a recent incident that happened. Now, everyone knows there has been millions of recent incidents so I don't exactly know which one this person is talking about nor would they tell me, so they're really trying to stay quiet about something! But whatever it is, it sounds like Blair is involved in some deep shit when it comes to this case, and all I have to do is wait on another email from this person with all of the details which is what they told me to do, so you all know what to do—keep it here because this is the exclusive stuff only Beverly can bring to all of you!"

"*H*ey, Mom," Jodie said, as she walked into my office with her backpack and school uniform on.

I clicked off the screen. "Hey, honey," I said, as she kissed me on the top of my head. "How was study group at the library?"

"Just fine," she replied with a smile. I could tell how hard she was trying to stay on my good side.

I looked at her Walgreen's plastic bag she had in her hands. "What's in the bag?"

"Oh, hygiene products since I'm running low on them. I also got you a large Hershey's candy bar."

"You've read my mind," I said with a smile.

She started looking for it and then started dumping the products in the bag out on my desk . . . *and there was a pregnancy test.*

I looked at her. I picked up the test. "Is this for me, too? Or Lorie? Or you?"

She lowered her head. "Mom, *please.*"

I sighed. I got on my phone.

"Mom, *please* don't call Dad!" she begged.

"I'm not calling your dad, I'm calling Lorie in here," I informed her. "Lorie? Come to my office right now. Jodie's in here with me."

"Why do you want her in here?" Jodie cried.

I sat staring at her with the test in my hand.

Lorie came into my office minutes later. "Mom? What's going on?"

"Is this test for you?" I asked, as I showed her the pregnancy test.

"What? No! Not at all! I'm still a virgin! I've never been with a boy like *that*!" Lorie said, as if it was the most offensive question I'd ever asked her.

"And I know it's not for me," I said. I sighed as I shook my head. I handed the test to her. "Take it right now, Jodie. Go on into my bathroom in here. Read the instructions carefully. Oh, and if it's positive, your party is cancelled."

Tears welled up in Jodie's eyes as she took the test and went to the bathroom here in my office.

"Lorie, you stay here with me because I want you to see the results as well. I want you to learn from this," I said.

"Okay, Mom," she said with a smile.

Minutes later, Jodie emerged from the bathroom as tears streamed down hard from her eyes as she held the test in her hands. She gave it to me.

Negative.

I nodded and showed Lori the results.

"Then why is she crying?" Lorie asked.

"Because she's happy she can still have her party," I said, as I glared at her.

"Mom, *please* don't tell Dad," Jodie pleaded again.

"There's nothing to tell him since it's negative. You both go to your study rooms and do your homework. I got some things I need to take care of in here," I informed them.

They left without any arguments.

I turned it back on Beverly's latest video. As I rewatched it, I knew that it was in fact someone close to me that'd written that email to her and was trying to get back at me for whatever reason when there was nothing I'd done to anyone. Someone close to me was trying to sabotage me and they could very well do it. I just didn't know who this person was, but what I did know was that it was the same person who was sending me these texts talking about how they knew it was me as to why Cecilia Sinclair was dead.

I got on my phone and looked at the last text this person had sent me . . . and sent them a text back:

Okay, you win. Tell me what it is you want.

I breathed heavy as I waited for a response:

Meet me at that old mini mall off of Garrison Street. You know which one I'm talking about.

When?

Tonight. Tonight only.

I'll be there.

CHAPTER TWENTY

And here I was. At a badly lit old mini mall off of Garrison Street, where all of the stores were either closed permanently or barely open for business if they were still in business. The night seemed darker than usual with the only light coming from a few tall, tattered light poles in the empty parking lot. I even saw how in the past 20 years that this place had gone to hell just as much as someone was trying to make my life hell, and it was clear that it was more than one person. I sat in my car as I waited for this person to arrive as "Smiling Faces Sometimes" by The Undisputed Truth played on the radio, and if anyone tried it with me, well, I had a nice hard fully-loaded piece of protection waiting for them.

I looked in my outside rearview mirror and noticed a dark-colored SUV come riding up into the parking lot. I didn't recognize it. It parked one spot away from my car leaving an open space between us. It had dark-tinted windows so I had no idea who was in it, and if there was more than one person in it, that concerned me since it was only me here in my car.

The SUV's lights turned off and I could see whoever it was step out of the car and I did the same as I put my gun in my purse and guarded myself with extreme caution.

"Hello, Blair."

It was Yusari! Maxi's assistant!

"Yusari?!" I asked, as if I didn't know it was her as we stood face-to-face in the one parking spot that was between our cars. "What the . . . *why? Why* are you doing this?"

She sighed as she slightly lowered her head. She then glared up at me, and I'd never seen her look at me like this before. I felt like I didn't know her anymore; like I was looking at a whole other person, a person who turned on me for no good reason other than the fact that she could, all because she claimed she had something on me but had yet to prove it to me. And whatever she had on me and could prove it, she knew she could get as much as she wanted out of me for it. "I really didn't wanna have to do this, Blair, but I think Cecilia Sinclair is owned justice for what you did to her."

"I didn't do anything to her! Where is your proof that it was me who went to her room that day?"

"Right here," she said, as she held up her iPad Mini and showed me the surveillance Maxi had been waiting on.

I saw myself in a light I'd never wanted anyone to see me in, especially myself, but there was still no way anyone could absolutely know a hundred percent sure that it was me. "You can hardly prove that is me, Yusari, and you know it! That could be any woman!"

"Yeah, Blair, but it's you; and you know it's you. It's clear you abruptly left Maxi's firm that day when you found out some info about how Cordelia Sharpe was in that room, huh? Well, so you thought she still was, because Maxi was out of the room for a while that day, then all of the sudden you had to up and leave when she came back into her office. You had on that exact black Burberry trench coat, and I've seen you wear that black Burberry baseball cap a few times to the firm. It's clear you went there thinking Cordelia was still in that room, and obviously thought Cecilia was her. Wow, Blair. I didn't think you had it in you to actually end someone's life because they claimed to be sleeping with your husband, only except you ended the wrong woman's life."

"I didn't end her life, Yusari! What the fuck is wrong with you? You weren't there! You only have what the video surveillance has shown to you, you have no video of what went on inside that room."

"I know you went in and then Cecilia went in several minutes later, and that only one of you came out alive, which was you—video surveillance shows you leaving as well. I know you thought you killed Cordelia, but you didn't. But I can make all of this footage go away for a great price."

"And Maxi will just get more footage of it so why should I give you anything?"

"Because you're a murderer," she said with a wicked smile. "Beverly will get a copy of this surveillance as promised to her if we can't negotiate some kind of settlement. I mean, you're Blair West, wife of billionaire Langston West. How much is your freedom worth is what you should be asking yourself right now and—"

"You're fired," Maxi said, as she walked up on Yusari!

Yusari jumped around as if she couldn't believe that her boss had snuck up on her! She looked at me as I smirked back at her. "What is this shit?! You set me up?"

"Sure did. Did you really think I was gonna come here all by myself? Are you kidding me?" I asked.

Maxi shook her head. "Should've known something was up with you, Yusari, when I never received the footage of who went to Cordelia's room that day; I knew you were behind it, but I just couldn't prove it. You stole that footage right out of my emails and sent it to yourself and erased it from my inbox so it looked as if it was never sent to me. How could you do some shit like that, Yusari? I really trusted you. You had absolutely *no right* to interfere in my investigation. *No right*!"

"She killed Cecilia Sinclair because she thought she was Cordelia Sharpe!" she cried, as tears welled up in her eyes.

"There's no proof of that and you know it!" Maxi said.

"That surveillance is all the proof you need! Your best friend is crazy! It's clear she'll do anything to hold on to that fucked-up husband of hers!"

Maxi looked at me as I stared back at her. I could tell she didn't know what to say to me. "Did you really kill Cecilia Sinclair because you thought she was Cordelia Sharpe?"

"No! I didn't kill her, Maxi, *I swear* I didn't!" I said, but didn't even know if she believed me at this point.

Maxi looked at Yusari. "You're not getting a dime from Blair. You get the fuck out of here. I'll have someone on the staff send you your things. And I suggest you get the fuck out of town, Yusari, because I have connections all over this city and state and other places as well where I will make sure you never work anywhere near here again. You did the unthinkable, so you're very lucky that I'm just firing you. And you are never to say anything about what has happened here tonight to anyone or you're gonna find yourself at the receiving end of some very bad karma—got it?"

"Yes," she said with her head lowered.

"Put that iPad down on the ground since it's property of my company so you know it's not yours anymore," Maxi ordered.

Yusari put the iPad down on the ground, turned around and got into her SUV, and left.

And just like that, she was gone. Just as much as Maxi had hoped, I hoped I would never see her again as well.

Maxi sighed as she shook her head as she looked up into the night sky, she looked down at the iPad and picked it up off the ground. She began working on it.

"What are you doing?" I squeaked out.

"Sending an email to my staff letting them know that Yusari no longer works at my firm. I'm also deleting her email so she can't use it. She better do what I say because I mean everything I say." She threw the iPad in her bag and stomped off.

I followed her as I almost had to catch up with her since she was walking so fast. "Where are you going?"

"To my car. Where do you think?" she asked as she shook her head.

"Maxi . . ."

"YOU INTERFERED IN MY INVESTIGATION, BLAIR! YOU COULD'VE BEEN KILLED RIGHT ALONG WITH CECILIA!"

I jumped back from her as tears welled up in my eyes. "I can't tell you how sorry I am that I did what I did, Maxi. I'm just a big fuckin' mess right now. I haven't been in the right state of mind since getting that very first text. It really fucked me up and has had me fucked up ever since. Please, I need you, Maxi. *You know* I need you in more ways than one. Please don't abandon me, *please*," I begged.

Tears welled up in her eyes. "I don't know what I'm gonna do, Blair. I honestly don't."

"Look, we need to talk about this."

"Damn right we need to talk about this."

Several minutes later, we sat in my car as we sipped on coffee in a well-lit Starbucks parking lot not too far from where both of us lived.

Maxi carefully looked at the surveillance on the iPad since this was the first time she was reviewing it. "I'm not gonna lie, Blair, I would've suspected that this was you, too, since I knew you were wearing that coat that day, as well as I've seen you wear that baseball cap more than once, so that little bitch is right."

"But you two were really the only ones that had. I tried to hide myself the best I could."

"I know you did, and I think most would not have known it was you because you did. How did you get into her room since it was clear she wasn't there since you let yourself in?"

I sighed. "I stole a maid's lanyard out of her cleaning cart that had the scanner on it. She came into the elevator and just had it laying on top of the cart and wasn't paying any attention to me; she was looking up at the numbers on the elevator. I guess she didn't think I would do something like that, but it was a one-and-a-million chance happening and I took advantage of it. Trust me, Maxi, I didn't even feel like the same person doing what I did."

"I know you didn't, Blair. I knew this had you fucked up, but I didn't think you were gonna go to these extremes."

I shook my head. "Neither did I."

She put the iPad back in her bag. "How did you know exactly what room to go to?"

"You shuffled around your papers on your desk that day and I saw one that said, *'POI—Person of Interest—Cordelia Sharpe Rm: 2609.'* My mind just went fuckin' crazy thinking she was still there, and I didn't wanna wait until you told me about her since I thought you were gonna bring her up when I first got there. But since you didn't, I felt I needed to go see her and confront her myself since I obviously thought she was still there."

She shook her head. "Good Lord, Blair. Okay, I'm listening. What happened in that room?"

I took a deep breath. "I did knock on the door to see if someone would answer, but when no one did, I decided to put the scanner to the test. It was like I couldn't believe it when I saw that it actually worked. I knocked on the bathroom door to see if she was in it after seeing that she wasn't anywhere in the room. When she wasn't in the bathroom, I decided to check out the room without touching anything."

"You touched the door to go in and out of there, Blair. And since you have no criminal record, your prints didn't come up in the criminal database because I asked the management and that's what the cops had told them. I didn't tell them at all that I was looking for your prints because at that point I had no idea it was you, and I would not have told them that anyway, of course. But I felt Cecilia's death was connected to your case, but never did I think it was a connection like this. So, what happened while you were in the room?"

"I looked around and noticed all of the high-end designer shoes and everything and the Louis Vuitton personalized luggage with the initials "CS" on them with pink and green stripes going down the middle of the luggage. Now you tell me, Maxi, would you have thought that was Cordelia Sharpe just by seeing that alone and by what I saw you had written on that paper? I just knew it was her!"

"Yes, that's hard not to believe that it wasn't her, Blair, I will admit that. But the fact is, *it wasn't her.* And you had no business in that room even it was her. You weren't invited up to her room, and you stole a maid's lanyard with her scanner on it to get into her room, only to find out it was someone else's room because the person who you really went to go see had already checked out. This has gotten you more messed up than I even thought you were gonna be over it. But no matter how messed up you were, Blair, you went way too far and you know it. There is now an official connection to Cecilia Sinclair's death and you and Lang's text scandal, and you're that direct connection."

"But no one has to know, Maxi! You know I trust you more than anyone else in this world not to tell anyone what I'm telling you."

"But you haven't told me everything, so I'm still listening."

I sighed once again. "Well, just judging by her luggage and all the nice shoes and clothes she had in her room, I knew this was Cordelia; I just knew she was being taken care of by Lang. You never told me about her when I was waiting on you to tell me and I especially was waiting on you to tell me that she checked out the morning before."

"Don't blame that shit on me, Blair. *Don't*. You interfered in my investigation, and you know it. You took matters into your own hands and acted on instinct and not facts and now a woman is dead because of it who had nothing to do with anything concerning you and Lang and the woman he's sleeping with that's sending you those texts."

"I know, Maxi. And now I'm gonna have to live with this shit for the rest of my life. But I didn't kill her."

"Then what happened?"

"She came into the room while I was still checking it out. I was yelling at her that she was sleeping with Lang and everything and she said I was crazy and pulled a gun out on me! *I swear* she did!"

She nodded. "And then what happened?"

"I threw a large tote bag at her that was heavy and full—a Christian Dior Lady Dior tote—and knocked the gun out of her hand, but she got a shot off at me before I did. She ran towards me and slipped and fell and hit her head on the floor and she hit it *hard*. The floor was hard flooring—not carpeted at all—in that area. I heard how loud it was. I thought she was just unconscious, so I looked at her driver's license since it fell out of the bag I threw at her . . . and that's when I saw she was Cecilia Sinclair, not Cordelia Sharpe. And I left."

She let out a huge sigh as she shook her head. "My goodness, Blair. You really have lost your damn mind. This investigation just turned into a nightmare. None of this had to happen. None of it."

"Are you still gonna investigate it? Because I still need to know who was in the penthouse and everything and I still don't know who sent me the text that started all of this shit."

"I promised you I would. But you've caused more shit than needed to be caused and you know it."

"Yes, I know." I nodded with a smile as tears once again welled up in my eyes. "But thank you for still investigating it."

"But you've made things a lot more difficult, Blair. A lot more difficult. So I'm gonna give you your final warning—you are *not* to interfere with my investigation on this anymore. I don't even know how we're gonna right this wrong when it comes to Cecilia Sinclair because in a lot of ways, we just can't. Her husband wants answers and now I feel very guilty about having all of the answers he needs."

"You don't realize how bad I feel about this, Maxi. This is why I was scared to tell you. This is why I didn't want you to see that footage of the person going to her room and was glad they were taking long in sending it to you. But of course, I had no idea Yusari was withholding it from you so she could blackmail me with it."

"Well, as you see, that backfired on her and rightfully so. I was wondering why you wanted me to meet you there since I knew there was really nothing in that area. I kept my guard up about it the whole time, but knew something was up when I saw the other SUV there. I had no idea that was her, either. It must've been her man's SUV because she's never driven it until now since she has her own car. I can't believe she tried to do that to you. I'm so sorry."

"It's okay, Maxi. I'm just glad you fired her and I hope she gets the fuck out of town like you said she better. I think she will."

"If wants to start her life over then she better do exactly what I say. And if you want me to keep investigating this for you then *you* better do exactly what I say, too."

"You know I will, Maxi."

CHAPTER TWENTY-ONE

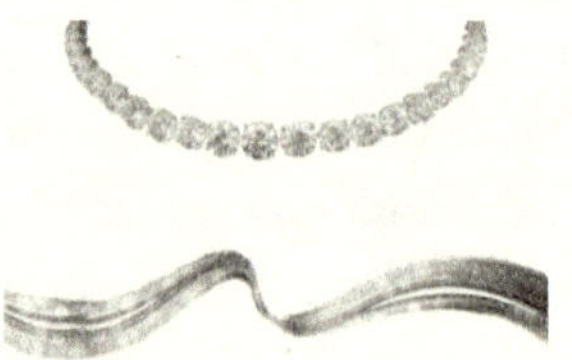

"My Cece loved the luxury life. She loved everything about it. That's why I'm standing here today because this was where she always loved to go shopping when she was in town —right at this luxury shopping center. She had plans to go here when she was in town on business, but while she was in town, her plans got derailed forever. But she also understood the luxury of love and family which was what she cherished most of all. It meant everything to her. Look, everyone, I *still* don't have any answers as to what happened to her and why. All I know is that someone else was in that room with her that morning and had a problem with her and thought that problem with her was big enough to kill her. I just don't know what to think of all of this and I'm just as confused as everyone else out there, so please, please give any information you have about this case to the local authorities because the hotel where she was killed is no longer cooperating when I feel they know more than they are willing to say just to protect themselves and their 150-year-old reputation. Thank you. Now, I'll take a few questions," Omar said.

"Yes?" Omar's lawyer said, as he pointed to a reporter.

"Do you know if Cecilia knew her killer?" the reporter asked.

"I have no idea. That's a big hotel with a lot of rooms so I'm gonna assume she did know because I just can't get myself to believe that it was random. My lawyer doesn't believe it was a random act, either," Omar replied.

"I sure don't. We just need more information on who was in that room but unfortunately the fingerprints on the doorhandle on the outside and on the inside did not match anyone's, so whoever did this obviously doesn't have a criminal record. That's all we know so far," Omar's lawyer said. He pointed to another reporter. "Yes?"

"THERE'S BLAIR WEST!" a reporter shouted out.

"Oh, shit! Here they come!" I said, as the media went from being at another press conference for Omar Sinclair to charging all over to me like some raging bulls!

"I got you, Blair," Blythe said, as she jumped out of the car and tried hard to protect me from them as she ran and stood by my driver's side door. "GET BACK! NOW!!" she screamed as her hands and arms were up and fully extended out in front of her as if she was already defending herself and me against the media.

The cops and other security ran over to my car and placed themselves in front of the media to let me get out of the car as Blythe held open the door for me and I reluctantly got out when all I wanted to do now was go back home. I looked over at Omar and his lawyers as they were now completely deserted as Blythe and I were heavily escorted into the luxury shopping center without no one ever knowing just how connected I was to his wife's case. I was the cause of him being here, and here was my chance to talk to him—but I didn't have my lawyers here. I was a cowardly, fucked-up mess at best. Even though no one knew I was the person they were looking for, all the media and others cared about was who sent the text to me about sleeping with my husband and if I was ever gonna find out who it was. Omar probably would not have guessed it in a million years that his wife was mistaken by me for a woman my husband was sleeping with who was in that exact room just that day before, and she had every reason to defend herself against me.

You just couldn't make any of this shit up.

. . .

"Well, it was not a bad shopping trip," Blythe said, as we carried some of the bags we got from shopping while I had ten security men and women carrying others as well as even more cops and other security made sure the media stayed away from me.

"Yeah, at least I found an outfit for the ABWS meeting that's gonna be held in my conference room in my office. It's a private meeting and I'm gonna be meeting some new members from different chapters in different cities so I can personally get to know them," I replied with a smile.

"Mrs. West?"

I looked up.

And there was Omar Sinclair staring at me with his lawyer right by his side!

"Yes?" I replied, as if I didn't know it was him.

"Do you have a few minutes?" he asked.

I looked at Blythe as I tried not to show any fear. I had no idea why he wanted to talk to me, but then again, he had every right to wanna talk to me. Maybe he already knew something I didn't know, something that was the last thing I wanted him to know.

"Yes, I have a few minutes," I replied. I signaled for Blythe to get into the car as security respectfully stood back.

"I just wanted to introduce myself to you. I'm Omar Sinclair. I'm the late Cecilia Sinclair's husband." He held out his hand for a shake.

I shook his hand as I'd hoped it didn't feel cold and clammy, but especially shaking. "Nice to meet you, Mr. Sinclair. And I'm so sorry for your loss."

"Thank you, Mrs. West," he said with a weary smile. "This is my lawyer, Mr. Peter Izawa."

"Nice to meet you, Mr. Izawa," I said with a smile.

"It's an honor to meet you, Mrs. West. Your husband Langston and yourself have done great things for the Black community. We appreciate it."

"Thank you," I replied with a smile. They didn't realize how bad I'd felt since I was the one responsible for why they were standing here;

still standing here. And they stood respectfully for hours to let me do my shopping to wait to talk to me. I was practically speechless.

"Did you know my wife?" Omar asked.

I looked at Mr. Izawa as he smiled at me. "No, I'm sorry, I didn't. I heard about her at the same time everyone else had."

"Okay, because I just don't know why I thought she knew you personally because she had mentioned you to me before."

I felt like I was gonna faint. But I knew I hadn't known her previously. "She . . . she did?"

"Yes," he said with a smile.

I looked at Mr. Izawa once again as he nodded with a smile. "When?" I squeaked out.

"Right before she left for her trip here. She said mentioned something about how people were talking about you and what your husband did to you—and I'm sorry about all of that. She was talking as if she knew you."

"Oh, okay. Yes, I'm sorry that so many people had to find out about this text scandal that was very private but became so public. I'm sorry they all ran over to me when they saw me here as if it was more important."

"That's the media for you. Well, we have to get going. Thank you for your time, Mrs. West. It was very nice meeting you," Omar said.

"Nice meeting you, too."

Several minutes later while we were away from the shopping center, I pulled over.

"What are you doing?" Blythe asked.

"You drive. I just can't right now," I said.

"Okay," she said, and we got out of the car and switched seats. "You haven't said anything about your conversation with Omar."

I sighed as I laid my head back on the headrest. "He thinks I knew Cecilia. He's claiming she was talking about me as if she knew me just before she left to come here on business."

"Are you serious, Blair?" she said, as she stared at me at a stoplight.

"I wouldn't lie about this, Blythe. This is just getting so fuckin' strange!"

"You're telling me, as well as a little confusing to me."

"And I can't blame you for thinking that. But when I was up in that room she claimed she didn't know who I was just as much as I didn't know who she was, and that was pretty obvious because I thought she was Cordelia Sharpe and didn't know who she really was until I saw her driver's license."

She sighed as she looked at me. "Blair."

"What?"

"You just confessed to me that you were the one in Cecilia's room that day she was murdered. Did you really kill her?"

"No! No, Blythe, *I swear* I didn't! I told Maxi the whole story. I didn't kill her, if anything, she tried to kill me and I couldn't blame her because I was in her room when I should not have been, thinking she was someone else."

"Good Lord, Blair. I knew you wanted to find the woman who sent you the text boldly claiming to be sleeping with Lang, but I didn't know you would even go this far in trying to find her."

I sighed. "Blythe, you've known me your whole life. You know this is not the person I really am. I didn't wanna cause any harm to the woman I thought was Cordelia—I just wanted to talk to her—but she got the acting just as fuckin' crazy as I was for being up in her room. I don't blame her for acting that way and saying the shit she said to me because if it was the other way around, I would've been acting just as bad as she did."

"Yeah, I would've, too."

"But, Blythe, you can't tell this to *anyone*. Not Nathan, not Mom and Dad. No one. You're the only person besides Maxi who knows I was up in her room for sure."

"What do you mean for sure?"

I sighed once again. "I'm saying that because the person who was texting me with those threats about knowing it was me who was in Cecilia's room that day was Yusari."

She shrieked! "What?! Are you serious, Blair? It was *Maxi's assistant* texting you those threats?!"

"Yeah, it was her. I didn't know when I wanted to tell you, but since you know for a fact that it was me then there was no reason for you not to know it was her who was sending me those texts. She's the one who anonymously told Beverly about the epic tea she had—well, she doesn't have it anymore because I had Maxi come with me unbeknownst to Yusari—and she fired her and told her to get the fuck out of town. I hope she listens to her because Maxi has a lot of power in this city when it comes to what she does and told her she will never work in this city again."

She smiled. "Good for her. That little bitch. And I actually liked her even though I rarely saw her. Thought she was gonna get some money from you, huh?"

"Yeah, that's exactly what she thought since she stole the hotel footage of me going up to Cecilia's room that day out of Maxi's inbox because she wanted to blackmail me with it."

"How much did she ask you for?"

"She never had a chance to ask me for anything because Maxi stepped up behind her and gave her a nice surprise."

"Good for Maxi!" she laughed.

I nodded, and then shook my head. "But none of this shit would've happened had I not went up there to begin with. I can't bring Cecilia back, and I just don't know if it's actually Cordelia who's sending me those texts now."

"Well, I think it's her, Blair, and I'll be convinced of it until it's proven that she isn't. It's clear she doesn't live here in this city since she was staying at the hotel that night Lang went to see her the night y'all were at the charity event, so it's much easier for her to taunt you through a text about sleeping with him when she knows she's not gonna see you anywhere here in this city."

"I think you're right about that, Blythe. But damn, I never knew I was gonna come face-to-face with Cecilia's husband. I think there's something about him."

She looked at me. "What do you think?"

"That's just it. I really don't know. I'm definitely gonna have to tell Maxi about him."

CHAPTER TWENTY-TWO

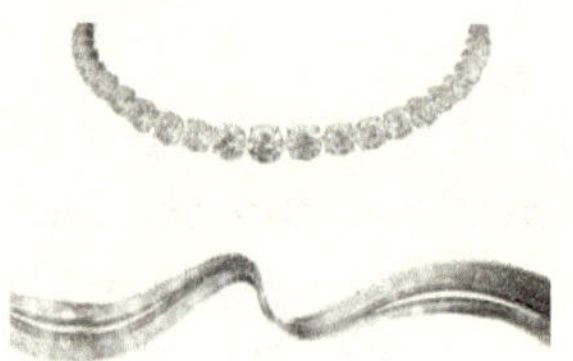

<u>WILD BLACK TEA WITH BEVERLY</u>
AN UNEXPECTED MEETING
OMAR SINCLAIR MEETS BLAIR WEST AT LUXURY
SHOPPING CENTER AFTER BEING ABRUPTLY CUT
OFF FROM HIS PRESS CONFERENCE DUE TO HER
UNEXPECTED SHOWING

"Well! This should show people once and for all whose case people prioritize! Omar Sinclair is a man in mourning, and he wants nothing more than to find out who killed his wife Cecilia since as of today, there are no suspects in custody. Today, he was standing outside of one of Cecilia's favorite places to shop when she was in town, but he told us that she never got to go there this time around for obvious reasons. But it seemed like the timing was absolutely perfect that Blair happened to roll up in her shiny white Rolls-Royce Cullinan SUV with her younger sister Blythe in tow, and a reporter yelled out that Blair was there, and the media came charging to her car like her story about having a woman text her about sleeping with her husband was the utmost important, as they clearly deserted Omar and his lawyer as you can all see from the video.

"Now I admit that I have done a lot of tea about Blair and Lang and this text scandal mess, but for the media to abruptly leave when she arrived just to do some shopping with her sister clearly showed what story they thought was a priority. Well, that's the kind of effect being a Black billionaire couple can have on the media and just on people in general—people seem so obsessed with them, including me, I'll admit!

"But Omar clearly had no hard feelings about what'd happened because him and his lawyer stuck around for hours, and I mean *hours*, after Blair and Blythe went in to do some shopping and left with the whole center and an entourage of security to help them with all of their bags of goodies. That's how a billionaire wife and the sister of a billionaire wife get down! It's great to be them!

"But it was clear Omar wanted to meet Blair, and he did introduce himself to her as you all have seen from the video, but no one really knew what the two of them talked about. Maybe he was asking her for money to help in the investigation of his wife's murder inside that hotel room . . . or maybe it was something else? I have a feeling there is some tea coming about this interaction so of course, keep it right here!"

I looked at her other videos, something that I rarely did since I'd seen all of the recent ones . . . and gasped. The previous one that she gave the tea alert out about and that someone had info about me that they were only sharing with her *was completely deleted from her page*. I got on my phone and called Maxi.

"Blair, hey," Maxi said.

"Hey, Maxi. I just wanted to know have you seen Beverly's latest?"

"No, I haven't seen it yet."

"Okay, but I'm not calling about that one, I'm calling about the previous one, the one where she had issued that lame-ass tea alert because someone had info about me that they wanted to share with her?"

"Yeah, I remember looking at that one."

"Well, it looks like Yusari contacted her and told her that she wasn't giving her any info about me because she took the whole video down—I searched for it and everything and it's no longer online. You really put the fear in that bitch!"

She chuckled. "I sure hope I did because I meant what I said. She had no right interfering in my investigation and especially talking to people like Beverly about it."

"Thank you so much again, Maxi."

"You're welcome."

"Um, have you found out anything more about my case?"

"I have some new info about Cordelia Sharpe."

I perked up! "What about her?"

"She's gonna be back in town next week, Blair, but she's not staying at the same hotel."

"Are you serious? Do you know why she's coming back in town and what hotel she's staying at this time?"

"No, not yet. That's what I'm trying to find out. You know I'll let you know everything when I find out. But when I find out what hotel she's staying at, Blair, *don't you dare fuckin' go there*. You're in enough shit with the Cecilia Sinclair case, but only I know that."

"And Blythe," I informed her.

"You told Blythe?!"

"She's my sister, Maxi. I trust her like the way I trust you in the two of you not telling anyone that I was the one in that room."

She sighed. "Yeah, I believe she's very trustworthy since I've known her just as long as I've known you. But don't you tell another person, Blair, I mean it."

"I won't," I promised.

"But I can't believe Omar waited for you for hours at the shopping center just to meet you!"

"Do you think he may know something?" I asked with panic in my voice.

"Only he knows that, Blair. But if I had to go on instinct, I would say he doesn't suspect a thing."

"Okay, but the only thing that bothers me about him was him asking me did I know her and that he thinks she told him that she knew me—it was right before she came here for her business trip. The whole interaction was strange like what I told you earlier today."

"Well, I know it's gonna seem like it, Blair, since you had the worst interaction with his wife and she wasn't even the person you wanted to confront. I know what happened to her was fucked up, but I believe you when you told me you didn't kill her. But you know you're gonna have to come clean with Omar about what really happened to her."

"I know I do, Maxi, I just can't do it yet. I had a chance to do it there when I met him, but I was a fuckin' coward. I hate myself for ever even going to that room that day, Maxi."

"And prove it by not going to Cordelia's room when she's back in town. You know what? In fact, I'm not giving you the name of the hotel she's staying at; I'm just gonna confirm to you when she checks in."

I sighed. "Actually, I think that's best, Maxi. I'm just too much of a mess and I'm capable of doing anything so as you know, I can't promise you that I won't show up there. At this point, all I want her to do is just admit to me that she's sleeping with Lang and that she's the one who's sending me these texts that started it all. I just want an end to all of this as fast as it began."

"Yeah, me too. Well, let me get back to working on your case. I'll talk to you later."

"Okay."

Maxi hung up the phone as there was a knock on her door. "Come in!"

"Maxi, there's someone here to see you," Kanesha said, her new assistant.

"Who is it?" she asked.

"Omar Sinclair."

CHAPTER TWENTY-THREE

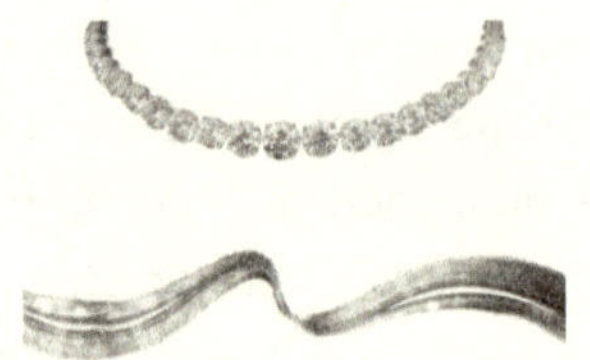

"Hello, Mr. Sinclair, I'm Maxi Bailey," Maxi said, as she and Omar shook hands.

"Very nice to meet you, Mrs. Bailey," Omar said.

"Very nice to meet you as well. Please, have a seat," Maxi said.

Omar sat in front of her desk. "I hope I didn't come here at a bad time."

"Absolutely not," Maxi replied. "So, what can I do for you?"

"I want to hire you to investigate my wife's death. Have you heard about her murder?"

"Yes, I heard about her death, and I'm sorry for your loss."

"Thank you."

"But what makes you think she was murdered?"

"My lawyer—who has connections to the police department—told me that a cop who was on the scene inside the hotel room where my wife was staying had told him that he saw my wife's gun out lying on the ground not too far from her body—which she was licensed to carry —and there was one bullet lodged in the wall. That information has never been reported to the media and my lawyer advised me to keep quiet about it as well. The cops think her attacker might have over-powered her to get the gun out of her hand and then strangled her."

"Has there been an autopsy done? Because it would show if she was strangled."

"I haven't gotten anything done and they haven't done anything. They haven't even showed me pictures of her body and of the crime scene. I believe everyone who is involved in this case are on the hotel's side, that's why I need someone independent to investigate it. My lawyer is just some smalltime city lawyer with really no power up against a hotel that has stood its ground for 150 years. This is the most attention he has ever got for representing a client."

"Does he know you're here?"

"No, he doesn't know I'm here, and I'm not sure if I wanna tell him. I think he's more in this for the attention that my wife's case is getting than seeing that I get justice for her demise. I just wanna know what happened, who did it and why, and I'm just not getting any answers."

"I understand. But how did you know about me?"

"It's been said all over social media that you're a great private investigator and the best friend of Blair West, who, by the way, I met outside of the luxury shopping center my wife loved to shop at. I was doing a press conference there with my lawyer and she just happen to drive up and the media went crazy in seeing her. I know she's got a lot going on in her own life with a text scandal and everything, and it must be pretty bad if the media wanted to hear from her instead of from me that suddenly."

"I'm sorry about that, Omar. That's just the annoying media for you. Yes, I am Blair's best friend, and besides her sister Blythe, I'm the closest to her. She's a great woman, and she is having a very rough time right now with everything that's going on, but she's trying her best to deal with it the best she can."

"I can tell she is," he said with a smile. "So, are you interested in taking my case? I can't see anyone that's a better fit for it."

You don't know the half of it, she thought.

Over an hour later, Maxi got on her phone as she was leaving her office. "Blair? We need to talk. I'm coming over *right now.*"

CHAPTER TWENTY-FOUR

I followed Maxi as she walked fast to my office. "Maxi! Are you gonna tell me why you needed to see me right away? Now you're making me very nervous and you know how bad my nerves are on edge to begin with."

"Well, wait, because your nerves are about to go off a fuckin' cliff when I tell you this."

"Oh, shit!" I said, as we walked into my office. I closed the doors to them. I followed her into the conference room where she put her bag down and went over to my Breville Oracle Touch coffee machine.

"I need to put some alcohol in this," she said, as she waited for her cup to fill up.

At this point, I just sat down in my seat. This was obviously something big and she clearly wanted to take her time telling me what she had to tell me, and when she did this, I knew it probably wasn't anything good.

She brought her cup of coffee over to the table and sat down. She took a sip and leaned back into her seat. She let out a long, loud sigh. "Blair. You have to be *very honest with me* now more than ever when it comes to what happened between you and Cecilia in that hotel room the day she was killed."

"It was purely accidental. You know I'm not lying about that, Maxi. You know I would never lie to you about anything and especially with something as serious as this. What? What is it? What is it that you have to tell me?"

"That Cecilia's husband, Omar, came to my firm today."

My shriek left an echo in the room. "What? *WHAT*?! Maxi, are you serious? He came to *your office*? Why did he come to your office?"

She jumped up! "Why the fuck do you think, Blair? Come on, stop acting like a fuckin' airhead because that's the last damn thing in this world you are! Yes, he came to my office and you know what he came there for!" She slowly sat back down and took another slow sip of her coffee.

I sighed. I shook my head as tears welled up in my eyes. "And what did you say?"

"Yes," she informed me as calmly as she could. "Yes, I told him yes that I would take on his case. Yes I did."

"Maxi! How could you? This is a HUGE conflict of interest and you know it! Why are you doing this? Do you need money? Because you know I can pay you anything if your firm is in trouble or whatever!" I said in a panic.

"I'm personally doing fine financially, Blair. The firm is doing fine financially. Look, I know this is not right and I'm really risking everything by doing this, but no one knows I'm investigating your case except for a person who is no longer employed at my firm, and since she isn't, she has absolutely no idea about me taking on Omar's case while I'm investigating yours. Remember, she has no proof that you had anything to do with Cecilia's death."

"I still don't trust that girl, Maxi, even though she doesn't work for you anymore."

"Well, karma's a bitch, so I hope she remembers it."

I sighed. "How did he know about you?"

"He found out about me through social media and saw how we're best friends. And he found out about all of this through the text scandal, Blair, a scandal that he has no idea that his wife unintentionally became connected to. But most importantly, he has no idea that you were in that room with her."

"And he's never gonna know, right?"

She sighed. "He's only gonna know what I tell him. Look, I got half his case solved already and he doesn't even know it. Look, Blair, you *can't* blame the man for hiring me to find out who did this to his wife. He's grieving, he wants answers. Now you said it was an accident on her part, and I believe you. He said he has not gotten back anything from anyone about any autopsy findings or anything. It's clear the cops, doctors, and everyone else are on the hotel's side like he told me, and I believe him because it's clear that they are. He just has a feeling his lawyer is just in this for the publicity he's getting on himself; he really feels like he's not gonna do anything for him that's why he hired me. His lawyer doesn't even know he came to me. He did his research on me and doesn't want anyone else working on his case."

I shook my head. "I just can't be okay with this, Maxi. I know you're doing your job, but you're investigating me for him since you already know it's me who was in the room with his wife that night."

"Blair, you were completely covered up, I can easily say I don't know who you are. But I have to do this for him. He may be paying me, but in a lot of ways it's also not about the money."

"I never knew I was gonna get myself into something like this. Never knew what I was in for. Now I'm really up shit creek without a fuckin' paddle, as they say."

"Well, there's a way I can cancel the whole investigation."

I looked at her. "And what way is that?"

"By you telling Omar exactly what happened, Blair."

I shook my head once again. "I just can't do it right now, Maxi. I just can't. I didn't kill her, I have way too much shit going on right now, and I still don't know who is sending me these texts and they've sent some more to me since—did you get them because I did send them to you?"

"Yeah, I got them, Blair. I'm still working on trying to trace them but as I suspected, they're from a burner phone, and probably not the same phone that the first ones were sent to you on. I gotta be very honest with you."

"Please, because I can't take any lies."

"You may not ever find out who's doing this to you. Are you able to accept that?"

"No," I replied matter-of-factly. "I'm too deep in all of this shit to accept that, Maxi. You're now investigating the case for a woman's husband that's dead because of me and you're investigating my case since there's still a bitch out there taunting me about sleeping with Lang."

"Where is Lang?"

"Probably skeeting on some bitch's pussy."

She chuckled. "Blair."

"Look, Maxi, there is no way I'm ever gonna feel comfortable about you investigating Omar's case for the most obvious reason. But I know you gotta to do what you gotta do and I know no one is gonna know, right?"

"Of course not, Blair. What is the point of being a private investigator if everyone finds out every case I'm investigating? It's called private investigating for a reason. No one is supposed to know except me and my client. Plus, me accepting the job of investigating his case also makes it look like you had nothing to do with it—can you agree to that? I have to throw him off as much as I can, and yes, it's unethical to do this, but this man is owed answers."

I sighed once again. "I just wish someone else could give them to him."

"And besides me? You're the only who can and you know it. I hope you reconsider, Blair. We can even tell him together if you want. At least you would know that's out of the way."

"Nothing is ever gonna be out of the way until I find out who started all of this to begin with because it sure as hell wasn't me. This has turned me into a person I never in my life thought I would become and unthinkable shit has happened because of it. I'll do anything to hold on to Lang and to my marriage and family, but I didn't think a woman who I mistook as another woman he was really sleeping with was gonna accidentally lose her life because of it and now you're investigating her husband's case which is pretty much investigating me because there wouldn't be a case if my fuckin' stupid ass didn't go up to that room that day. How did all of this shit come to this?"

"All I can say, Blair, is that we as humans should never ever say what we will never ever do."

"Yeah, you can say that again."

She looked around the room. "Those red roses are beautiful. Looks like you're all set for the ABWS meeting here tomorrow," she said, clearly trying to change the subject.

"They're too dark red. They look like old blood."

She grinned. "Blair . . . come on. They're gorgeous and some of the most expensive flowers in the world and this room is full of them as well as your office area. I also love how they're always sprinkled with that genuine 24-karat gold powder that looks like glitter. It adds that amazing sparkling touch to them. Lang got them for you like he always does when you have a meeting here, huh?"

"That and a whole lot of other things. Asshole."

"Blair, stop. I mean it. Now I'm gonna try and get through this investigation for Omar as quickly as I can—but I don't wanna lie to him. I may have to do some things you don't want me to do."

I shook my head. "As long as you don't prove to him that it was me who was in that room with his wife that morning then I don't care what you do. I just have to find the mental and emotional strength to tell him myself."

"And the sooner you find it, Blair, the better." She pulled out her iPad and looked through it. "Oh, and I forgot to tell you something else."

"What is it?"

"That Cordelia Sharpe is back in town."

"What hotel is she staying at?"

"Blair . . ."

"I know you fuckin' told me that you weren't gonna tell me but I wanna fuckin' know!"

"Blair, calm your ass down right now. I said I would let you know when she was back in town, but I was *not* telling you what hotel she was staying at—remember I told you that?"

"No," I lied.

"Bullshit," she replied as she put her iPad back into her bag. She could always see right through me.

I shook my head. "That's probably where Lang is at. In fact, *I know* that's where he is."

"That's why I didn't want to tell you what hotel she's at, and no, I'm not making it up about her not being at the Regalis Montemar, so don't go charging the fuck down there like you did last time and why you're in this shit that you're in and why I'm investigating some shit that should've never happened all because of you."

I lowered my head. The one thing I loved about Maxi was that she was always straightforward with me about everything. *Everything*. And if anyone said they didn't need a best friend like her was only fooling themselves. I needed her more than I ever needed her, but I knew I needed to stay out of her way and let her do a job she already knew the outcome of, and I knew she was praying like crazy that I would finally give in and tell Omar what really happened.

Several minutes later, Maxi was gone, so I continued to sit in my office as I stared at the flowers Lang had given to me for my meeting here for tomorrow as I drank a dirty martini while listening to "Eye Hate U" by Prince. And the last thing I wanted to do was hold this ABWS meeting here tomorrow because I just didn't feel like dealing with a bunch of bitches who thought their lives were so perfect and wanted to fake feeling sorry for me because of what'd been going on with mine.

CHAPTER TWENTY-FIVE

"Well, I will tell you all one thing. The Cecilia Sinclair case has been the case that has gotten the most attention at my hotel in a very, very long time," Astrid said, and took a sip of her water. "In the 150 years of its existence, there has been a lot of things that has happened there—a lot of deaths whether it was murders, suicides, murder-suicides, natural causes—all kinds of death, let's just put it like that, but this is the first one in recent years that has involved a Black woman."

I stared at Astrid Regalis-Dubois since she was a friend of mine that, of course, became a friend of mine through Lang since they'd gone to the same high school and college. Astrid was actually one of the heiresses to the Regalis Montemar Hotel since her White father, Winston Regalis V, was the great-great grandson of one of the creators of the hotel, Winston Regalis I. He married Astrid's Black mom in the late 1970s when she worked at the hotel in one of the gift shops at the time. She even admitted that no one really wanted him to marry her because she was Black, but he didn't care what they said and did it anyway, and they were still married to this day. We'd always told her that her dad was turning the history of the hotel Black by marrying her mom, and she had turned it even more Black by marrying her husband, investment financial analyst Merriman Dubois. The Montemar side was still all White.

"Well, Astrid, you should've known something was gonna happen there again sooner or later. But I just hate that it happened to a Black woman, and one with a family at that. It's like no one cares about us," Charlene said, a ABWS member who was married to a very prominent surgeon in the city.

"You got that right," Fayal said. "I honestly believe it was Omar who killed her."

"How do you know it was him?" Astrid asked.

We all looked at Fayal, especially me.

"Because it's usually always the husband who did it, and look how he's constantly in the media talking about it. That's usually the first sign that he had something to with it."

"Not necessarily," Charlene said. "I believe some janitor or someone who worked there did it."

"It's possible, ladies, but we will probably never know," Astrid said.

"What has your dad said about it, Astrid?" Fayal asked.

I looked at Astrid as I really wanted to hear what she said about this.

Astrid sighed. "Well, we really shouldn't be talking about it if you all want to know the truth. The hotel's lawyers are handling everything. They just haven't talked about it publicly and especially to the media because there is no suspect in custody and Omar has filed a huge lawsuit with the hotel that's yes, in the millions and millions. No one has really given him any information about how Cecilia died, either, everyone is just assuming she was murdered, but it's been said that she hadn't been."

"What?!" they all said in shock.

"Look, ladies, like I said, I should *not* be talking about this to anyone. I could possibly lose my part of the inheritance to the hotel if it gets out that I'd talked about this."

"And since we don't want that to happen then this conversation is over and is to never be brought up again," I ordered.

Everyone looked at me.

"Hey, fine with me!" Astrid said with a smile. "Thank you, Blair."

"You're welcome," I replied with a smile, even though I was more saying this because I was the suspect in this and just didn't feel like talking about it anymore. "So, who are we still waiting on to get here?"

Charlene looked at her watch. "We're still waiting on Heather to get here with the two new ABWS members."

The two new ABWS members was kept a secret from everyone until they met me. It had been a tradition in the ABWS since the creator of the organization, the late Fannie Livingston, wanted it that way. Her daughter, Mildred Livingston, who was in her late 80's now, was the active heiress to the organization. As the organization's national president, I had to answer to her.

I looked at my watch as well. "Well, they should've been here by now."

They all looked at each other.

"Is everything all right, Blair?" Fayal asked.

Everyone in the room looked at me since there were about ten of us in here.

"You know, I wonder how you all have been talking about me and this text scandal when I'm not around," I said.

Crickets.

They all looked in every direction except right in mine as some of them took a sip of their drinks while others stuffed gourmet hors d'oeuvres in their mouths to avoid saying anything.

"Yeah, that's what I thought," I said.

ABWS Secretary Heather Willard walked through the front doors of my office just in time. "Hello, ladies!" she said as she walked into the conference room with her enthusiastic smile as the two new members stood by her side waiting to be introduced.

"Hello!" everyone said with their fake voices.

Heather walked over to me as I stood up. "Blair, here are the two new members of the ABWS in their respective cities. This is Trina Bridgeton, from the Diamond Lake Chapter. Trina, this is Blair West, ABWS National President."

"Hello, Trina, nice to meet you," I said with a smile.

"It's an honor, Mrs. West," Trina said with a big smile as we shook hands.

"Thank you. Welcome to the ABWS," I said with a smile, and I always liked to welcome new members like this because it'd shown how far us Black women had come in a society that was against us, and that who a woman could marry could change her life for the better or for the worse, and we were proof it was for the better.

But it was far from perfect.

Heather smiled as Trina took a seat at the table as she got ready to introduce me to the next new member. "Blair, this is Cordelia Sharpe from the Saddle Hills chapter."

Cordelia smiled. "Nice to meet you, Mrs. West," she said as she held her hand out for a shake.

I punched her in her face!

Everyone in the room screamed as Cordelia fell back on the table as she held her face!

I didn't know how Astrid got so fast over to me as well two others as they held me back from her!

"GET HER PHONE! GET HER PHONE! THE TEXTS THIS BITCH SENT TO ME ARE ON THEM!" I screamed.

Fayal grabbed her phone which was on the floor and gave it to me.

"HOLD HER! THIS BITCH ISN'T GOING ANYWHERE! SHE'S SLEEPING WITH MY HUSBAND AND IS SENDING ME THOSE TEXTS TEASING AND TAUNTING ME ABOUT IT!" I yelled as it was so chaotic in the room as I looked at her phone at all of her text messages to see if there were any sent to me. "WHERE IS YOUR OTHER PHONE?! YOU HAVE ANOTHER PHONE! *I KNOW* YOU HAVE ANOTHER PHONE!"

"I'm not the one sending you those texts, Blair! *I swear* I'm not! And I don't have another phone!" Cordelia said, as she held her face as tears streamed down her eyes.

Everyone looked at me.

I threw her phone back her. "Get this bitch out of my house! GET HER OUT!" I yelled.

About five of the women escorted Cordelia out of my conference room and made sure she left my house. I sat calmly back down at the head of the table as I tried to contain my composure once again.

I looked at Trina as she stared at me with her eyes wide and full of fear. "Sorry you had to see that. That was very inappropriate of me to do."

"But I understand why you did it," she replied with a nervous smile.

CHAPTER TWENTY-SIX

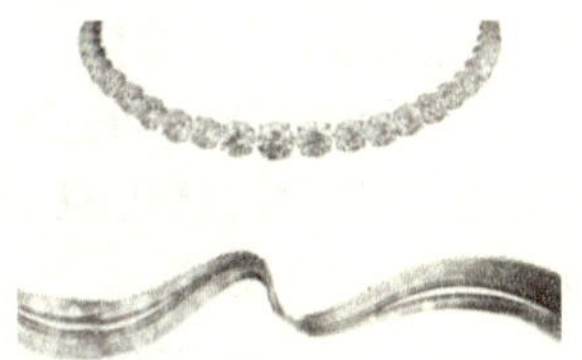

"JUST WHAT THE FUCK WAS THAT SHIT YOU DID AT YOUR MEETING, BLAIR?! HAVE YOU LOST YOUR FUCKIN' MIND?!" Lang yelled, as we stood in the hall between our master bedroom and down the hall from our girls' bedrooms.

"HAVE YOU LOST YOURS?!" I yelled back. "None of this shit had to fuckin' happen, Lang, if you didn't sleep with that bitch! And then you had the nerve to tell her she could walk through these fuckin' doors to this house to meet me?!"

He sighed as he looked up at the ceiling. "Blair, I didn't tell her she could come here, okay? I didn't know she was an ABWS member where she's from."

"Oh! So you're actually admitting to me that you do know her, huh?"

He kept staring at me.

"HUH?!" I yelled!

"Stop yelling! I don't even think you even realize the kind of shit you've caused by assaulting her like that, Blair! You'll be lucky if you're just sued!"

I let out a sarcastic laugh. "Yeah, sued by one of your hundred

145

lovers, should I really be surprised? I was wondering why I haven't had to do what I did a lot sooner!"

"And you won't do it again, and I mean it. You really messed up the rep of this family, Blair, by doing what you did! How the hell did that look to the other members and to Trina Bridgeton whose husband is the president at my company in Diamond Lake!"

"LIKE REALITY!" I yelled.

"*I SAID* STOP YELLING!"

"YOU STOP FUCKING OTHER WOMEN AND I WOULDN'T HAVE TO KNOCK THEM THE FUCK OUT AFTER SHOWING UP AT THIS HOUSE AND ACTING AS IF THEY DIDN'T SLEEP WITH YOU!"

Jodie and Lorie came slowly walking down the hall.

"Mom? Dad? What's going on?" Jodie asked.

We looked at them, and then looked at each other.

"I'm sleeping in one of the guestrooms tonight," I informed him. I looked at Jodie and Lorie. "You two, go back to your rooms. The fight is over."

They looked at each other and turned around and walked back down the hall to their rooms.

I stormed past Lang to go change into my pajamas. He followed me.

"You know we need to talk about this some more, Blair. Now you don't have to believe me when I say that I did not know Cordelia Sharpe was gonna come to this house."

"Yeah, I just bet you didn't because you would not have tried to stop her if she had anyway so why does it really matter, Lang? You know I know that you're sleeping with her and you haven't even admitted it to me. At least you can do that."

"Look, I'm worried about how our girls are being affected by this, okay? This isn't only about your hurt feelings over what you think I did."

"What I *think* you did, Lang? What I *think* you did?! Are you fuckin' kidding me?!"

He continued to stare at me as I changed into my pajamas.

"ARE YOU FUCKIN' KIDDING ME!?" I yelled.

"I told you to be quiet about this! You see how you were so fuckin' loud that our girls heard you all the way down the fuckin hall and around the corner from their bedrooms! You know how big this house is, but your mouth is twice as big as this house!"

"FUCK YOU!"

He shook his head. "Okay, where is your proof that I slept with Cordelia Sharpe or any other woman out there?"

"Where is my proof, you ask?" I said, as tears welled up in my eyes.

"Yeah, where is your proof, Blair? Because you couldn't find it on Cordelia's phone when you checked it yourself that she's the one who's been sending you those texts about sleeping with me, that's what Astrid told me."

"Then she has another phone," I concluded.

He shook his head as he grinned. "I doubt that, Blair. A lot of people only have one phone and she's probably one of them."

I honestly didn't know what to think at this point. I did not want to admit for the life of me that it wasn't Cordelia who was sending me these texts. I wanted it *so bad* to be her so this part of this text scandal could be over with, but something in me had told me that it really wasn't her and that the phone I'd checked was the only phone she had.

I stormed out of my closet room after changing into my pajamas and headed towards one of the guestrooms. I looked back and saw Lang staring at me from a distance as he stayed where he was; it looked as if he was a mile away down this wide hallway. It was amazing to be living in a house that resembled a royal palace, but it felt so cold and empty, and so fake and dishonest. And as I entered one of the guestrooms, I thought about the one thing he never said. He never said he *didn't* sleep with her.

<u>WILD BLACK TEA WITH BEVERLY</u>
BREAKING NEWS!
THE PUNCH HEARD AROUND THE WORLD!
BLAIR WEST KNOCKS OUT HUSBAND'S CONFIRMED
LOVER CORDELIA SHARPE AT FANCY ABWS
MEETING!

CORDELIA ALSO CONFIRMED *NOT* TO BE THE INFAMOUS TEXTER WHO STARTED IT ALL

Beverly started the show by sipping her tea. "Chile! I knew this story was gonna start making those teapots whistle off the stoves! This is what I was waiting for! I couldn't believe this when I got this video! And if you're gonna knock a bitch out for sleeping with your husband, do it in style like Blair did in her $6,300 Bottega Veneta silver intrecciato leather woven skirt, black silk-cashmere sweater, and black Manolo Blahnik heels. But it's clear that Blair is not playing with any of these women out here who are fooling around with her husband, and if she has proof that you are, she's gonna give you what you rightfully deserve if you have a nerve to step into her 40,000 square foot royal home—for business or not!

"Welcome to the show, everyone, I'm Beverly, the only one you need for all of your wild Black tea, and we had some wild-ass shit go down at the home of billionaire wife Blair West at a rare home ABWS meeting. For those of you who don't know what that stands for, ABWS stands for Affluent Black Women's Society, and yes, you can only get in if you're married to a man of some big affluence in your city. The philanthropic organization has been around for 90 years and has a lot of chapters in cities all over the country. One of the most notable members besides Blair is her good friend Astrid Regalis-Dubois, one of the heiresses to the 150-year-old Regalis Montemar Hotel. Yes, that hotel has a Black history on the Regalis side starting with Astrid's Black mother Jewelle!

"But Blair happens to be the ABWS National President, and we all know it's because she's married to one of the richest Black men in the world that the job was just given to her for that reason alone. But we don't know how long Blair is gonna keep that job because of what happened today at a rare in-home conference meeting that she only has a few times a year, and this one was to meet two new members, and one of those two new members was Cordelia Sharpe, a member of the Saddle Hills Chapter, and wife of a prominent older businessman who owns a string of Black banks across the country. And yes, we can confirm with friends of Cordelia that she was having an affair with Lang West, but she's *not* the one who's been sending the texts to Blair, and Blair wanted to make sure of that because after punching Cordelia's lights out seconds after meeting her, she demanded her phone and checked through it and saw no texts sent to her from her phone.

"It's unclear how Blair found out Cordelia was one of the women sleeping with Lang, but she was so sure she was one of his many lovers that she made sure she would never sleep with her husband again! You go, Blair! You've known Lang for 20 years and you've built an 18-year marriage with him and have raised two beautiful girls. Do what you gotta do to not let any woman try and take that away from you!"

"And that's exactly what I'm doing," I mumbled to myself and took a sip of my drink.

A chime came into my phone.

You're gonna lose him for good now! You can't stop him from sleeping with me or with anyone!

I turned off my phone. I had enough of all of this for one night. I knew this was not Cordelia Sharpe, but at least now everyone knew I was not playing in the least bit about these women sleeping with my husband. I was on a mission to keep my marriage and family together, but in reality, I really didn't know if what I'd done earlier just made it all fall apart.

CHAPTER TWENTY-SEVEN

"*L*ook, I just acted on instinct, all right? I mean, what would the two of you have done if a woman that was proven to be sleeping with your husband would've showed up in your house for the first time and met you like she wasn't doing a damn thing with him?" I asked, as I wiped tears from my eyes.

Maxi and Blythe stared at me, and then looked at each other.

"Well, truth be told, Blair, none of us could really say what we would've really done unless we're right there face-to-face in the situation like the way you were. Maybe I would've punched the shit out of her, maybe not, but she would've definitely have been escorted out of my house," Maxi said.

"I agree," Blythe said.

"You both know I just haven't been myself," I said.

"And you need to stop using that excuse now, Blair, and I mean right now. You're better than this shit. This should not have gotten you to this point," Maxi said.

"Oh, yeah? Well, I think I would be myself again if I could bring back Cecilia Sinclair, but I can't do that. I can't undo anything that's been done, and the person who started all of this is still out there teasing and taunting me. They know what I did to Cordelia and it's like they're getting a kick out of it, as the old saying goes. I just don't know who the fuck this is."

"I think you should just forget about who she is, Blair. I think it's time to block this bitch and any other contact she tries to make with you through emails and all of this other shit. This is getting you into trouble you should not be getting in and otherwise would've never gotten in," Blythe said.

"I agree," Maxi said, as she stared at me like only a best friend who really cared about me could stare at me. "You know I'm still working on this, Blair, and telling you everything you need to know. I didn't think things would get this out of control with you."

"Well, everything would be in control if Lang was just honest with me about everything. It's like he *still* couldn't tell me to my fuckin' face that he slept with that Cordelia bitch! And I find out that she's married, too? Because you have to be married to be an ABWS member, but you both know that."

"What has Mildred said about your status as the national president?" Blythe asked.

Maxi stared at me.

I sighed. "I got a personal email from her acknowledging that she is aware of what happened here and that she saw the full video of it. She's flying in to talk to me here so I will know then. Look, I know I'm in trouble, okay? I just don't wanna think about this shit right now."

"And that's exactly why you need to talk about it, Blair. We don't want you getting into any more trouble. How do you know that Cordelia won't sue you for assault?" Blythe asked.

"She's lucky I'm not suing her for being a homewrecker. Cause and effect," I said, and took a sip of my drink. "I just need to find out who this other bitch is who keeps texting me."

"So you're sure it's not Cordelia anymore?" Maxi asked.

Blythe looked at me.

I sighed. "Yeah, I guess I can cross that bitch off the list. But if she crosses me again she's gonna be even more sorry."

"Don't go making threats, Blair. You showed her you weren't playing by physically assaulting her; and you hit her *hard*, Blair. The sound and look of that punch made me lightheaded!" Maxi said.

"Me too! The way she fell back on that table made it seem like it was a movie!" Blythe said with a slight chuckle.

"I have a lot of strength since I do a lot of weight training," I said with a slight grin.

"And now we want you to use your mental and emotional strength to fight through all of this stress and madness you've been feeling, Blair. We can't afford to have you in jail; your girls can't afford it," Maxi said.

"Exactly," Blythe said with a smile.

"My girls mean everything to me. *Everything*," I stressed.

"Speaking of them—and Lang as well—where are they?" Maxi asked.

CHAPTER TWENTY-EIGHT

"You must've really loved the movie from the start, Dad, you didn't fall asleep once throughout it," Jodie said with a smile as they left the movie theater.

Lorie laughed. "Yeah, I noticed that, too!"

"And I think that's one of the first times you haven't in a long time, so this was a great Daddy-Daughter Date Night," Jodie said with a smile.

"I agree," Lorie said.

Lang smiled. "I agree, too, and it was a great movie. Had my attention from the start. Great job, Lorie, for picking it."

"I've been wanting to see it since it first came out," Lorie said with a big smile.

"Now, where do the two of you want to go eat?" he asked.

"TACO BELL!" they replied with excitement.

He laughed. "Taco Bell it is!"

They began walking towards the exit of the casino where the movie theater was in.

"MR. WEST!"

They all looked around.

"Girls, stay right here. Don't go anywhere," Lang replied, and walked over to the two women. He spoken to them for a minute when one of them suddenly walked away.

Jodie and Lorie looked at each other in confusion.

"Do you know who they are?" Lorie asked.

"No, I've never seen them before," Jodie said. "Dad will tell us."

After a few minutes, Lang walked back over to his girls. "Sorry that took long."

"Who are they?" Jodie asked.

"They work at my company," he replied as they walked towards the exit of the casino.

Jodie and Lorie looked at each other and nodded with a smile.

<u>WILD BLACK TEA WITH BEVERLY</u>
LANG WEST AND DAUGHTERS JODIE AND LORIE SPOTTED OUT ON MONTHLY DADDY-DAUGHTER DATE NIGHT AT THE MOVIES
LANG SEEN TALKING TO TWO FEMALE COMPANY EMPLOYEES

"Well, there seems to be some kind of normalcy restored in the billionaire West family household with one of my sources spotting Lang West out with his daughters Jodie and Lorie on what the three of them have as a monthly Daddy-Daughter Date Night. But what I was really tripping off of was Jodie's $3,800 Louis Vuitton LV x YK Faces Patches denim jacket along with a matching pair of denim jeans on—and the pieces are sold separately, by the way. Lorie looked cute in a Madeworn Salt-N-Pepa tee shirt with jeans and sneakers. Lang's fine, cheating ass looked good as well in his plain long-sleeved black tee and jeans and sneakers. And since this was a date night for just him and his girls, the scorned wifey Blair was nowhere to be found.

"But word has it that her job as the ABWS National President is hanging in the balance since she knocked out one of her husband's lovers and new ABWS member, Cordelia Sharpe, so I just don't think we will be seeing much of her. And it has also been said that Cordelia is confirmed *not* to be the one who has been sending her those texts that started this whole text scandal, but at least Blair got her revenge on one of them!

"But back to this date night Lang had with his girls. After the movie they saw, two unidentified women called him over to them, and he made his girls stay back while he went over to talk to them. It was confirmed later to be two women who work for him, but why wouldn't he introduce his girls to two women out of the hundreds and thousands of people who work for him all throughout this country since these people are also responsible for how well these girls live? But it's clear Lang didn't think they were that important for his daughters to meet. And I gotta feeling that some things are about to be exposed about Lang himself because this man is a piece of work. He has taken absolutely *no accountability* for what he has done and is just letting his wife act up in ways no one has ever seen her act up in all over him. This is far from over, y'all, so you know to always keep it here!"

I walked out of the guestroom and into the master bedroom . . . and found Lang sitting up in bed staring right at me.

He patted my side of the bed. "Sleep with me tonight."

"As long as you're not sleeping with other women," I replied.

He grinned as he refused to say a word as I got in bed.

"How was the movie?" I asked, as I sat up in bed with him.

"We all loved it," he replied with a smile.

I nodded. "Lang, *you know* we need to talk."

"About what?"

I sighed as I shook my head. "Don't start asking questions like that, Lang, because you know damn well about what. I'm tired of being made a fool of, okay? You haven't taken any responsibility for what's been going on; you haven't even wanted to talk about it. I mean, where the hell did I go wrong in our marriage that caused you to do these things, huh?"

"Have I ever said you were a bad wife, Blair? Or a bad mom?"

"Well, because of what's been going on lately it really seems like I have been, Lang! And that hurts because I'm trying to do the best I can at being the best I can at everything, and it's now taking a toll on me. It's like my best is no longer good enough for you. It's clear this is about me that's making you do these things."

"It's not about you, Blair."

"Then what is it about, Lang? Somewhere in our marriage something went wrong. This woman who sent me that text that started it all would not have sent me anything like that if something wasn't going on. Why would she have a reason to do that, huh? She turned our lives upside down and you're acting as if everything's okay. Like I said, we haven't personally talked about this. I think we need to go to marriage counseling."

"We don't need any damn marriage counseling, Blair. I'm not wasting my money on that shit."

"Well, I just think we're not talking enough, and you're especially not talking to me. It's like I don't even know you anymore. You're not being honest with me about a lot of things, Lang, and this is hurting me a lot and it's like you don't even care that it is."

"I care about how you're making this family look, Blair. You know as my wife you have a rep to uphold no matter how much shit this family is going through right now. You have not been holding it together like the way you used to do."

"This family's personal business was not put on display for the world to see until now either, Lang! I admit that I don't know how to handle it, okay? This is all new to me. For 18 years we managed to avoid having our personal lives in the spotlight, but all of the sudden, one text changed everything overnight. And you *still* won't admit to me the obvious."

"Well, if it's so obvious then why should I have to admit it to you?"

"See! Here you go! I'm not gonna go around in circles with you! *You know* I need to hear you say it, Lang, and you haven't said it. You know you're the one who caused all of this shit. *I've never cheated on you,* and you know it."

He smirked. "Damn right I know it."

I looked at him. I knew right at this moment that he'd hired a private investigator to track my moves in the past, especially when we first got married. "So, what is so wrong with you admitting to me what you've done? That's all I want is for you to admit it to me, Lang, and how long you've been doing it. I just don't know how much longer I'm gonna be able to take any of this. I don't even know if I'm gonna have a job much longer."

"When are you supposed to be meeting with Mildred?"

"Soon, I guess. She hasn't given me a specific date when she'll be flying in to see me. I can't afford to lose this job because I love it. It gives me something to do."

"And it's your fault if you lose it, Blair. You lost your temper towards a woman that you can't prove that I slept with."

I shook my head. I just didn't think he was ever gonna admit to me that he was sleeping with her, and if he was never gonna admit to me that he was sleeping with her then I might as well have said fuck all of the other ones as well. "Who were the two women you ran into after the movies?"

"Who told you I ran into two women after the movies? You must've been looking at that tea woman Beverly again."

"Yeah, I was," I said with a glare.

He smirked once again as he shook his head. "They're women who work at my company. They even addressed me by Mr. West like everyone is supposed to. They recognized me even though I didn't recognize them. What's the big deal?"

"That's what Beverly said in her video about how they worked for you."

"Yeah, everyone is following my every move. This is not fair to me or my girls."

"And what about me, Lang? Am I somehow left out of all of this?"

"You seem to be in your own little world about all of this, Blair. I told you when all of this first went down that we needed to still be as private as we could about everything. But when you're knocking out women in this home that you meet for the very first time and just in general not being yourself, well, that's a problem. I never said handling these changes in our lives were gonna be easy. Hell, I sometimes even have trouble concentrating on work, but I'm still getting things done because I pretend that none of this shit is going on."

"Yeah, shit that you started."

He turned off his light and rolled over. "Goodnight."

I still sat upright in the bed as tears welled up in my eyes. I felt at this point he was never gonna admit to me that all of this was his fault. He just expected for me to still act like the beautiful little Blair that he fell in love with and married, as if everything in our lives was still perfect and were never gonna change. I couldn't believe just how delusional he was being about all of this. I honestly thought he saw absolutely nothing wrong with what he was doing but thought there was something wrong with how I'd been rightfully reacting to it. Yes, there were some things I went way too far about, and the Cecilia Sinclair incident was definitely one of them which was completely unexpected. But all I wanted him to do was admit his part in all of this which led to everything that I'd done which was completely the opposite of the kind of person I really was.

I looked at my phone and saw that there was a text from Maxi:

Just found out some mind-blowing information. Meet me at my office first thing tomorrow morning.

CHAPTER TWENTY-NINE

"So that's the independent autopsy findings. It wasn't a murder, it was a head injury caused by a bad slip and fall. She obviously couldn't break her fall when she slipped and fell backwards and hit her head hard on that very hard floor. It may or may not have been a different outcome had she been on carpet, but you just never know. I'll give you more updates as soon as I get them."

I stared at Maxi with my eyes as wide as I could get them as she still spoke on the phone. She'd been in here talking on it since I'd gotten here.

She hung up. "Well, you heard it for yourself. And you were right all along, Blair. You didn't kill her. It was a freak accident."

I shook my head. "I wish it didn't happen at all. This is still all my fault for going there to begin with."

"There's nothing we can do about that now, Blair. I just wanted you to hear it for yourself as I told it to him, and I have to let you know something else."

"What is it?"

"I did show Omar the video surveillance of you going to Cecilia's hotel room, and he said he did not recognize you."

"*He said* he didn't recognize me?!"

"Relax, Blair. I mean it in the way that he did not know it was you; I never told him it was you and never asked him did he recognized it as being you—you know I wouldn't do that. Remember, you were all covered up and if you didn't tell me it was you and especially if you didn't come into this office that day with that black trench coat on and I had never seen the black baseball cap you had on when you went to the hotel room, I would've never thought it was you, either. To the average person, you covered yourself very well."

"Well, I hoped that I did, even if I never got into her room that day. I just wanted to see if what I'd seen written down on that paper was in fact real, and I saw how it was. Only little did I know at the time that Cordelia checked out of there the day before. Had I known that, Cecilia would still be alive."

She sighed. "Look, Blair, there's something you need to know about that room."

"What about it?"

"It's not an ordinary room there."

"What do you mean it's not an ordinary room there, Maxi? Well, I guess it's not an ordinary room because someone did die in it and it's all my fault that she did since I was up in there when I shouldn't have been."

"That's not the only reason," she said. "Look, I don't know how to tell you this and I don't even know if I should tell you this because I don't want you flying off the damn handle and doing shit that you shouldn't be doing."

"I'm in enough shit, Maxi, so just say it."

She sighed once again. I knew what she had to tell me was something pretty serious. "Blair, that room, Room 2609, the room you were in when everything went down with Cecilia, the room Cordelia Sharpe was in . . ."

"Yeah?" I asked, as I stared with wide-eyed suspense.

She shook her head. "Room 2609 is a reserved room."

I gave her a look of confusion. "*Reserved room*? Okay, but aren't all the rooms reserved for guests? I mean, it's a hotel, isn't it?"

"Very true, Blair. But this reserved room is different from all of the other ones."

"How is it different?"

"It's different in the fact that it's only reserved for . . . for certain people."

I sighed. "I'm afraid I'm not following you, Maxi. It's a fuckin' hotel room. You need to reserve a room or rooms so you can stay there; it's the fuckin' Regalis Montemar. You can't just walk off the street and get a room."

"Yes, you're right about that."

"So, what are you getting at?"

"I gotta admit, Blair, this even surprised me, and things rarely surprise me."

"Oh, shit! If you say that something surprised you then this was obviously a surprise, so stop holding me in suspense and tell me what rarely surprised you. I could barely sleep last night when you texted me and told me you had some mind-blowing information. So? What's the mind-blowing info?"

"That Room 2609 is a private room that's only available to . . . "

"To? To . . . who?"

She took a deep breath. "To people who personally know Lang."

I jumped up out of my seat! "What? *What*?! Why does he have a hotel room that is only available to people who personally know him? Is it for business purposes? Does he have a contract with the hotel?"

"Only a contract with Astrid," she informed me. "And you know that's all the contact and contracts he needs."

I slowly sat back down in my seat. "What the fuck are you trying to tell me, Maxi?"

"I'm trying to tell you, Blair, is that Lang has had Room 2609 for more than 20 years. This is before he met you. He has paid Astrid a lot of money to always have that room available for women he flies into town. Remember, Astrid is one of the heiresses at the hotel—she can pull many strings there, and that was one of the strings she has pulled. I don't know if she knew about Cordelia Sharpe beforehand or not, but when Lang has a woman he wants to personally see and whether she's from here or out of town, he always has Room 2609 privately booked for her."

I shook my head as tears welled up in my eyes. "And I thought she was my friend. She's been a hundred percent complicit in his affairs."

"She's been his friend longer, Blair. And money is everyone's best friend. Even though she doesn't need it, he's been paying her to keep that room unavailable to other hotel guests for more than 20 years—*more than 20 years*—so you know that's before the two of you officially met."

"So, the other woman was obviously at our penthouse the night of the charity event because Cordelia was in the hotel room he always has available for women he's having affairs with."

"Exactly, Blair. I still don't know who the woman on the elevator at y'alls penthouse is, but you know I'm still working on it." She sighed. "So, Blair, in knowing this, here comes some more bad news."

"I . . . I don't wanna think about it. Please . . . PLEASE don't let me think what I'm thinking!"

She sighed. "If what you're thinking Blair is what I wanna tell you, I'm gonna apologize to you ahead of time."

I sat with my right had completely covering my forehead. "Just say it."

"There are text exchanges between Lang . . . and Cecilia Sinclair."

Tears instantly welled up in my eyes. "Let me see them."

She stared at me as she slowly shoved her iPad towards me. I looked at the phone records of Cecilia Sinclair and the texts she had that were between her and my husband:

Hey, I just arrived in Room 2609. And it's beautiful just like you said and what I've seen in the pictures and video of it.

Glad you like it. So, when can I see you?

Right after my talk. Shouldn't take that long. Are you sure you can't attend? It's open to the public?

No, I have to work. Just let me know when I can come see you. You know I've been waiting to see you in person ever since you slid into my DMs on social media a while back.

I can't believe this is finally gonna happen. Can't wait. It's all I can think about. But business before pleasure.

And I'll be there for the pleasure. See you then.

Tears streamed down my eyes as Maxi stared sympathetically at me. I could tell she really felt sorry for me.

"I know this hurts, Blair. And I admit I couldn't believe it when I was reading these texts. I knew there had to have been something much more to Cecilia Sinclair than what you'd told me. The texts are proof that she lied to you about knowing who you were and who Lang was."

"Yeah, she was a great actress; a fuckin' great actress. A great liar. I really believed her, Maxi, I really did. And she had the nerve to come after me when she knew damn well she was in a room that Lang had reserved for her and paid for, even though it was put in her name. Wow, this has been an incredible twist in this story that I never saw coming. Does Omar know about all of this?"

"No, he doesn't. And I just don't know when I wanna tell him, but I gotta tell him. Cecilia's phone has been in police custody ever since her body was found in the hotel room, but they gave me the records to it since I'm investigating his case since it's clear they're not doing anything with it; I don't even think they looked at her phone. And now they're not going to since her death has been officially ruled accidental. When I saw this text exchange, I knew it was between her and Lang; her mentioning the room number gave it away. It was just on one of his other many phones. She was careful not to say his name in them."

"Wow. I would have known all of this had I picked up her phone and looked at it, but she had me so convinced that she didn't know him or me that I didn't even bother to look at it. She never even had a chance to meet him in person, and it was all because of me."

"It was because of her being in that room that Lang gave her money to pay for when the only business that she had being there was for a talk she was supposed to give, but it was clear that wasn't the only thing she was there to give because she would not have been in room 2609 if that was the case. It's also clear he always wants the room in the woman's name so he looks like he has nothing to do with the room or her. You know how expensive the least expensive room is at that hotel even for one night, and that room is one of the more expensive ones as you personally saw for yourself."

"Yeah, I know. So, I basically stopped her from sleeping with him before she did."

"You sure did."

"And thinking she was Cordelia Sharpe at that. You can't even make this shit up."

"And I have to admit this, Blair. Never in all of the years I've been investigating have I ever had anything like this happen. Your case and Omar's case end up being connected in a way I never thought it would be even after you'd told me it was you as to the reason why he opened up a case with me to begin with because he wanted his wife's death investigated. I honestly don't think he knew she was gonna meet up with Lang later on that day after her talk."

"I just don't think he knew, either. He seems like such a nice man. And she was cheating on him through sex texts with my husband after all and was gonna meet him in person for the first time. I mean, you honestly cannot make any of this shit up. That 2609 room shit has just freaked me out to an unexplainable level, Maxi. It makes me wanna see the list of every woman who has been in that room since the two of us have been married."

"I could probably get it for you if you want it, Blair. But I suggest you don't think about that right now. We still need to figure out who's been sending you these texts because that's the main thing because we want it to stop, and I don't think this woman is gonna stop because she simply doesn't think she's gonna be caught."

"She's gonna catch my fist when I find out who she is."

"No she's not, Blair. You stop talking that shit. You're already in enough trouble for knocking out one of the women Lang was sleeping with, and hopefully she'll never do it again knowing what you did to her and knowing as well that all of it was caught on video. She was humiliated as hell so I don't think you have to worry about her anymore."

"I better not have to because I've been through enough already. A woman should not have to fight this hard to keep her marriage and family together, Maxi. And when a woman ends up doing shit she would've never done otherwise, then that's a problem, a problem she never started."

"You're right, Blair. Lang definitely started all of this, and I definitely believe you when you said that you have never cheated on him. You've been a very loyal wife and mom, and that's what you want people to see you as again. You have to admit you have put yourself in a bad light for right now, Blair, but I know you can restore your rep among people."

"And that's just it, Maxi. I end up with a fucked-up rep now and it was all because of what Lang did, and his rep is still just fine. If anything, he's the one who should have the fucked-up rep, not me. I'm the one out here doing shit I would never do and had never done before that very first text came to my phone, but it's like he's going unscathed except for maybe the media bumping into his car trying to ask him questions about our private lives which are now very public while Charrod is driving him to and from work and taking our girls to school almost every day. Why is that?"

"Because he's Langston West, Black billionaire. He really never has to worry about his rep with anyone, but you're the one who has to because you're the one who married into the family."

"Yeah, Maxi. You know how it is. You've always known how it is." I looked at my phone. There was an email from Mildred Livingston. I took a deep breath and read it.

Maxi looked at me in curiosity. "What is it, Blair?"

"Mildred is flying in tomorrow to talk to me about what happened at the meeting with Cordelia Sharpe."

"Let me know how it goes."

CHAPTER THIRTY

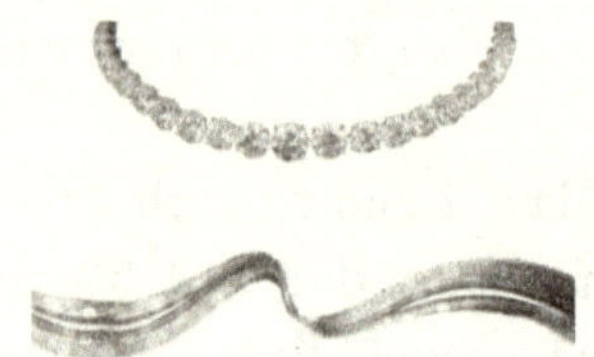

$\mathcal{I}$ didn't think I could hide my nervous smile as Mildred Livingston stared around my conference room with a warm, seemingly genuine smile with her Herend teacup in her hand at this very peaceful and quiet environment, which was a huge contrast to how it was when I held a meeting in here that'd never had anything like it ever happen in the ABWS history. And I was gonna learn my fate in this prestigious Black historic organization today.

Mildred Livingston was in her 80's and had been married for 60 years to a wealthy now-retired doctor. She was the daughter of the founder of the ABWS, so she inherited the position of the organization as well as the organization itself, and her oldest daughter who was in her late 50's was next in line to inherit it.

I continued to stare at her as she was always dressed like she was headed to Sunday church services with her fancy, colorful skirt suit on and big matching hat, and Chanel classic medium black bag. I let her continue to take in my conference room since this was the first time she'd been in here. She'd been to my house on numerous occasions before.

"I must say, Blair, that this a beautiful room, as well as your office. Maybe you should consider having all of the ABWS meetings here."

"Thank you, Mildred, but I do prefer having them at the Regalis Montemar Hotel since the conference room we have our meetings in are much bigger than this one." *Now more than ever do I prefer to have them there,* I thought.

She nodded with a smile as she took another sip of her tea as she still looked around the room. "Hard for me to believe that such a tragic event took place in here."

"Tragic event?" She made it sound like it was a shooting or something. I only punched the bitch in her face and rightfully so.

"Well, I'm sorry that everything had to go down the way it did, Mildred. It's just that I have so much going on in my personal life lately and it's been everywhere when I always wanted mine and Lang's lives to stay private for the sake of us and especially for the sake of our children. It's just that I'd found out the information I'd received about my husband's infidelities was correct and verified information, and it came as a surprise to me that when out of all people I was meeting, one of the new ABWS members happened to be a woman who my husband is having these infidelities with. Since it's ABWS tradition for me to meet the new members without knowing who they previously are, I couldn't hold back my composure when Heather said her name. I'd never seen Cordelia up until that point, even though I knew she was the one who my husband had been cheating on me with. I knew her name, but not what she looked like even though I could've easily looked her up. I just didn't wanna see her, so it was a great surprise when I was introduced to her face-to-face like that. I honestly never thought I would be."

"I understand your surprise and shock, Blair, but as the ABWS National President, you conducted yourself in an extremely unprofessional manner. This is something that just can't be ignored or swept under the rug. Something must be done. Never in the 90-year history have we ever had a president, much less a national one, behave in the way you did, Blair."

"And I can't even say I'm sorry enough about it. Ever since this text scandal has put my family into a spotlight I never thought we would be in, I have not been my usual self because of it, and everyone close to me have noticed it. I'm pretty much accusing all of these women Lang has been having these affairs with as being the one who has started all of this. Come to find out, Cordelia didn't start any of it, but she is one of the many women who is the cause of why my family is having all of these problems now. Lang is definitely the cause of it as well. He doesn't have to do the things he's doing."

"You're right, Blair, he doesn't. But he's the reason why you're in this organization and why you were appointed to the highest position in the organization because of the person you are and what you have stood for since being married to him. We are a philanthropy organization and we take our members and their positions in the organization seriously. This does not look good to our charities as well as other businesses we deal with. We are who we are, and we want women who reflect the morals and values of who we are and have stood to be for 90 years."

"I understand," I said, as I lowered my head.

But it was like she wasn't even trying to hear me. I felt that all of the blame was still falling on me and not on Lang, and it was clear she wasn't even blaming a brand-new member, who happened to be Cordelia, for her lack of morals and values since she was the one sleeping with Lang. And I wasn't sleeping with anyone but him.

"Now, you know I have to ask you this."

"What is it?"

"Are you having any extramarital affairs?"

"Absolutely not," I replied and felt good saying it. "I take my marriage to Lang seriously. I took my vows seriously. I've never done anything to make him do the kind of things he's been doing. I've never done anything to any woman to make her want to harass me with texts about sleeping with my husband."

"I am sorry all of this is happening to you, Blair, and I'm sorry I'm gonna have to say this."

Just say I'm fired, I thought. "Okay," I squeaked out.

"You are required to make a statement about what happened that day at that meeting and make a public apology for it—a written one and a videotaped public apology so everyone can see it. And you are suspended for 90 days effective immediately. The ABWS National

Vice-President Astrid Regalis-Dubois will be the interim president while you serve out your suspension. Do you object to any of this?"

"No, I don't," I said with a smile of relief.

"No marriage is perfect, Blair. And you know after me being married for 60 years, I know a lot about that. But you are one of the luckiest women in the world to be married to a Black billionaire, and you're the first one to be married to one who has been a part of our organization. That means something. But we have to keep up what our organization represents. I expect your written apology emailed to me this week, and your videotaped apology in a few days. Any questions?"

"Yes."

"What is it?"

"What happened to Cordelia Sharpe?"

"She's no longer an ABWS member. She was expelled."

<u>WILD BLACK TEA WITH BEVERLY</u>
BLAIR WEST SUSPENDED FOR 90 DAYS FROM PRES-
TIGIOUS ABWS JOB FOR PUNCHING OUT HUSBAND
LANG'S LOVER CORDELIA SHARPE: A NEW AND
NOW EXPELLED ABWS MEMBER!

"Yes, what you see in the title has all been verified by me personally! Blair West is still in as ABWS National President, and Cordelia Sharpe, brand-new ABWS member, is OUT! Welcome to the show, everyone, my name is Beverly, the only one who brings you all the wild Black tea, and this is some wild Black tea, everybody! For those of you who still haven't seen that now-viral video, please go look at it. Blair, I must say, has a mean right hook, and that was that type of right hook that meant business, the 'I know you're sleeping with my husband, bitch!' right hook! Okay, let me stop!"

She laughed some more and took a sip of her tea.

"Okay, yes, like I said, all of this has been verified personally by me about the status of the two of them after ABWS Organization heiress Mildred Livingston paid Blair a personal visit to her 40,000 square-foot mega billionaire royal palace and had a nice little chit chat with her about her inexcusable behavior that day, but it obviously wasn't bad enough for her to fire her from the most prestigious position this Black historic organization has.

"According to my sources who got information from Mildred's account of the meeting between her and Blair, that Blair said she has never cheated on Lang, even though it's clear he's done it—and everyone knows he's still doing it—to her. But Cordelia admitted to Mildred when she talked with her that her and Lang were having an affair, and after she admitted this, she was immediately expelled from her ABWS membership. She had one of the shortest memberships ever! But it was her fault. Everyone knew Blair didn't do that shit for no reason at all. Blair has always kept it classy until all of this text scandal stuff has come out and has had her acting in ways she normally wouldn't act in, but it's all a part of being human. We're all not perfect and will lose it on things at times, and this is Blair's time!

"But she didn't go without any kind of punishment whatsoever. She's been suspended for 90 days effective immediately and fully agreed that the suspension was 'fair.' She's also supposed to be issuing a public apology on a video so we'll all be looking out for that, of course. But I still have a feeling that everything is far from over when it comes to the West Mess, as I've called it. After all of this, remember, it's been confirmed that no one still knows who sent the text to Blair that started all of this mess to begin with, but what's also been confirmed was that it wasn't Cordelia Sharpe, and Blair made sure of that herself since she checked her phone to see and saw for herself that it is definitely someone else out there. I have a feeling this is not gonna end well."

She looked at her phone. "Oh my god, everyone! Oh my god!

TEA ALERT! TEA ALERT!" She pressed a button that made an earsplitting sound of a teapot whistling. "I just received an email from someone that I never knew I was gonna hear from! I gotta get this verified because if I do, I will have an epic Wild Black Tea interview to give to all of you. Gotta end this show early! But please stay tuned!"

"Tea alert, my ass. That's what you said the last time and ended up having to take down the video because my BFF ran that little Yusari bitch out of town for trying to blackmail me. And you never told your viewers why you took it down either because you know they asked," I mumbled to myself.

I walked out of my office and to my clothes closet to find something to wear for my date night with Lang tonight. We had a lot to talk about whether he wanted to talk about it or not.

CHAPTER THIRTY-ONE

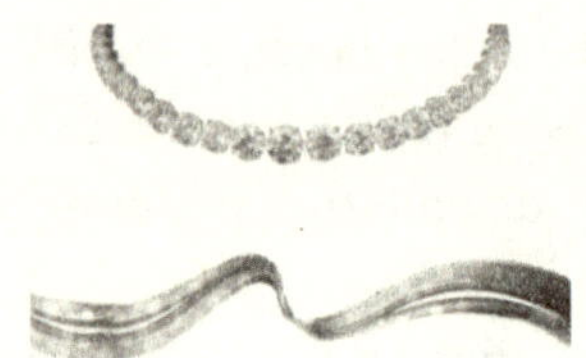

I reluctantly grabbed on to Lang's hand as he helped me out of the car while we were here on one of our date nights for the month at a Mexican restaurant . . . and somehow the media found out all about it as we held hands and walked towards the restaurant as the restaurant's owner led the way inside while security kept the media back as they shouted questions and lit us up with the flashes from their cameras.

"Blair! How do you feel about your 90-day suspension from the ABWS?" a reporter shouted out.

How the hell do you think I feel? I thought, as I checked out my date night casual but sexy Dolce&Gabbana black lace trim deep V-neck blouse, Dorothee Schumacher cropped flare indigo blue jeans, and Dolce&Gabbana black nappa leather sandals with a beautiful baroque gold D heel on one shoe and a G heel on the other. But what I loved most of all about this look was my beautiful Dolce&Gabbana black and gold multicolored embellished jeweled box clutch, and since it was $11,000, I was glad to finally be carrying it.

The reporters tried throwing every question at us to get us to answer something that would satisfy them.

"Don't answer them," Lang said.

"I wasn't going to," I informed him.

"You look beautiful, Mrs. West!" another reporter shouted out.

"Thank you," I replied with a smile since I was glad that someone noticed my date look instead of just being flat-out nosey about our personal lives, as we were finally led inside and into a private dining room.

Minutes later, I sipped on my margarita while I stared at Lang while he ate an appetizer of gourmet chips and salsa. "Lang, things are not getting better when it comes to everything that's been going on, and I'm tired of you acting as if you don't wanna talk about it. We've never had a problem with the media following us around like this, and the size of them wherever we show up at is just getting bigger and bigger."

"What do you want me to do about it, Blair? They have a right to do what they do."

"Turning our lives upside down because of one text? None of this shit had to come to this and you know it. Now you know damn well you haven't even admitted to me that you've slept with Cordelia Sharpe, and what I did to her cost me a 90-day suspension from a job I actually love."

He ate some more of his chips. "We all make mistakes, right?"

I stared at him. I knew he was not gonna come out and admit he had cheated on me with her, and I was tired of going around in circles like this. "Mildred told me Cordelia told her she admitted to having an affair with you, and she was expelled as an ABWS member because of it. Now if you didn't have an affair with her, Lang, and Mildred told me Cordelia specifically said *you*, not anyone else, why would she make something like that up and cause me to do what I did?"

"I don't know? Because she wanted your job if you hit her and thought you would be fired from it?"

I sighed. "That made no damn sense, and you know it. Why do you have such a hard time admitting that you slept with her, Lang? As well as with all of the women you slept with since we've been together because at this point I don't even wanna know how many. But everyone knows you slept with Cordelia but you're still blocking about admitting to me that you did. All I wanna hear you say is that you did. Don't you care at all that I'm suspended for 90 days?"

He took a sip of his water, and then sighed. "You're a grown woman, Blair. You're old enough to know how to control yourself in stressful situations. Wow, I guess I really gave you the ultimate life of fantasy and prestige and privilege that you really lost sight of the real world, huh? Since you haven't had to live in it since we met?"

"Now you're trying to make me feel guilty, huh? And you have no right to do that, Lang. You've been doing what you've been doing with cheating on me for so long that you're the one who has lost sight of reality. You're talking like it's normal to get married and then cheat on your spouse just because you're the one who has provided a lifestyle for me that yes, went beyond my wildest dreams. But do I have to take your cheating in exchange for it? What example does that set for our girls and especially when they get married? Would you want their husbands to do to them what you're doing to me? You know damn well we never agreed on an open marriage, and I will never agree on it. I just feel like you lost respect for me for some reason, and I just don't know what it is I did if you have."

"I haven't lost an ounce of respect for you, Blair. You know you're the love of my life because if you weren't then I would've never married you. I said you were the one for me and I think since we've been married for 18 years and have known each other for 20 years that I mean what I say. But I'm not perfect in any way. I have always had a problem with women, and yes, I thought I wouldn't anymore when I met you. If you want me to admit that I slept with Cordelia then yes, I slept with her, okay? And I'm sorry I did it and I'm sorry it caused you to lose your temper and hit her when you met her. She'll never be better off than you are, Blair, and you know it. No woman can take your place, and they know they can't."

"Yeah, but they'll try," I said as I shook my head. "But I'm glad you admitted to sleeping with her, Lang, but she's not the one who's been sending me the text that started this text scandal. So, who is she?"

He took another sip of his water and ate some more of his chips and salsa. "Honestly, I don't know, Blair. And if you really want me to be honest, I just don't wanna talk about this anymore. This has caused enough crap in our family. I wanna look forward to bigger and better things, things that matter. We got my company's 25th Anniversary Gala coming up as well as Jodie's sweet sixteen party. There is a lot more to life than some text some woman sent to you about sleeping with me. As far as I'm concerned, I'm not sleeping with her. Did you ever think of that? Did you ever think of the fact that she could be making all of this up?"

"And if she is, Lang, why would she do it?"

"Why do people do stupid things, Blair? Come on, let's just drop this, okay? I want to have a nice date night tonight, and I'm tired of talking about this."

I took another sip of my margarita as my phone chimed in with a message from Maxi and a link. "But it's clear that the woman you finally admitted to me that you slept with is doing a live interview with Beverly."

He stared at me. "We'll see about that."

CHAPTER THIRTY-TWO

<u>WILD BLACK TEA WITH BEVERLY</u>
LIVE AND IN STUDIO!
EXCLUSIVE INTERVIEW WITH CORDELIA SHARPE
THE EXPELLED ABWS MEMBER SPILLS THE TEA ON
THE FIGHT WITH SUSPENDED ABWS NATIONAL
PRESIDENT BLAIR WEST, AND HER AFFAIR WITH
BLAIR'S HUSBAND, BILLIONAIRE LANG WEST; AND
WHETHER OR NOT SHE REALLY SENT THE TEXT
THAT STARTED THE WEST MESS!

"Hello, everyone! And welcome to Wild Black Tea with Beverly
and as you all know I am your girl, Beverly. And I just may have
the show of the year here right now because the West Mess has
been going on for some time now, and things just got even more
interesting with it."

Beverly took a sip of her tea while Cordelia tried her best to
smile since her face still hurt from being punched in it, but
what happened to her did not break her style as she was head-
to-toe in Gucci starting with her $565 black round frame inter-

locking GG sunglasses that concealed what had left to be healed; her $1,100 black fine rib wool turtleneck tucked into a $4,300 red python print long leather skirt. She topped of her look with a pair of $850 black Gucci heels and her hair swept up in a high blowout thick and long faux ponytail.

"Before we get started, I gotta say how much I love your whole look you wore today—you didn't come here to play!"

"Thank you," Cordelia said with a smile, and took a sip of her tea. "I respect your show very much."

"And I respect you very much for that," Beverly said with a smile. "And people have been waiting to hear all about you and everything that has you all involved in this West Mess, because I have a record of over 50,000 people in here and the numbers are flying higher and higher as I speak! Thank you, everyone, for tuning in and please, come on in, come on in, because we got Cordelia Sharpe right here in my studio and she's gonna give us the wild Black tea, everybody!"

"It's been pretty wild," Cordelia admitted.

"So, how did you meet Lang since you live in the wealthy city of Saddle Hills which is out of town?"

"I met him when I toured his company here. My husband actually knows his dad, Langston West II. They're around the same age so yes, my husband is a lot older than me—30 years older, actually. Long story short, one thing led to another with Lang and me, and I know it was wrong since I'm married as well, but it happened, and I can't take back anything that has happened."

"Do you wanna take back what has happened?"

"Not really, because like I said, it just happened. We were clearly attracted to each other and acted on it."

"So you knew he was married when you met him?"

"Yes, of course. Any woman who says she doesn't know that Lang West is married is a liar. At least I'm being real about everything. I didn't expect for him to leave her for me unlike what a lot of other women he has slept with had hopes of him doing."

"He said that he has slept with other women?"

"Of course, he has. Lang has no shame. He's a rare Black billionaire who acts as if he's single. I mean, he has had so many affairs I just don't understand why he married Blair to begin with."

Beverly sipped on her tea. "Well, okay. You are all hearing it here first. So, you really never had any serious relationship with Lang?"

"Not at all. He was just someone I would see when I was here in town. My serious relationship is with my husband; Lang's is with Blair."

"But someone out there is trying to ruin their relationship by boldly sending her a text taunting her about sleeping with him which is what started the West Mess, as I call it and what everyone else is now calling it. Are you telling the truth when you said it wasn't you sending the texts to her in the video when Blair got a hold of your phone and looked through it?"

"I'm absolutely telling the truth. I am not the one who is sending her those texts. I have only one phone and that was the phone she looked through on the video. I have no time for that childish crap. I have a husband and four kids. He has older kids that I don't consider my step kids since they're pretty much around the same age I am. I also have an educational company. I have a busy life."

Beverly nodded with a smile. "Well, everyone, you heard that from Cordelia Sharpe herself. She is not the one who sent the text that started this all. Well, I have to say that I do believe you, but you know some people probably won't."

"That's not for me to worry about," she said, and took a sip of her tea.

Beverly once again nodded with a smile. "So, let us talk about the day you met Blair since the two of you were in the ABWS. Were you nervous about meeting her since you knew you were one of the many women sleeping with her husband?"

"Not at all. I figured she didn't know. I was so confident that she didn't know that I really didn't give much thought to it."

"I'm gonna have to slow the chat down because it's going crazy right now," Beverly informed her and her audience. "So, were you gonna tell her you were having an affair with her husband?"

Cordelia gasped with disgust. "Beverly? What kind of a question is that? You really think I was gonna tell another woman—the ABWS National President—that I was screwing her husband? Are you serious?"

"I had to ask," Beverly said, and flashed a grin and took another sip of her tea.

"Well, as you know—and what everyone saw—that I didn't have to tell her even if I wanted to because she already knew when she was introduced to me, and I could tell she didn't know who

I was until Heather said my name. My name has obviously been brought up in her circles. It was probably that Astrid woman who's currently the active ABWS national president who told her since they're friends, and she's been friends with Lang for over 20 years."

Beverly sipped some more of her tea. "Astrid could be the culprit, most definitely. But you know I only like to report facts on my show that's why I never mentioned Astrid being the one who told Blair that Lang was sleeping with you."

"Someone told her and it obviously wasn't Lang because I personally asked him. But it doesn't matter anymore because none of this is worth it anymore. I have a bad mark on my face that will eventually heal from doing something I had no right to do, but that video is forever out there for people to see and make fun of me. No one realizes just how humiliating this has been for me, my husband, my kids, and friends and other family. My rep is ruined and it may be irreparably ruined, but it's something I have to work on and I'm willing to put in that work."

"What would you like to tell women out there about your experience?"

"That it's not worth getting involved with someone who is unavailable to you, and especially if you're unavailable as well. I don't blame Blair for punching me in my face, but then again, I felt she could've handled it better. She could've simply told me to leave and yes, I would've left, especially since it was her house. But for the ABWS to expel me as a member but only suspend her from her job therefore she keeps her membership? That was very unfair—but I can't undo what has been done. I admitted to Mildred that Lang and I were having an affair which I knew was an offense worthy of expulsion from the organization since she knew Blair didn't just punch me like that for absolutely no reason. But I believe that anyone who commits any type of physical assault towards another member —especially one who has the highest position in the organization—should be expelled as well. It shows just how much power she has of being the wife of a billionaire."

"Well said. One last thing. What message do you have for the woman whose text started all of this?"

Cordelia took a deep breath. "All I wanna say is that you need to come clean. Your actions have caused a lot of crap and even had me accused of being the one who was doing it. Like I said before, I don't have time for that childish nonsense. Whoever is doing this seems to have a much bigger and personal problem with Lang that I have nothing to do with. I only slept with him, but this woman is holding something much deeper and personal against him and probably against Blair."

"That's what it sounds like to me, too, and a lot of people in the chat room agree with you, Cordelia. I know you have a flight to catch soon so thank you for being here."

"Thank you for having me."

"*D*amn, she fine with those sunglasses on since I know her face is still fucked up," Jamichael said with a huge grin, and took a sip of his drink while in Lang's personal area of his office at his company.

"She knows damn well I didn't want her to do any interviews that had anything to do with me, Blair, or all of this text shit. I honestly think this is her way of getting back at me because I didn't feel any sympathy for her for what Blair did to her. I told her she should've seen it coming."

Jamichael laughed. "Yeah, she should've! But do you think it you did the right thing by telling Blair about you sleeping with Cordelia?"

Lang stared at the big screen. "Yeah, I think I did. I feel it was about time that she knew so she would stop bugging me about it. I didn't want her to think she punched her in the face for nothing."

"Yeah! That's definitely true!" Jamichael laughed.

Lang laughed. "But has Blair been trying to get anything out of you about my involvement with other women?"

"No, she hasn't," he lied. "I just think she wants an end to all of this just as much as you do; just as much as all of us do."

"Yeah, we do, man. But Blair knows that I don't like to talk about any of this. She thinks she's gonna get something out of me about all of the other women, as if I know who this is who started all of this. I think this shit has just gone way too far, farther than it ever should've. I shouldn't have had to watch one of the women that I'd slept with whenever she was in town on some gossiping-ass woman's tea show."

"I agree, man. But do you have any idea who could be sending those texts to Blair that started all of this?"

"I have no idea, man. But there is one thing I do agree with that Beverly said."

"And what's that?"

"That whoever it is definitely has a big problem with me or Blair, or with both of us. And since I believe that to definitely be true, then I don't know where to start."

Maxi and Blythe stared at me after we got done watching the live interview Cordelia Sharpe gave to Beverly as we sat in my upper-level recreation room that was specially reserved for family and close friends. The lower-level recreation room was more for first-time guests.

"Okay, so what is it that the two of you want me to say?" I asked as I had my arms crossed.

"What did you think?" Maxi asked.

Blythe looked at me as she raised her eyebrows.

"That she's full of shit and that she's still sleeping with my husband even though she's trying to make the whole world believe that she isn't anymore," I replied.

They looked at each other and grinned.

"You're probably right about that, Blair, but you probably won't hear anymore about it. She's probably not gonna have another rendezvous in the 2609 room," Blythe said.

"Yeah, well, probably not for a while since Cecilia's demise happened in there," I said. "Do they still have it where no one can book it? Oh, I'm sorry, where Lang can't have it booked for some bitch," I asked Maxi.

Blythe's grin broke out into a full laugh.

"Actually, it's open again. But the last time I checked, Blair, he doesn't have anyone staying in it."

"So it must've been true about her going back to where she belongs today." I sighed. "I just don't think Lang is gonna stop seeing her or any of these other women out there. My main concern is finding the one who started all of this because there is a big reason as to why she started it, but now it's getting ridiculous where one of the women he slept with is now going on a thot tour giving interviews? This is what I didn't want to happen."

"Thot tour! Love it!" Blythe said with a laugh.

Maxi chuckled. "Well, she only did because of what you did to her, Blair. Had that not been caught on video then no one would know who she is."

"I believe that, too," Blythe said. "But Blair, do you believe Cordelia when she says that whoever did start all of this with that first text that was sent to you about sleeping with him does have a much bigger problem with you and Lang? Or with one of you or both of you?"

Maxi looked at me.

"I don't see who would have a problem with me. I haven't done anything to anyone. If they have a problem with someone then it's obviously with Lang but they're taking it out on me since I'm his wife," I said, but I honestly just wasn't sure or even knew what to really think at this point.

Maxi looked at her phone as it rang. "Excuse me." She went outside to talk.

Minutes later, she came back in.

"What's up?" I asked.

Maxi sighed. "That was Omar Sinclair. He just informed me that he fired his lawyer and has no plans anytime soon to get another one."

Blythe and I looked at each other.

I sighed. "What is going on?"

Maxi once again sighed. "Your guess is as good as mine."

CHAPTER THIRTY-THREE

Wearing a Chanel black and silver glitter tweed jacket and jeans on that no one could see since I was being shown from the waist on up like a TV news anchor, I stared unassumingly into the camera as I got ready to make my official statement as the ABWS National President about the incident involving Cordelia Sharpe. I wanted to tell it like it is, but I knew I had to keep my professionalism.

"Ready when you are, Mrs. West," Talia said, my ABWS assistant.

I checked out my Chanel Fil De Camélia necklace and earrings and then straightened my jacket. "Ready," I replied with a forced smile since I felt there was no reason why I had to do this. I'd already sent the written version of my apology to Mildred, and she said it was lovely and professional. I hardly meant a word of it. Now it was time for me to bullshit my way through my apology video version so people could see just how 'sincere' I really was when I made a statement about something I still felt was very personal and therefore, I felt forced to do this. I felt that the written apology was enough.

"You're on," Talia informed me.

"Hello, everyone. I'm Mrs. Blair West, the AWBS National

President. I'm here today to make a formal public apology for my inexcusable behavior I displayed right here in my own home in my conference room in my office towards Mrs. Cordelia Sharpe, a former ABWS member. My actions were unprofessional and inexcusable; therefore, I have accepted my 90-day suspension which I have no objections whatsoever in serving out. I extend my deepest and sincere apologies to everyone who was affected by my actions, and I hope that everyone, including myself, can move forward from this unfortunate incident. Thank you."

"Okay, it's off," Talia said with a smile.

"Thanks," I said, as I got up from my chair since I was sitting in a media room we used to for interviews which showed a beautiful life-sized recent picture of my family hanging in a baroque gold frame right behind me on a soft white cashmere wall. "The family picture behind me was in the video, right?"

"I would not have left it out," Talia replied with a smile as she let me look at the video.

"Perfect," I said. "And that's all the apology I'm gonna give about this shit. You know I'm really not sorry for what I did to that bitch. I just wanna keep my job and restore my rep as well as my family's rep since Lang thinks I ruined it so bad."

"Well, I don't think you ruined anything, Mrs. West. If someone was sleeping with my husband—and I'm not even married yet—and came to my house and acted all sweet and kind and so innocent to me like she wasn't doing anything? She would've gotten more than a punch in her face!"

I laughed. "Yeah, I think any woman would've lost it, no doubt! But that was as far as I was gonna go with an apology. I hope I didn't sound too insincere."

She laughed. "You looked and sounded great, Mrs. West, as if all is forgiven."

"That's the last thing everything is," I replied with a grin, but I was serious.

"Well, I'll send this to Mildred and if she approves of it then I'll upload it to the ABWS website, as well as all of the social media accounts. See you after your suspension."

"You bet," I replied with a smile, and then took a sip of my water.

<u>WILD BLACK TEA WITH BEVERLY</u>
A BEAUTIFUL APOLOGY
SUSPENDED ABWS NATIONAL PRESIDENT BLAIR
WEST APOLOGIZES IN CHANEL WITH FAMILY
PICTURE IN BACKGROUND
BUT SHOULD SHE HAVE BEEN FORCED TO GIVE A
PUBLIC ONE?

"Yes, it has been great to hear from Blair since she is still under a 90-Day suspension from her job as the ABWS National President for punching Cordelia Sharpe for acting as if she didn't sleep with her husband. But as you all had seen that I was able to get an interview with Cordelia while she is still in a physical, mental, and emotional healing phase of what'd happen to her, and I asked her today during a FaceTime talk about Blair's apology to her and to everyone involved in the incident or affected by it. She told me that she doesn't believe Blair is even the tiniest sincere in her apology to her, only that she was caught on video doing what she did. She told me that she believes, however, that she's sorry to her husband and the ABWS because she doesn't wanna lose him or her job there, but not lose him most of all.

"But how anyone looks at it and what they think of her apology, that Chanel look Blair had on was a hundred percent on point! The woman knows how to convince people that she is sorry for what she did even if she really isn't sorry, and you can't blame her if she isn't. She's going through a lot right now but still knows how to put a professional look together from head to toe and had that professional voice to top everything off! Oh, and she wanted everyone to see that big, beautiful picture of her family in the background—*that* was sending a message to all of you thots out there who think you're gonna steal Lang from her. Never gonna happen! And you, secret texter, who everyone has yet to find out who you are, that includes you, too!"

"Damn right it includes that bitch, especially her," I mumbled as I got up out of my seat. I turned around and found Lang staring right at me. "You're home early."

"Not much to do, but always something to do," he replied as he continued to stare at me. "I leave the always something to do to everyone else."

I nodded with a smile, and left the room.

He followed me. "Where are you going?"

"To check on Jodie's gifts to make sure everything is here. They said this was the last shipment."

"That much stuff, huh?" he said with a grin.

"Well, it is her sweet sixteen and she only turns that age once," I replied, as it seemed as if where this room was where I had her gifts hidden was about a mile away from my office. I did this so she wouldn't go snooping around looking for them. "Do you think this house is too big?"

"Never," he replied with a smile.

We approached the room. I put my phone up to the QR code and opened the door.

"Damn! How much did all of these gifts set me back?" he asked, as the room was full of boxes all the way stacked up to the ceiling, all unopened.

"You know none of these gifts set you back, Lang."

"Whose gonna open these boxes and wrap the gifts?"

"I hired a special gift-wrapping crew to come in here and wrap them, you know, the same ones I hire for Christmas. Most of the boxes are already wrapped with bows and everything, but I want professional wrapping paper put on all of them."

He smiled. "You love this, don't you?"

"Of course! Don't you?"

"Of course!"

We laughed. We continued to smile at each other.

He slowly grabbed my hand. "Blair, this is what I miss."

"Me too."

We held hands as we walked over to the table I had set up for the gift wrapping crew.

"It's nice that we're holding hands in private instead of public," I said.

"What?" he asked, as we sat down at the table.

"I didn't mean it in a bad way, Lang. It's just that us holding hands like this makes it more authentic because there is no one else around. With everything that has been going on, us holding hands in public on our date nights when all of that media is around and taking pictures and videos of us just seems forced now."

"I don't think it's forced, Blair. We're married. We love each other. I don't think it's fake when we display public affection now just because of everything that's been going on. We were always holding hands and everything before all of this shit went down."

"And we still don't know who caused all of this shit to go down, Lang. Now I know you saw that fake public apology I had to give on video and in writing. I'm tired of lying about how I really feel about everything, Lang. This isn't fair to me or to our friends and family. I just want all of this to be over."

He sighed. "So do I, Blair. And I'm sorry all of this has happened. But we need to move on like you said in your video apology."

"You know I was full of shit when I said that, Lang. The only way I would ever feel like we have moved on is if this bitch who started all of this shit to begin with will admit to me who she is, and I don't ever think she's ever gonna do that."

"Maybe, maybe not, Blair. But we have too many important things coming up. I mean, look around this room? This is a room reserved just for gifts for our baby's sweet sixteen. This party means the world to her and we have the financial means to give her the best party ever."

"I know, Lang. But life is not a damn party, and hopefully she will understand that when she gets older, and Lorie, too, because you know we gotta do this again in two more years."

He laughed. "Yeah, I know, and I wanna enjoy it just like I wanna enjoy Jodie's upcoming party, and not have to have her worry about us fighting about all of this shit that's going on right now."

"I know when to put her first and not ruin her day, Lang. Hopefully we'll find out who this is before then and this will all be behind us."

"Yeah, I hope so, too. But for right now, let's just enjoy the events we have coming up, like my company's 25th Anniversary Gala. Everyone's looking forward to it this weekend; they can't stop talking about it."

I'm sure that's not the only thing they can't stop talking about, I thought. "I'm looking forward to it as well. I remember when I met you, you told me your company was only 5 years old."

"I remember that, too. Time flies, baby. But it's been a great ride."

I smiled as I continued to look around this room at all of Jodie's unboxed gifts as I reminisced about my fantasy lifestyle since being married to Lang, but the same one who'd gave me this lifestyle was the same one who'd caused the fantasy part to completely fall off into a raging dark sea of reality.

CHAPTER THIRTY-FOUR

"*L*ang! The man of the gala and his beautiful wife, Blair! Look this way, please!" a photographer shouted out as Lang and I stood in front of the backdrop where his company's logo as well as with the 25th Anniversary logo was splashed on it—and of course, the logo of the Regalis Montemar Hotel and their 150-year stamp of their existence splashed all over it since they had been hosting this gala for all the years the event had been going on. It seemed like it took forever for the business to get to this point, and it was still very hard for me to believe that when I met him, his company was only 5 years old. He'd definitely built it up to a multi-billion-dollar business while taking care of me and our children, and we were enjoying every moment of it—until the text scandal changed that.

But tonight was Lang's night; it was our night, his partner's night, and the company's night to celebrate 25 years in business. I wanted to forget about everything tonight and just enjoy myself, something I hadn't been able to do in a long while, and especially since we only had this gala once every five years. And each year here, I had to impress with my dress, and I'd hoped that I didn't disappoint at this year's event with an eye-catching gorgeous flamingo pink Carolina Herrera 3D floral embroidered strapless gown with a sweetheart neckline and silk floral appliqués and sequins. It was one of the most beautiful gowns I'd ever owned—so bling-bling sparkly and beautiful—and I felt I had attention on me in a good way and it'd felt like forever since I had. Lang looked gorgeous in his black Tom Ford tuxedo, white silk shirt and black bowtie, and it was something about a man wearing a suit that I could see drove all of the women crazy including myself.

"THE MOST BEAUTIFUL COUPLE! THANK YOU, LANG AND BLAIR!" another photographer shouted out.

"You're welcome," we both replied with a smile as we walked out of the backdrop and towards the ballroom as our private security followed us.

Several minutes later, Maxi, Blythe, and I talked in a group while Lang made his rounds of greeting people at the gala with his partner Rodney, as well as being introduced to people who were extended this exclusive invitation who worked at other companies.

"This is a beautiful gala and filled with beautiful people!" Maxi said with a big smile as she checked out the surroundings. "It just seems like so many more people are here at this one than at the gala five years ago."

"It does seem that way," Blythe said with a big smile.

"That's because it is that way. I think it's also because people wanna see Lang and me together in the same room because of everything that's been going on in our personal lives," I said.

"Can't disagree with that," Maxi said with a grin.

"Me neither," Blythe said.

"Have you talked to Omar lately?" I asked Maxi.

Blythe looked at me as she waited for her to answer.

Maxi sighed. "Come on, Blair. Not here."

"I'm just wondering, that's all," I said.

"Well, if you're wondering, then no, I haven't talked to him. The last time I did, he said he still had no plans on hiring a new lawyer."

"So, he's thinking about dropping the case against this hotel for what happened to his wife?" Blythe asked.

I looked at Maxi.

"Well, I don't want to say all that because that's not what he told me, but something strange is going on here with him. It's like since he found out it was accidental like you said it was, Blair, then I just think he lost interest in suing this hotel. This is a big hotel with a lot of clout and 150 years to its name. I think he knows he's not gonna win anything from it," Maxi concluded.

"I don't think he is either. But let me know if you hear from him," I said.

"I'm supposed to be talking to him soon, Blair, okay? And I'll let you know," Maxi said.

Astrid approached us. "Hello, ladies."

"Hi, Astrid," Maxi and Blythe said with a genuine smile, as they tried to make it look like they weren't talking about Omar and this hotel.

I flashed her a barely-there smile and began to walk away to find Lang because I could see him directly in my sight as women surrounded him and his partner Rodney, who was also married.

"Blair?" Astrid said, as she tried to keep up with me as I rushed towards Lang.

"What?" I asked.

"I love your dress," she said with a smile.

"Thanks," I said, and kept walking.

She looked at me as if she couldn't believe I was talking like this to her because I never had until now. "Blair, is there something wrong?"

I stopped since my feet were starting to hurt a little already. "What makes you say that?"

"Because you just don't seem like you want to talk to me. I mean, you're not mad that I'm the interim ABWS National President, are you?"

"It is what it is," I said, and started walking again towards Lang. "I'm rightfully serving my suspension. I just wish Lang was more honest with me about sleeping with that bitch and I would not have had to do what I did and none of this would've ever had to happen— none of this *ever* had to happen."

She kept staring at me as I glared down at her. "I understand, Blair." But she knew there was something much more than just Lang's cheating because she'd never seen me act this way towards her before.

"I need to talk to my husband, so excuse me."

"Sure," she said in a somber voice as she walked away.

I shook my head as I looked back and saw Maxi and Blythe staring at me. As I continued to walk towards Lang, a chime came into my phone:

I'm here.

It was her.

And I had no reason to believe it wasn't her. I looked up; Lang was gone.

I'm here. Beautiful dress you have on. Still no match to me and your hubby.

I put my phone back into my pink minaudière, turned and looked at Maxi and Blythe as they laughed and talked to their husbands Erwin and Nathan, and made a quick exit out of the ballroom and headed down the hall.

I believed the bitch was here. I believed it a hundred percent. But little did she know, I knew *exactly* where she was.

I looked both ways and got on the elevator . . . .

And headed to Room 2609.

CHAPTER THIRTY-FIVE

*a*s the elevator ascended to the 26th floor, I was hoping it wouldn't stop. I stood in here with my arms crossed wearing a $14,990 evening dress going up to a room that I knew my husband had snuck off to . . . again. He may have done this at the last event here, but he had no idea that it was different this time because I knew he was up here with that bitch in Room 2609.

Ding!

The 26th floor.

I was so glad I was able to make it all the way up here without the elevator stopping. I looked both ways and got off and headed to the room and I was ready to make my move. I felt that this was disrespectful to his company and especially to me that he would be up here in this room with a whore who would boldly text me to let me know that she was here.

Yeah, well, so was I.

And I had arrived . . . .

To Room 2609.

Again.

I honestly didn't think I would be back at this room so soon. I couldn't believe that I was here once again and couldn't believe even more as to what'd happened in there. I didn't know exactly what Omar was up to as to why he would fire his lawyer and not have another one by now, but in a lot of ways I was hoping he would just forget about the whole suing thing since it was ruled an accident . . . an accident that happened all because I was right in this room that I was standing in front of once again. But Cecilia didn't have a chance to sleep with my husband because little did I know, I stopped that affair before it got physically started . . . for good.

I looked both ways once again and knocked on the door. Without trying too much to touch the door, I tried to get my ear as close as I could to it; I couldn't hear a thing. But as I already knew, it was a big room, and I believed because of what'd happened the last time I was in there, that the walls were indeed soundproof because the argument between Cecilia and me was very loud and could've easily have been heard by anyone who was in the room next to us, or up above us or below us.

I looked at the text. I decided to respond to see if she would come out of the room:

You're here, huh? Well, so am I. I'm here right outside your hotel room door.

I sighed as I waited for her to respond.

"Ma'am?"

I turned around.

It was the maid who I rode the elevator with the last time I was up here!

I couldn't hide myself now! "Yes?" I squeaked out as I tried not to look shocked.

"There's no one staying in that room at the moment," she informed me!

"Oh, okay. Thank you for letting me know."

"What room number are you looking for? Maybe I can help you find it?" she asked.

"Um, no. I just realized I'm on the wrong floor. Thank you anyway."

"You're welcome. And your dress is absolutely beautiful."

I smiled. "Thank you."

She didn't recognize me.

I walked back to the elevator where it opened to *Maxi and Blythe staring right back at me*!

"BLAIR! See, *I knew* we'd catch you!" Maxi said, and got out of the elevator while Blythe held the door so it wouldn't close. She pulled me into the elevator and Blythe pressed the button to go back down to the ballroom.

"*What the hell* were you doing up there?" Blythe said.

"The bitch sent me a text while I was in the ballroom looking for Lang. See," I said, and showed it to them.

I'm here.

"Blair, how do you know if she's actually here, huh? She could've been just saying that shit because she knows you're here because this gala is all over social media and you're here with Lang," Maxi said.

"That's what I think, too," Blythe said.

"Well, I think she's here. I think she sent it to me because she didn't think I knew she could've been up there in that special room, Room 2609. She knows that I have no idea who she is that's why she's taunting me like this."

Maxi sighed as she looked up at the elevator ceiling. Her eyes panned down and met with mine. "Blair. *No one is in that room.* I told you that when you asked me the last time and that hasn't changed since I request updates on the guest list for that particular room since I found out that it pretty much belongs to Lang as long as he keeps paying Astrid for it."

I shook my head as I let out a sigh. "I feel like a fuckin' fool. The maid told me no one was in the room and it's like for a second I didn't believe her; I didn't wanna believe her. And would the two of you believe that she's the same maid who was in the elevator with me that first time I came up here?! Of all maids! You know there's a ton of them who work here since this is a big hotel!"

"Are you serious, Blair?" Blythe asked.

"For real?" Maxi said.

"Yes! I *instantly* recognized her! She's obviously working the evening shift now because remember I came here in the morning the last time I was up there."

"And you won't be going up there anymore, Blair. You're gonna end up blowing this investigation if you keep doing shit I clearly tell you not to do. You have no idea what you could *still* be getting yourself into," Maxi said.

"Look, I've gotten myself into enough shit, so after what happened with Cecilia Sinclair and finding out she and Lang were actually text lovers ready to be real-life lovers even though she lied to my fuckin' face about it, nothing surprises me. I never have any idea just what I'm in for, but I still take the chance because I need to find out who's doing this. And Lang still doesn't know that I know about the room. But I'm concerned about the bitch who started all of this and you see how she has no signs of stopping her bullshit. She says she's here, so I believe she's here."

Maxi sighed. "I don't think she's here, Blair," she said once again.

"Me neither," Blythe agreed. "She could be just saying that shit to make you crazy and have you searching this hotel for her, and that's exactly what you did."

Maxi looked at me as she raised her eyebrows.

"Yeah, but I knew exactly where to look for her if she was here so I actually didn't have to search the whole hotel like she probably thought I did," I said.

"And Lang is looking for you because he asked us where were you when you suddenly disappeared from the ballroom," Maxi said.

"And we told him that we would find you," Blythe said.

"But we knew *exactly* where you went," Maxi said. "Stay away from that room, Blair, I mean it."

"Hopefully when I find out who this bitch is I will be able to," I said.

We got off the elevator and headed back to the ballroom.

As we entered, I locked eyes with Lang.

He hurried over to me. "Blair! Where were you? We're about to make the 25th anniversary toast to the company!"

A waiter came over to us and gave us a glass of the most expensive champagne.

"Thank you," I replied with a smile as Lang said the same.

We held hands with one hand and our glasses of champagne with the other and headed up to the stage with Rodney and his wife Zendra, and other top executives in the company.

"My beautiful wife Blair and I would like to make a toast. To 25 years of building a strong tech company for the future of our families and all of the future generations to come. And here's to 25 more years and beyond and keeping West-Moore Tech Inc. strong with unbreakable bonds," Lang said.

Everyone nodded in agreement as they had their glasses lifted. "TO WEST-MOORE TECH INC.!" they said. And we toasted to a well-deserved celebration in terms of the company, but it was a whole other thing when it came to family.

"You didn't answer my question," Lang said, as everyone danced to Kool & The Gang's "Celebration" as we were still up on stage.

"I went to the bathroom," I lied.

"If that's true then you were in there for a while," he said as he stared at me. "Come on, let's dance."

I forced a smile as Lang and I walked off the stage and danced along with everyone else. It was better to act as if everything was okay than everyone seeing that it wasn't.

CHAPTER THIRTY-SIX

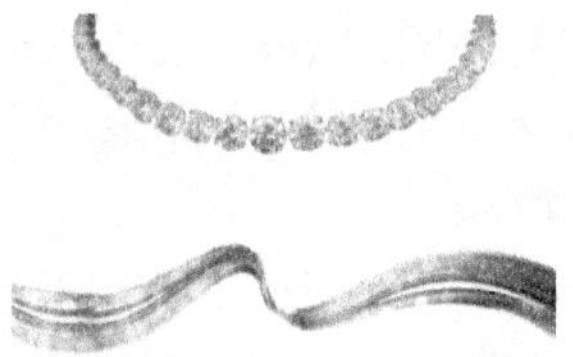

$\mathscr{C}$omfortably in my loungewear, I went to Lorie's bedroom where she sat in the suite area of her room watching TV.

"Hey, Mom," she said with a bright smile.

"Hey, honey," I replied, and gave her a kiss on the top of her head. "How was the gala?"

"Interesting, but fun," I replied with a smile.

"That's good to hear. Sorry Jodie and I didn't wanna go; we thought it would be boring."

I laughed. "Well, when you both turn 18 then you know you're required to attend whether you work for the company or not."

"I know, Mom," she said, as she was still focused on what she was watching.

"Um, did Jodie have Spearo over here while we were gone?"

"No, she didn't. She said he was out with his mom and older sister at his older sister's favorite restaurant since it's her birthday today. I'm surprised she didn't sneak him over here, either."

I laughed. "Okay, that's good to hear. She knows how close her birthday is getting and she doesn't wanna get into any trouble."

"With those truckloads of gifts for her coming in here for weeks, I wouldn't wanna get into any trouble, either!"

I laughed again. "Talk to you later." I walked down the hall to Jodie's bedroom. I noticed how her wardrobe room which was connected to her bedroom had its lights on. I opened the doors to find her taking selfies in her three-way full-length mirror.

"Mom! Hey!" Jodie said, as she suddenly tried to hide what was in the crook of her arm.

"Hey. And I've already seen what you have there, so don't make a pitiful attempt to try and hide it," I informed her as I stared at a brand-new Louis Vuitton LV x YK Painted Dots Capucines MM bag in black with multicolored dots all over it. I sat on the white sofa in this room. "Why did you buy that bag, Jodie, and not tell me or your dad?"

"I didn't think it was a big deal since I wanted a pre-birthday gift," she said with a nervous smile.

I sighed. "*A pre-birthday gift?* Jodie, you know you're getting plenty of gifts for your birthday like you do every year, but especially this year. Your debit card is not for buying $8,800 handbags that you'll probably only carry once. I'm trying to teach you—and Lorie as well—the value of a dollar because it doesn't matter if you're from a billionaire family. You should know better even more."

"I'm sorry, Mom. But everyone was wondering why I wasn't carrying anything new yet. Most of the kids get extravagant pre-birthday gifts, so I just wanted something as well."

"I don't care about those kids and what they spend their money on, I care about you and Lorie. I'm only gonna let this go because your birthday is coming up, but if you do it again without asking first, you're gonna be in trouble for it."

She gave me a hug and kiss. "Thanks, Mom."

"You're welcome. I'll be in my office," I said.

Several minutes later, Lorie walked into Jodie's wardrobe room as she still took selfies.

Jodie stopped what she was doing and looked at Lorie. "Did she ask?"

"Yes," Lorie responded.

"What did you say?"

"What you told me to say. If I didn't, would she have been in here being nice to you?"

Jodie sat down on her sofa as Lorie sat with her. "Well, she was upset that I bought this bag at first, but let it go since I said it's a pre-birthday gift."

"I love that bag."

"Thanks, sis. About liking the bag and the other thing."

"You're welcome. Look, you *can't* keep doing this, Jodie. You know I'm not always gonna be around to lie for you about having Spearo over here."

"Yeah, I know, okay?"

Lorie put out her hand with a grin as she raised her eyebrows.

Jodie dug in her pocket and handed her a $100 bill.

"Thank you. It's a pleasure doing business with you."

"Get out of here," Jodie said with a huge grin.

I sat at my desk and went to the site Lang had forbidden me from the start to look at:

<u>WILD BLACK TEA WITH BEVERLY</u>
BLAIR WEST KNOCKS IT ALL THE WAY OUT THE
BALLPARK WITH BEAUTIFUL DRESS AT HUBBY'S 25TH
ANNIVERSARY COMPANY GALA
WAS SEEN WANDERING ON TO AN ELEVATOR
DURING EVENT—JUST WHERE DID SHE GO?

Beverly started her show by sipping on her tea. "Well! As you all can see from the video and pictures from the gala, which is held once every five years, Blair certainly was the belle of her husband's ball with that beautiful $14,990 Carolina Herrera pink bling dress on! She was as close to a real-life Barbie doll as you could get!

"But it's clear that Blair wasn't herself, because people who have sent me texts and emails who were at the event said she seemed a little standoffish and her smiles did not seem genuine, and she even appeared to snub interim ABWS National President Astrid Regalis-Dubois—and in *her* hotel at that? Oh, no! Barbie Blair would've had to go!

"Well, I actually can't blame her because she is going through a lot and it's hard to keep a happy demeanor when all you got on your mind is who your husband is hammering from behind! Ooh, chile! Let me stop! Yes, I think I'm having way too much fun talking about an event I would never personally be invited to.

"But let me say this. People who did have the privilege to attend had sent me texts stating that Blair had left the ballroom and was seen getting on one of the elevators . . . *alone.* Take a look at the pic, everyone! That is Blair getting on the elevator at the hotel during the event, and check out the video, too, so you can see that beautiful Barbie bling that dress shows off! But I'm gonna have to inform you all that I have no idea where she was going, but wherever it was, she wasn't there for that long because she came back down and off the elevator with her best friend Maxi and her younger sister Blythe, who were also at the gala, of course. I contacted them to ask them about it and as usual, my request for an answer went unanswered. Well, something's definitely going on here so I'll definitely be keeping you all updated as I get more information."

"You're not getting a damn thing," I said, and then shut down my computer and headed back to my bedroom. Once I got there, the lights were off as Lang sat up in bed watching TV. I climbed into bed with him.

"I hope you're not tired," he said.

I sighed. "Yes, I'm tired, Lang. It's been a long day."

"Where did you go?"

I knew he wasn't gonna let this go. "What do you mean where did I go?"

He sighed as he shook his head as he still stared at the TV. "Blair, you know damn well what I'm talking about. You left the ballroom during the gala and went somewhere, and it wasn't to the bathroom so don't lie to me again." He looked at me. "Where did you go?"

His phone rang.

"Hey, Astrid," he said, as he stared at me. He got out of bed and walked around the corner and more than likely out of our bedroom.

I put my pillows down, laid down, and was fast asleep within minutes. And woke right up out of my deep sleep within minutes . . . .

To find Lang staring down at me as he stood by my side of the bed as I barely had my eyes open where it still looked as if I was asleep. I could literally feel him breathing on me. I slowly opened my eyes as I watched him walk back to the side of his bed and climb back in it. I could hear the clicking of the remote as I still had my back turn towards him. Whatever conversation he had with Astrid, it was clearly keeping him awake . . . and I had a feeling it had something to do with me.

CHAPTER THIRTY-SEVEN

The day had finally come. Our sweet little Jodie was sweet sixteen, and she'd practically been up since midnight celebrating. Everything was set for the party, and I was hoping it would turn out to be one that we all would never forget in the best way possible.

It was still an hour before the guests were to arrive, and Lang and I got ready together. He shook his head as he sprayed his cologne on him.

"What?" I asked, as I slipped on my shoes.

"Jodie's outfit," he said.

"What about her outfit?"

"She looks like a hooker."

"Like the ones you sleep with?"

He gave me a daunting gaze—but I was unfazed. "Watch your mouth. It's our daughter's day today."

"You're right, Lang. It is her day today, so I don't ever wanna hear you say she looks like a hooker in anything she wears. That's a Louis Vuitton outfit," I said, referring to her LV x YK Buttons leather bustier in black with colorful buttons going down the back of it along with a matching LV x YK Buttons leather mini skirt with an A-line shape and two rows of colorful buttons going down the front of the skirt. I thought the outfit was adorable.

"Just because it's expensive doesn't mean it doesn't make her look a certain way, Blair. You should know all about that."

"Would you rather see the outfit on me?"

"You're too old to wear something like that."

"Fuck you."

"I'm not in the mood," he said with a smirk. "Maybe later."

"Yeah, if you don't leave from here to go get it from somewhere else."

"We have a party to host."

We walked downstairs to check on all of the preparations for the party which was being held in the Grand Party Room, as we called it. We looked at all of Jodie's gifts which sat on a beautifully decorated table and looked like they were stacked as high as the cathedral ceilings in here. The DJ got set up on the stage and knew we only wanted tasteful music for tonight.

"Blair and Lang," Maxi said with a smile.

"Maxi, hey," Lang and I said.

We all hugged.

"Where's Erwin?" Lang asked.

"Already in the bar room," Maxi replied with a smile.

"That's where I need to be after seeing Jodie," Lang said. "Excuse me, ladies."

I shook my head. "Have you seen her?"

"I have, and I think she looks beautiful. I wish I could wear a leather LV outfit like that!"

"Lang said I was too old to wear it," I said, and shook my head.

"He's got a lot of damn nerve! You would look just as good in it!"

"I would hope so! But I don't compete with my girls."

"Exactly, you don't." She looked around. "Um, I was gonna wait to tell you this."

I gave her my curiosity stare. "Tell me what?"

"It's about Omar."

Now she really had my attention to the fullest.

"What about him?"

"It's about his case."

"Uh, oh! What about it?"

"He just dropped it," she informed me.

"*What?!*" I said, as I tried to be quiet about it since the DJ was still getting set up.

"Yeah, Blair. He just dropped the case; just like that. Paid me for what I'd done for him and thanked me graciously. What the hell is going on here, Blair? It's clear he didn't wanna fight the hotel for money anymore even though his wife's death was ruled accidental rather than being a murder, and he wanted me to investigate it to find all of the evidence he needed to do it. But despite it not being a murder, I still think he could've gotten something out of them."

I sighed. "I have no idea what's going on, either, about why he dropped it. You know I would tell you if I knew. But you know for obvious reasons I'm actually glad he did."

"I know. So, Astrid hasn't said anything about it?"

"Not a thing from what I know. She's supposed to be here soon, by the way."

"Oh, I knew she was coming. But like I said, this is all so strange, but I don't wanna think about it anymore since today is Jodie's day."

"I don't wanna think about it, either."

And with that said, we mingled with all of the other invited guests as they started to arrive.

Over an hour later after everyone had arrived for the party, the music was stopped and Lang and I, as well as Lorie, stood up on this stage with Jodie was we all wanted to personally say something to her in front of her guests which from what I was looking at out in the crowd, appeared to be hundreds. Spearo had spoken first, then Lorie, and then I had, and now it was Lang's turn.

"As everyone knows, I'm Langston, Jodie's dad," he said, as he wrapped her in a black Louis Vuitton LV x YK Painted Dots monogram shawl. The room quietly laughed. Jodie looked up at him and smiled. "And I can't begin to tell you all how proud I am of my beautiful daughter here that she's sweet sixteen today. It seemed as if it was just yesterday that I was holding her in my arms the day she came into this world 16 years ago today, and she has grown into a beautiful young woman ever since. I'm proud of you, baby." He kissed her on the top of her head.

Everyone smiled and clapped.

"Thank you, Dad," Jodie said with a smile, as she adjusted the shawl on her shoulders. "I can't believe I'm actually 16 years old. I have amazing parents, an amazing sister, an amazing boyfriend, and an amazing amount of endless friends and family. I am beyond blessed to live the life that I live, and I don't take it for granted at all and I never will. I love you all."

Everyone once again clapped.

"With that said, everyone please follow the birthday staff to another room since the gift giving is not over with yet," Lang said with a smile.

Jodie screamed with delight, and everyone once again laughed.

Lang and I held hands as we all walked to this special room to give Jodie her last gift, the gift she'd really been highly anticipating as she joyfully skipped ahead of us as she held Spearo's hand as our social media manager took video of her and of all of us.

Enjoy your little spoiled snobby daughter's party while it lasts! Because Lang is all mine at our personal after party!

We reached this special room that we called The Showroom. And it was used to showcase extravagant gifts. We had the guests stand in large groups on two sides of the room leaving a big space in between them.

"Okay, everyone. Since Jodie passed her driver's test today since today is her birthday, we don't have to wait to give this last gift to her," I said.

"YES!!" Jodie screamed.

Everyone laughed.

"So, it's pleasure to present the gift we know *all* 16-year-olds are waiting for—and I, by the way, had to wait for mine almost a month later after my birthday since I failed my driver's test on my 16th birthday."

Everyone once again laughed.

"I passed mine on the first try a few weeks after my 16th birthday," Lang said with a grin.

"Don't rub it in!" I said with a laugh.

Everyone once again laughed and then clapped.

"Okay, here's your gift from your entire family, Jodie!" I said with a big smile.

The lights shut down and a single bright light shined towards the entry into this room as Charrod slowly drove a beautiful brand-new Mercedes GLC 300 4MATIC Coupe SUV in the Diamond Metallic White color into the showroom!

Jodie screamed as she jumped all around as she hugged Lang and me, as well as Lorie, and then Spearo. The lights came back on as Charrod got out of the car and smiled, and Jodie gave him a big hug as well. Flashes from the cameras of people's phones lit up Jodie's new car as she jumped into the driver's seat and Spearo got into the passenger's front seat and Lorie into the back.

"Oh my god this interior is so beautiful!" Jodie said, as she checked out her new ride while recording it on her phone.

"Is it exactly what you wanted, baby?" Spearo said with a smile as he recorded it on his phone as well.

"*Exactly* what I wanted! The outside color *and* the inside!" Jodie said with excitement.

Spearo nodded and then got out and Lorie got up front. He walked towards the entrance of the showroom as guests surrounded Jodie's SUV.

"Mom?" Spearo said.

"Hey, son. What did I miss?" Gwendolyn, his mom, said.

"Mom? Did you just send me this?"

"Send you what, dear?"

CHAPTER THIRTY-EIGHT

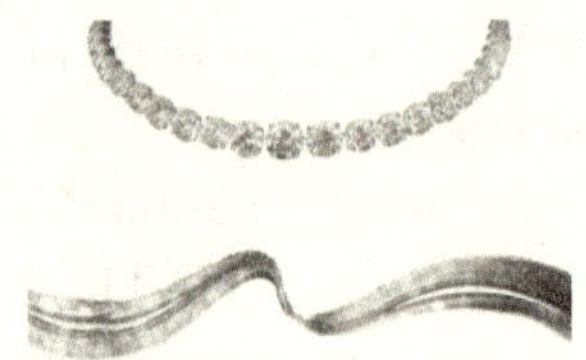

As Lang and I held hands while Jodie posed in front of her SUV as her guests turned into a frenzy version of the paparazzi, I noticed Spearo talking to a woman.

"MOM! Don't play dumb with me! What the hell is going on? Did you send this to me?!" Spearo said.

"What are you talking about, Spearo?" Gwendolyn said, as she looked around the room.

"I'm talking about this, Mom! THIS!" he yelled, and held his phone up to her.

I began walking towards Spearo and the woman he was talking to since it was clear to me now that their argument was getting pretty heated. Lang stayed back and spoke to Erwin and Nathan.

"What's going on with Jodie's boyfriend and that woman?" Maxi asked, as she followed me.

"That's what I wanna find out because I don't want any fighting in here," I asked. I looked back at Jodie as she was now taking pictures with a famous social media fashion influencer as they stood at the back of her SUV.

"Yeah, we need to find out what's going on. I want don't want my niece's party ruined," Blythe said.

Gwendolyn looked at what Spearo had shown her since he had his phone all shoved up in her face, and then turned away from it.

As we approached Spearo and this woman, I looked down at the ground. "Excuse me? Where did you get those shoes from?" I asked, reacting to the $1,995 Jimmy Choo Saeda 100 pumps all embellished in multicolor candy pink crystals!

Spearo held up his phone again to her face:

Enjoy your little spoiled snobby daughter's party while it lasts! Because Lang is all mine at our personal after party!

"Was this text for Blair, Mom? Was it? And you accidently sent it to me?"

Maxi and Blythe gasped as they looked at each other and then looked at me.

I noticed how security for this birthday party stepped in. "Get Lang over here right now," I told them as I stared at this woman. I looked down at her shoes. "Who are you? Where did you get those shoes from?"

"Jimmy Choo," she replied as she couldn't even look at me.

"Mrs. West, do you recognize this text?" Spearo asked.

I took his phone from him and looked at it. "Yeah, it looks like the one someone has been sending to me about sleeping with my husband," I informed him as I once again stared right at this woman.

"This is my mom, Gwendolyn," Spearo informed me. And if there was ever a time a young man seemed so ashamed to introduce me to his mom, then it was now.

"Let me see your phone. *Now,*" I demanded.

"I don't have to let you see anything," Gwendolyn said as she glared at me, and it was a look in her eyes that showed all kinds of hurt inside.

"What's going on?" Jodie asked as she walked up to us along with Lorie. "Wait! *She's the woman* Lorie and I saw at the movies that night talking to Dad! Wasn't she?"

"Yes," Lorie said, as she had a look of confusion as to what she was doing here.

"This is my mom, Jodie," Spearo said.

"*This is your mom?*" Jodie said, completely in shock. She turned to me, "Mom! What is going on?"

"LANG!" I yelled, as I looked around for him.

At this point now, the music had stopped and everyone at the party had their attention focused on us, and not in a good way.

One of the men on the security team walked Lang up to us as he stood by his side.

I looked at her. "Let me see your phone, Gwendolyn. *Now.*"

"Show it to her, Mom! She has a right to know it's you who's been doing this!" Spearo said.

"Doing what?!" Jodie asked. She looked at me. "Wait a minute! What? *She's the one* who's been texting you about sleeping with Dad, Mom?"

"We'll know as soon as she shows us her phone," I said, as I still glared at her.

Spearo snatched her purse from her and pulled out her phone!

"SPEARO! Give me back my phone!" Gwendolyn yelled, as a guard held her back from him.

He pressed a few buttons on it and gave it to me. "Does this look familiar?" he asked me, as he handed me her phone.

And. There. It. Was.

All of the texts I needed to see that made his mom a hundred percent guilty.

She was in fact the one who'd been texting me from start to finish from:

I'm sleeping with your husband. And you're not stopping me, and you're especially not stopping him.

To:

Enjoy your spoiled little snobby daughter's party while it lasts! Because Lang is all mine at our personal after party!

And every *single* text in between.

I sighed. "Yeah, it's her," I said as I stared at her. I gave Spearo back her phone as a security guard still held her back.

Maxi and Blythe stood like human shields in front of me.

"Mom, how the hell could you do this? You started all of this? Why? *Why?*" Spears asked.

She continued to stare at her son as if he was the one who did something wrong. She then turned and looked at Lang. "Lang knows."

"Get this woman out of my home," I said as calmly as I could. I think I even shocked myself with how I was, and knew I was doing this for Jodie.

"Come on!" Gwendolyn said to Spearo.

"Yeah, go with her," Jodie said to him.

"What? Why?" he asked.

"Because it's over between us. Your mom tried to ruin my mom and our family. I can't forgive her and I can't continue to be with you because you have way too much stigma attached to you because of her. Please leave," Jodie said, as tears streamed down from her eyes.

"You're wrong for this, Jodie! You're wrong!" Spearo said.

"Not as wrong as your mom was. Blame her," Jodie said.

We all watched as our team of security guards for this party escorted them out of the room and out of our house.

I turned around as I tried to look for Lang.

He was gone.

CHAPTER THIRTY-NINE

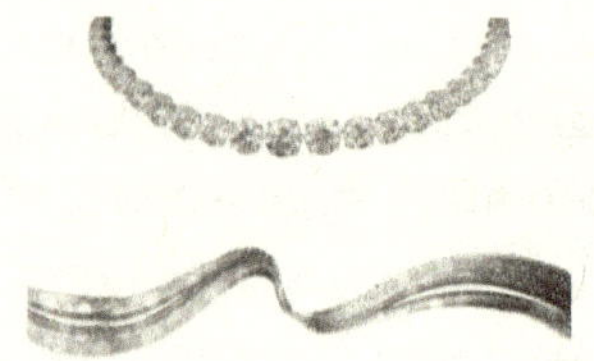

Gwendolyn sped off down the road with Spearo in the car.

"Mom! Slow down! You need to tell me what is going on with you and Lang right now!"

"SHE STOLE HIM FROM ME!" she yelled, as tears welled up in her eyes.

"What?! Mom, c'mon. What the hell are you talking about?"

"Blair stole Lang from me! He was supposed to me mine! MINE! It could've been us celebrating our 18th wedding anniversary, not her!"

"My now ex-girlfriend's dad used to be *your* boyfriend? Mom, c'mon now. Stop making stuff up."

"It all started 20 years ago."

20 Years Ago

"Hello?" Gwendolyn said.

"Hey, baby. Just wanting to see what was up with you," Lang said.

"Nothing much. Just gonna escape to Escape tonight for Ladies Night."

"Gotta get away from your three-month-old baby for just a few hours, huh?"

"Yeah, I do. My mom is babysitting her for tonight because she knows how much my time means to me since I work and all."

"You know you gotta do what you gotta do, baby."

"So, you're not coming to the club tonight?"

"Naw, you know clubs are really not my thing. I gotta work tomorrow."

"Come on, Lang. I really wanna see you there. It's been over a week since we've seen each other. I miss you."

He sighed. "Okay, I'll come there just for you since I've never been there before. I'll see if my boy Kamden wants to come since he's always into going to the club."

"Great! Can't wait to see you there."

"Can't wait to see you."

"He ended up coming there just to see me, and leaving with Blair. He knows he heard me calling him that night when he was leaving with her—pretending like he didn't hear me. But he can't pretend now that we've been seeing each other off and on the whole time he's been married to her, and I just couldn't keep quiet about it anymore. We would spend time at his penthouse, he would fly me out to different cities where he had business meetings at so we would spend time there. He even had me stay in the Regalis Montemar Hotel for weekend treats. Room 2609 was the room I was always in. I felt it was like my second home. He always wanted me to be in one of the best rooms there where we could enjoy ourselves without any interruptions.

"But Blair interrupted everything, even though she didn't know she did at the time. And Lang just got richer and richer, and built his wealth to billionaire status a few years into his marriage to her. *It was me before her,* and he knew it. I lost out on a lifetime of great wealth and prosperity and luxury opportunities I would've never had otherwise, and now I don't have them and never will because of him being with that bitch and marrying her instead of me, and no one cares; always telling me that he was never my boyfriend and to get over it and move on."

He sighed. "Mom, is there *any chance* he's really my father because *you know* I was Jodie's boyfriend? Because if there could be a chance that Lang is my father then that's fuckin' *sick,* man!"

She shook her head. "No, Lang is not your dad. It's been proven through DNA. Your father ditched me just like your sister's father did who wasn't shit. I thought I had a chance with Lang but then he ditched me, too, and said it was because he wanted a woman with no children to be in a serious relationship with when I confronted him a few weeks later after he left with Blair that night at Escape. Your father said the same thing, too, before he got me pregnant and then ran off to Europe for his basketball career and started a family with a woman over there, and his family and friends said it was because he wanted nothing to do with me or you, and you know that all too well by now. I'm always being left behind when I haven't done a damn thing wrong to anyone."

"But you took all of this out on Blair and caused all of this mess in their family which caused them to be in a spotlight they never wanted to be in. Jodie just broke up with me because of it and I just don't know when I'm gonna get over it, but I understand why she did even though I told her she was wrong for doing it. I'm just so hurt by it, that's all. This was very immature of you, Mom."

"You just don't understand how I feel. No one understands how I feel. Lang was my ticket to a life I should've had. Blair just had to show up there that night. I could see he was not interested in any other woman there that night especially since he only showed up there to see me. He was only there because of me, but he leaves with someone else and marries her two years later."

"That sucks, Mom, I agree. But that's life."

"AND SHE STOLE MY LIFE FROM ME! HER LIFE SHOULD'VE BEEN MINE! MINE!!"

"Good Lord, Mom, calm down, okay?"

Tears streamed from her eyes. "I can't take this anymore. We're starting over. We're moving far away from here and no one knows where we're moving to. I have put up with too much in my life to stay here for the rest of my life. I need a fresh start. Your sister agrees with me and she's moving with us."

"And what about *me,* Mom? You wanna run away now after Blair and Lang and everyone else found out it was you who started the West Mess with that first text? *You're the one* who caused all of this shit between Blair and Lang and ruined my relationship with Jodie because of it! Just because you thought Lang should've married you and not Blair? C'mon, Mom. Look at the way you're acting, you're acting like a scorned woman."

"*I AM* A SCORNED WOMAN!"

"Over a man you never had."

She smacked him hard!

His eyes welled up with tears. "You didn't have to do that!"

"I'm sorry. Lang was never officially my boyfriend, you're right, and I'd been led on by him long enough. He wants to keep in a way that I don't wanna be kept anymore; I'm tired of being his side whore. And I know I'm not the only one and it's been proven I'm not the only one. Cordelia Sharpe and me are one of many; maybe hundreds. I don't know, but I just don't wanna be a part of any of this anymore. So, we're starting over. Your sister, you, and me. We're leaving tonight. I have enough money."

"So this is what we're all gonna do? What about school?"

"What about it, Spearo? Do you honestly think you can go back there and face your now ex-girlfriend after what happened tonight? Huh? Yeah, it's all my fault and maybe it was good you caught me and called me out on it. I fucked up and sent you that text by accident, but it turned out to be my karma—and I got my karma. You don't realize how much you opened my eyes, Spearo, to a man I spent decades wanting him to still want me even after he got married. I should've taken everything for what it was—nothing. He was never leaving Blair for me and only gave a shit about me when he just wanted to have some fun with me. And the only way I felt powerful against Blair was doing the shit I was doing. And where did it get me? Nowhere. I just can't with this anymore, Spearo. I wasted 20 years of my life chasing a man when I could've had someone else in my life and settled down with him and started a family. He may not have been as wealthy as Lang, but how many men out there are? But I was blinded by the delusion that Lang would somehow leave Blair and finally be with me because after all, he knew me before he knew her. Please say you forgive me."

He wiped tears from his eyes. "I forgive you, Mom. But I think you seriously need to see a therapist wherever we're going. I actually don't want to know where we're going until we get there. After what happened tonight, I think it's best that we get out of here as well. We need a new beginning."

"And we're leaving to our new beginning tonight."

CHAPTER FORTY

"Well, Jodie's party is definitely gonna go down in our family's history," Blythe said, and took a sip of her drink. "I honestly don't think there will ever be another one like it."

"Me neither," I said, as we all sat in the recreation room.

"Well, as you know, I have officially closed your case since Spearo told on his mom. I thought that was very brave of that young man to do. I hope his mom goes easy on him," Maxi said.

"I hope so, too. But I just don't remember her at all. She knew Lang before I did, but I never stole her from him, so I hope you all are not believing that shit all over social media about me stealing him in the club from her 20 years ago."

"I saw that crap and knew it wasn't true, especially since I was with you that night when you met him and left with him. I didn't see him talking to any other girls, but it was clear he was talking to Gwendolyn before we got there," Maxi said. "Wow, you can't make any of this shit up."

"Sure can't," Blythe said as she shook her head.

"And I was wondering why I'd never met her before. I felt that Jodie and Spearo were together for a while that I would meet her by now, but she said Spearo always said his mom would tell him that she was always busy. I guess she was really trying to protect her secret relationship with Lang, and he was obviously trying to protect it, too, because he never had an interest in 'meeting' her."

"But then wanted the world to know that she was sleeping with him and taunting you about it," Maxi said.

"Yeah, that's how it went," I said. "But I'm glad I know who it is now. It's like I couldn't believe it when I looked down at her shoes and saw they were those crystal pink Jimmy Choo's. My mind immediately flashed to the video of the penthouse with her getting in the elevator and holding the shoes in her hands."

"And she had a nerve to imply to you that she bought them from Jimmy Choo herself," Blythe said with a grin.

"Of course she was gonna say that; I was expecting that," I said.

"Me too," Maxi said. "But that is what happens, ladies. One slip-up could change everything, and that's exactly what happened in this case. She accidentally sent the text to her son when she meant to send it to you, Blair. But I just could not trace her number for some reason. She must have connections or something because I should've been able to get those phone records and would've known it was her and this would've been solved some time ago."

"Well, it's solved now, and I thank you, Maxi, for all of the hard work you did on my case. I'm forever indebted to you because it."

"I was just doing my job so you're not indebted to me for anything," Maxi replied with a smile.

"And who was the other woman with Gwendolyn that night she saw Jodie and Lorie and Lang at the movies?" Blythe asked.

Maxi looked at me.

"Her daughter, that's what Jodie found out. And she was only three months old when Lang and Gwendolyn first met," I replied.

"Wow. He did know her for a while, but it was clear he fell in love with you, not her. He didn't owe her anything, especially since Gwendolyn's child was not his," Blythe said.

"Exactly. Doesn't matter if she knew him first. He fell in love with me and I fell in love with him," I said.

"That's right," Maxi and Blythe said with a smile.

Blythe took another sip of her drink. "How's Jodie doing?"

"She's still upset that she ended her relationship with Spearo over this and on her birthday at her party that, but she said he has too much stigma now. She doesn't know how she's gonna handle seeing him at school."

"Yeah, the first few days are gonna be hard, but she'll do just fine," Blythe said. "She's a West, so she's strong like her mom."

I smiled. "Thanks, sis."

"Um, that was really fast," Maxi said, as she looked at her phone.

"What are you talking about?" I asked.

"It's being reposted everywhere that Spearo sent out a message confirming that his mom was the secret texter to you, Blair, and that him and Jodie are no longer together. And that he no longer attends their school."

"Damn! That was fast!" Blythe said.

"Well, it is what it is, huh? I'm glad the boy is more honest than his mom could ever be. I hope he grows up and really learns from this so he can be a better person than her," I said.

"We all hope so," Maxi said.

WILD BLACK TEA WITH BEVERLY
JODIE WEST'S WILD SWEET SIX*TEA* PARTY WILL GO
DOWN IN HISTORY!
HER NOW EX-BOYFRIEND SPEARO'S MOM, GWEN-
DOLYN WARD, EXPOSED AS THE WOMAN WHOSE
TEXT STARTED THE WEST MESS!

"Oooh, chile! It went all the way down at Jodie West's sweet
sixtea, I mean, sweet *sixteen* party! If you were lucky to get an
invite then you were very lucky because only close friends and
family were invited to the billionaire daughter's extravagant
party which did not disappoint in how the party was set up with
the beautiful colorful flowers, the Mount Everest amount of
gifts sitting on a beautifully decorated table, the hottest DJ in

the world spinning tasteful hits—all the bells and whistles for the belle of the ball, little miss Jodie. And a person from her school must've been pretty special to be invited to this party as she had not only classmates there, but some of the hottest teen social media beauty and fashion influencers there as well.

"But all was well as Jodie received some of the most extravagant gifts in the world that a teen could ask for, but she got what all teens want when they turn 16, a car. But Jodie didn't get an ordinary car, she got a freakin' brand-new Mercedes SUV, one of those expensive ones. You can check it out on videos and pictures I have posted of it on my social media pages as well as Jodie's social media pages which are linked below.

"Okay, everything was going fine and everyone was having a great time, until after Jodie received her SUV. Spearo went to greet his mom when she came in and all hell broke loose then. Well, I'll let you all look at the short video from a person who attended the party."

She sipped on her tea while the video played in its entirety.

"Can you all believe this shit?! Spearo's mom, whose name is Gwendolyn Ward, is the one who was behind the secret texts that started the West Mess! I am shocked! No one knew about this! She was on no one's radar! But once her name was brought up, I didn't have to look that hard anywhere to find out that she had an on-and-off again relationship with Lang dating back 20 years, and thought Blair had stolen him from her! I mean, Black social media is going off about this! Something about a club called Escape back then that Lang and Blair first met at and Gwendolyn was there the night they met and everything and that Lang was there only because Gwendolyn had told him to come there that night. I guess when he saw Blair it was love at first sight. Yeah, it must hurt a lot—I'm not trying to be funny about that, either.

"But Gwendolyn, if you're reading this, that gave you no excuse to taunt Blair with texts bragging about sleeping with her husband just because he obviously never became yours. Well, Jodie didn't like this at all, so she broke up with Spearo because of the hell his mom caused to their family—and that break-up video is linked down below!

"But all I have to say is this. Gwendolyn, you need some serious therapy, and so does Lang for his infidelities. It's not worth chasing a man for 20 years who'd been married for 18 of those years to another woman when I think he made it clear that night he met Blair and didn't give a shit about you that he clearly showed his true colors to you—only you were too blind to see them. No one likes to be hurt, and we all think we're deserving of a great life, and yes, Gwendolyn, you were very close to getting it.

"I've never been in Gwendolyn's situation, so I can't say what I would and wouldn't do if you wanna know the truth, but what I do know is that most men out there don't have half of even a tiny of a fraction of the wealth that Lang has, but have all the love to make up for it and could give you the decent life you feel you deserve. I should know because I've been married to a man like what I just described for 8 years. It makes no sense to waste 20-plus years thinking that some man is gonna come to his senses and want to finally be with you. If he showed you 18 years ago by marrying another woman that he didn't want to be with you the way he wanted to be with her, then you should've taken that as your biggest hint and ran in the opposite direction with it. No man is worth that many years wasted because you can't get those years back, and taunting the woman he decided he wanted to spend the rest of his life with does nothing but cause what you caused. I wish you the best of luck, Gwendolyn. And to the West family, I hope you all find some kind of peace and solace now that this mess has finally been cleaned up. Best wishes to you all."

I nodded with a smile as I sat in my office. "And I could not have said this any better myself."

CHAPTER FORTY-ONE

*I*t'd been months since I took a dip in our indoor swimming pool since it was getting colder outdoors so I couldn't go swimming in that one. I swam my laps as I found it very relaxing and therapeutic, and it felt like it'd been forever since I'd felt this way. I swam up to the side of the pool and looked up and found Lang staring down at me.

I took off my goggles. "What's up?"

He stared down at me. "Get yourself cleaned up. I wanna take you somewhere."

Well over an hour after I got myself ready for him to take me wherever he wanted to take me, we walked out to one of the garages. I stopped dead in my tracks.

There sat his yellow Lamborghini Murcielago he took me to his house in for the very first time after we left the club 20 years ago!

"Lang! Oh my god! I haven't rode in this car in soooo long!"

He grinned. "I know. Get in."

Minutes later, we were on the road.

"So, where are we going?" I asked with a smile.

"You'll see."

"Am I dressed for it?" I asked.

He sized me up. "You look just fine."

As he drove us wherever he was driving us, the area started to turn worse.

"Lang, you know I don't like being in these areas at this time of night. It's not safe, especially with us being in a car like this, and it doesn't matter how old it is now."

"I know," he replied.

I continued to stare at him because it was something about the way he was acting that started to make me uncomfortable. I stayed quiet for the rest of the ride.

Several minutes later, he turned into a parking lot.

I looked at him. "No! No way!"

And here we were, 20 years later, back at the now-defunct Escape nightclub. The whole business area had pretty much become defunct and looked spooky as buildings showed clear signs of urban blight, as Minnie Riperton's "Memory Lane" played on the radio.

"Where did all of these businesses go in these past 20 years?" I asked.

"Beats me," he said. "This is what happens when people just don't care about keeping businesses in business. I was one of the lucky ones who got into a business that is always lucrative. People are always gonna want and need technology and always want the latest and greatest at that and my company provides that."

"Very true."

We sat staring at a very blighted Escape as it looked like it was just a shell of itself as it had been through numerous name changes and different businesses, but now it was nothing.

"Look in the glove compartment."

"What's in it?" I asked with a smile, knowing that he had gotten me another gift since after all, it had been 20 years since we met each other. I opened it. A small box sat in it, along with some papers. I pulled both of them out.

He took the papers out of my hands. "Open the box first."

I looked at him, and then opened the box. I saw there were two items but couldn't see them clearly since the lights were off in the car. I pulled out what was inside of it as he turned on the lights in the car . . .

And dropped them!

It was the lanyard with the scanner on it as well as Cecilia Sinclair's driver's license!

"Yeah, I thought those items would cause that kind of reaction in you," he said, as he stared me into a frozen fear. "Talk, Blair. I'm listening."

Tears welled up in my eyes as I stared straight ahead.

"I'm. Listening."

I was still too frozen in shock and fear to even get one word out. I couldn't even look at the papers that I still managed to have on my lap. Now I had a feeling what they were about.

He shook his head. "You had absolutely *no fuckin' business* going to that woman's room and confronting her about sleeping with me, and it was the wrong woman! THE WRONG WOMAN!" He slammed his fist down hard on the glove compartment!

I screamed! "This was your fault, Lang! You weren't honest with me! I've never cheated on you! NEVER! I tried to talk to you about this and you never wanted to talk about it. All you had to do was tell me who it was and none of this would've ever happened!"

"But Cordelia wasn't the one who was sending you the texts, and I think you know that by now, too, but you still punched the shit out of her in our house, Blair! You lost your fuckin' mind!"

"Not as much as you lost yours."

He laughed! "Oh, yeah, of course." He glared at me. "But I didn't kill anybody."

"I didn't kill her, Lang! She shot at me! I threw one of her bags at her and the bag knocked the gun out of her hand! She then came charging at me and slipped and fell backwards and hit her head on the hard-ass floor—I thought she was just unconscious from the fall, but the fall obviously killed her."

He continued to stare at me. "Is that what really happened?"

"Yes, that's what really happened, Lang, I *swear* it did!"

"Omar still thinks she tried to defend herself against her killer that's why she fired the shot that obviously missed you."

"I'm not a killer, Lang! It was a freak accident that she slipped and fell like that running towards me! I didn't know she wasn't Cordelia until *after* she fell, and I saw her driver's license on the floor and looked at it to see who she really was. What was I supposed to do?"

"Turn yourself in."

I sat as tears streamed from my eyes as I stared at Escape as I wish I could escape back to the past, back to the time when we first met, and I'd really thought hard about who I was getting involved with and why. But no woman would've turned down a relationship with Langston West III, no woman at all. I just wish I would've made better decisions about how I handled his infidelities because now 20 years later, a woman was dead because of me, and another one thought I'd stolen her life from her and tried to destroy me because of it, causing me to almost lose complete control of myself.

"How can things start off so good and end up so bad?"

He looked at me, and then stared straight ahead at what used to be Escape, the club we met at 20 years ago. "Because people let them."

"Exactly. Nothing had to get as bad as it did, Lang. Like these businesses being gone. Somewhere along the way, something got bad and they ended up closing and never reopening and ended up in this condition. And then it spread to other businesses and they ended up the same way, resulting in this whole area looking like this now."

"Our marriage was never a business agreement, it's a real marriage."

"I know, Lang. But the two have a lot of similarities."

"I won't disagree with that."

We continued to sit in silence for a few seconds.

"Have you ever wondered why no one has heard from Omar anymore?"

"Yes," I replied without hesitation. "Why haven't we?"

"Because I paid him off."

I gasped as I looked at him. "*You?!*"

"Yeah, me, Blair. Except he doesn't know that it was me. As soon as I found for myself what you thought you had hidden so well for so long that belonged to Cecilia, I knew it was you who was in her room that morning and obviously mistook her for Cordelia. You must've gotten her name through Maxi's private investigation on me, huh?"

I stared dead into his eyes. "Yeah, I did. But I was snooping on her desk in her office and saw a person of interest name and the room number she'd written on a piece of paper and knew it was at the same hotel we were at the night of the charity, Lang, so I acted on it. She had no idea I did it until I told her, so now I'm telling you."

"Thanks for the confession. Finally." He shook his head. "Damn, Blair. Look, my lawyers went directly to Omar since he fired his lawyer, and everything was settled that way. But like I said, he has no idea and he will never know that it was me who gave him the money, since the money was sent to him as a private donation to his family; set him and his kids straight for life, and even though they were pretty well off to begin with, they're very well off for life now. They're gonna suffer for the rest of their lives because of their mom not being around anymore because of you."

I wiped tears from my eyes. "I didn't kill her, Lang. I told you the truth about what happened."

"Yeah, *your* truth."

"*It is* the truth, Lang! How many times am I gonna have to say it?!"

He sighed. "Look, Blair. It's gonna take me a long time to process all of this, okay? I just don't know if things will ever be the same between us. That's the reason why I had a new agreement written up." He gave the papers back to me. "Read it and sign them."

"You know I don't understand all that legal stuff, Lang."

"There are no lawyers involved in this. I personally wrote this up. This is between you and me and the future of our family."

I stared straight ahead. I didn't wanna know what it'd said.

"Read it. *Now*," he demanded.

I sighed as tears streamed from my eyes. "What if I don't?"

"Then I'm turning you in for what happened, Blair. I'm trying to keep you out of prison because you could possibly go to prison for this even though you said it was an accident, and only you know that. I want an understanding to this new agreement with the understanding that if you read it carefully and sign it then I'm bound by this secret as well. Since yes, this all started because of my infidelities so I'm taking some of the blame for why this happened—but not all of it. You crossed the line when you went to that room thinking it was still

Cordelia in there, Blair, and you know it. You should've just let Maxi do her job and not interfered in her investigation and you wouldn't be in this shit and you know it."

"And neither would you," I said.

"What? What the hell are you talking about, Blair?"

I sighed. I put the papers back in the glove compartment.

"What the hell are you doing? You need to read those papers, Blair, and sign them. I'm not moving this car until you do."

"Well, then we can sit here all night and talk, because there are a lot of things I have to say about the whole Cecilia Sinclair thing."

He stared at me. "And what about it, Blair?"

I got my phone out. "I know, Lang."

"You know what, Blair?"

"I know."

"Know *WHAT*?!"

"There's no reason to yell. Remember, it's just us here. I know about Room 2609, you know, the room Cordelia Sharpe was in, *and* Cecilia Sinclair was in right after?"

"Yeah, so you remembered the room number. Big deal?"

"*It is* a big deal, Lang. A very big deal. You have a long history with Room 2609 dating all the way back to when this area was thriving and surviving."

He'd never given me the kind of look he'd given me at this moment. It was a look of shock. A look of intimidation. A look of disbelief. "What the fuck are you talking about, Blair?"

"I'm talking about you having that particular room and only that room reserved for your in-town and out-of-town whores that you have paid your friend Astrid a lot of money for! *That's* what I'm talking about, Lang!"

He shook his head. "Where's your proof?"

"You never saying that it's not, that's my proof, Lang. It's just that the one I thought was Cordelia was very good at pretending she didn't know who you were or who I was when I confronted her, so good that I actually believed her—until Maxi showed me this." I shoved my phone into his face that had the copy of the text exchange between the two of them the day before I confronted her which led to her unfortunate demise. "The one you didn't get the chance to sleep with is the one who ended up dead in all of this. And she pursued you. Wow."

He shook his head. "I guess Astrid was right."

I looked at him. "Right about what?"

"Right about the fact that you found out about the room, Blair."

I sighed. "How did she find out?"

"Video surveillance shows you knocking on the door to that exact room during the gala, Blair. Couldn't miss you in that sparkling pink dress. I knew you went somewhere other than to the bathroom like you'd told me, but the last thing that would've ever crossed my mind was that you went to Room 2609 because it's obvious you thought I was up in there with a woman."

"Were you? Because Spearo's mom did text me that night and said she was there at the gala. But of course I thought she was up in the room even though she didn't know that I knew about the room. Was she ever up in that room during the gala?"

"No, she wasn't. She did come to the gala, but she pretended to be a guest at the hotel since some other event was going on in another ballroom there. But that room hadn't been used since Cecilia died in it."

"So you're just gonna get another room, huh?"

He sighed. "No."

I didn't believe him, but I didn't feel like arguing anymore. "Look, I say we forget about this new agreement you wrote up and just move on with our lives, okay? For the sake of ourselves, and especially for the sake of our girls. They don't need this shit. They've been through enough. We've all been through enough. I just want to move on from everything with a clean slate and not have some papers you wrote up always hanging over my head that's now dictating my life. You were the force behind my bad behavior, Lang, as well as Spearo's mom, and you know it. I'd always been good to you and for the millionth time, I've never cheated on you. And I never did a damn thing to her because I didn't even know she existed until now. But now it's over. What's done is done about everything."

"Give me the papers."

I took them out of the glove compartment and handed them to him.

"So Omar officially knows the truth about what really happened to his wife?"

"I watched for myself in Maxi's office that day when she was talking to him about the findings. And she told him his wife's death was officially ruled as an accident."

"He knew he was no match for the Regalis Montemar. Even Astrid said it."

"That's why you paid him off in a form of a private donation. Did you pay off Spearo's mom to leave you alone? To leave us alone?"

"Why the hell would I do that? I'm just glad he knows the truth about his mom, and that Jodie broke up with him. I don't ever wanna see her again. She sent me a text saying that she's moving far away from here and that she never wanted to see me again so that works out fine for all of us."

"Well, I'll believe it if I never hear from her again."

"I don't think you will, Blair. It's over. But there's something that isn't over yet. And how this is handled is how I decide what I wanna do with these papers."

I sighed. "What isn't over yet, Lang?"

"I need for you to tell Omar Sinclair that you were the one who was in the room with his wife that day she died. You need to tell him face-to-face what really happened, Blair. And I want you to do it now if he's available."

"Now?" I squeaked out.

"Yes. Right now. Do you have his number?"

"No, I don't."

"Get your phone out and I will give it to you right now."

My hands shook as I got out my phone. I looked at the papers sitting on the dashboard.

"Dial this number," he instructed.

I did what he said, hoping that Omar wouldn't answer.

"Hello?"

He answered.

"Hello? Is this Omar Sinclair?" I asked as I pitifully failed in my attempt not to sound nervous.

"Yes, who is this?"

"This is Blair West."

"Blair West? Are you serious? Hey! How are you doing?!" he asked with a clear excited tone to his voice. He didn't even ask me how I got his number.

Lang looked at me and smirked since I had it on speaker.

"Just fine," I lied. "Um, I wanted to know if you had time right now to talk?"

"My goodness, sure! That's no problem at all."

"Okay, I actually want to do this via FaceTime right now. Is that okay?"

"Of course, Blair."

"I'll call you back in a few seconds."

"Sounds good."

I sat for more than a few seconds trying to gather up my strength to say what I had to say.

"Well, what are you waiting for? Get the FaceTime session with him going. He'll never know I'm here."

I took a deep breath, and FaceTimed him.

CHAPTER FORTY-TWO

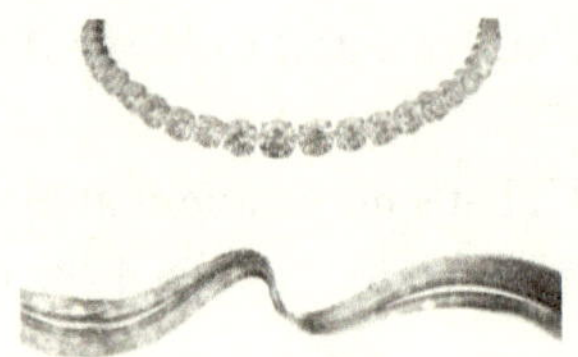

"Hi, Omar," I said with a nervous smile that I couldn't even hide, as well as my voice cracking under mounds of pressure.

"Hello, Blair! I must say that you look beautiful."

"Thank you," I replied with a smile. I took a quick look at Lang; a slight smile formed on his face. I knew he wanted me to get to the point of why I called him, but he didn't know just how hard this really was for me to say what I knew I had to say to him.

"How are you doing, Blair?"

"I'm doing okay, Omar. But I was calling you to ask you how you were since no one had heard from you in a while?"

"I'm doing better each day, Blair. I don't think I'm ever gonna get over what happened to Cecilia, but I have learned to move on because my kids need me. We're all in therapy because of it and I think that it's been helping us."

He was making it very hard for me to tell him what I had to say. I looked at Lang as he raised his eyebrows at me as his way of wanting me to get to the point of why I called him.

"That's great to hear, Omar. And I was actually calling you about what happened to your wife."

His eyes widened with curiosity, and I knew he was wondering why I was asking about it. "Okay, what about it?"

"Um . . . what was her death officially ruled as?"

I had to ask because I wanted to see if he would actually tell me the truth despite what everyone on social media was saying and what I'd heard with my own two ears what Maxi had told him.

"They ruled it an accident, Blair. A head injury from a very bad slip and fall on a hard floor."

Tears welled up in my eyes. "I'm sorry, Omar."

"Oh, Blair. It's okay. It was an accident. I actually thought someone murdered her, too. I guess no one was in her room after all. She probably thought she heard something in there and fired a shot warning the person. My Cece was very paranoid at times."

"I'm sorry," I said, and broke down and cried.

He kept staring at me. I could see it all in his eyes that he couldn't understand why I was crying so hard about a woman I didn't know. "Blair, it's okay."

"No it's not, Omar. It's not okay," I sobbed.

He kept his eyes glued to me. I was somehow making him feel so bad about my crying. He had no idea . . . until I'd told him. "Blair, I'm so sorry this had made you so emotional. I'm sure Cece would appreciate it."

"I thought she was Cordelia!" I blurted out.

He gasped in shock! "Blair! What the hell?! What are you talking about? Please explain what you just said to me because I'm confused."

I cried hard as I looked at Lang.

"Tell him," he mouthed to me.

I breathed heavy as I gasped for air as I tried to get it out of me.

"Blair, please calm down and tell me what you're talking about. I'm listening."

"I was in her room that morning, Omar. I was in Cecilia's room. I had no right to be there. I was in there thinking she was Cordelia. She came in after being out of it for a while and I surprised her by snooping around in there. She tried to tell me it wasn't her, but I wouldn't listen. She was just defending herself against me when she shot at me because I refused to leave when she told me to. When she fired the shot at me, I threw one of her bags at her and it knocked the gun out of her hand and she ran after me after firing the shot and that's when she slipped and fell backwards and hit her head on the hard floor! I saw how she really wasn't Cordelia when I looked at her driver's license that happened to fly out of the bag I threw at her. I just left. I never called anyone because I thought she was just unconscious and she would just regain consciousness sooner or later. I'm sorry, Omar. I'm sorry for everything. I'm so so sorry."

He sat stunned. I couldn't get out of him what he was really thinking. "Is this a joke, Blair? Are you making this up?"

"No, Omar, I'm not. I feel so bad. I feel so bad. I was not in the right state of mind with everything that was going on with the text scandal and everything. I thought Cecilia was Cordelia and she was the one sending the texts to me, but everyone knows now that it wasn't Cordelia. I had no business being up in her room that day, even if I was a hundred percent sure she was really Cordelia. I'm so sorry, Omar. I'm so sorry." I cried and cried as I gasped for air and hyperventilated like I never had before as he sat there still looking stunned. I honestly think he didn't believe it was really me who was up in her room. I knew it never even crossed his mind.

"Never in a million years did I ever think I was gonna hear this, Blair. I'm shocked. Stunned. But I also believe you didn't go up there with bad intentions. Now after what you'd told me, I believe you a hundred percent that it was an accident just as the independent investigation into her death showed. But it was said that there was no match to the fingerprints found on the door on the outside and inside. Don't worry, Blair. I don't think I will ever know how much courage that took for you to admit to me what you just admitted to me, and I respect you for it. I accept your apology. I forgive you."

I broke down and cried even harder. "Thank you, Omar. Thank you. Thank you so much."

"I won't tell a soul about this, you hear?"

"Yes, and I can't thank you enough for it."

"You're welcome. Please take care."

"You too."

I disconnected the call from him and cried my eyes out. I didn't think I had any tears left in me.

"I'm proud of you, Blair," Lang said, as he gave me some tissues. "What you did was what I wanted you to do. And I'm glad he forgave you for it. I can tell he really believed your version of what happened since Cecilia can't speak for herself."

"I'm just glad all of this is over," I said, as I tried to calm myself down.

"It's over, Blair. And he didn't have to know about my text exchange with his wife because a physical encounter between us never happened. He was paid off because of what happened to his wife, but like I said, it was a private donation so he still doesn't know it was me who did it."

"How much did you give to him?"

"$150 million dollars," he said like it was no big deal.

I gasped! "Wow, Lang. I knew it was a lot but I didn't know it was that much."

"Yeah, I felt he deserved it since no one had done anything for him when it came to his case because they just didn't care, not even that lawyer of his so I'm glad he fired him. I just wanted the man to be set for life because I knew the hotel was not gonna give him that amount if anything at all. $150 million dollars—$1 million dollars for each year they've been in existence. Couldn't have a better private donation than that."

"Does Astrid know you gave him that amount?"

"No, because it's none of her business. She's just lucky he dropped the lawsuit against her hotel, but she even said he was fighting a losing battle, but I made up for it."

I wiped tears from my eyes. "Yeah, you did."

He kept staring at me. "How did you get that lanyard with the scanner on it?"

I sighed. "I stole it off a maid's cart who happened to come in the elevator I was in while I was going up to the room. Had she not come in the elevator, I think the outcome in all of this could've been a lot different."

"Yeah, maybe, maybe not."

I looked at the papers on the dashboard. "What about those papers?"

He took them off the dashboard . . . and ripped them up.

I managed to crack a smile. "What did they say?"

"Well, it doesn't matter now since you confessed to Omar about what really happened to his wife. But when I wrote up those papers, Blair, I thought you'd murdered her because you thought she was Cordelia. You were right about what'd happened all along."

"I know I was. What did those papers say, Lang?"

"It was about a lifetime separation agreement."

"What? Are you serious, Lang?"

"Unfortunately, I was. I didn't want a divorce, but I just felt we couldn't be together like the way we used to, and nothing would be the same. Although we can't bring Cecilia back—and yes, she was in town to see me after she gave her talk that she never gave—the fact is that her death was accidental. I'm glad you came clean to Omar about it."

"But you didn't come clean to him about her being there to see you as well."

"Like I said before, he didn't need to know because it never happened and now it never will."

I sighed. "We just need to move on now, Lang. Really move on. We still have our whole lives ahead of us, especially our girls."

"And I agree to that. So, let's go home and be with our girls."

I nodded with a big smile. "Let's go."

We drove off and out of the parking lot as I looked back at Escape, where everything began for us 20 years ago. No one ever knows what the future will hold, but what we do know is that nothing is guaranteed just because you may think that it should be, and no one has the right to try and sabotage your life because they believe you stole a life from them that they believe should've been theirs. I became a person that I never thought I would become during this whole ordeal, and a woman ended up losing her life because of it, but her husband forgave me for something that changed his life forever, and my husband gave him a donation that changed his life once again forever because of it. And because of his forgiveness and this text scandal mess being officially over with, I finally felt that I could move on with Lang and my girls and we could restore our family back to the way it once was.

ABOUT THE AUTHOR

Sheila Murdock is a combination of her birth name and her late grandmother's maiden name on her mother's side. When she's not writing, she enjoys watching movies and TV shows—old and new—on YouTube, Netflix, and Amazon Prime Video, but always loves a surprising show she can find on cable TV. She also enjoys reading all kinds of non-fiction, but has a particular interest in African-American historical and contemporary non-fiction, but will read an occasional fiction book. She enjoys listening to old-school/throwback rap, hip-hop, and R&B, and jazz music from any era.